GREEN LAKE

GREEN LAKE

S.K. EPPERSON

DONALD I. FINE BOOKS

New York

DONALD I. FINE BOOKS
Published by the Penguin Group
Penguin Books USA Inc., 375 Hudson Street,
New York, New York 10014, U.S.A.
Penguin Books Ltd, 27 Wrights Lane,
London W8 5TZ, England
Penguin Books Australia Ltd, Ringwood,
Victoria, Australia
Penguin Books Canada Ltd, 10 Alcorn Avenue,
Toronto, Ontario, Canada M4V 3B2
Penguin Books (N.Z.) Ltd, 182–190 Wairau Road,
Auckland 10, New Zealand

Penguin Books Ltd, Registered Offices:
Harmondsworth, Middlesex, England

Published in 1996 by Donald I. Fine Books,
an imprint of Penguin Books USA Inc.

1 3 5 7 9 10 8 6 4 2

ISBN 1–55611–493–1
CIP data available

This book is printed on acid-free paper.

Printed in the United States of America
Set in Linotron Bembo

My sincere gratitude and thanks to Vinson and Kathy Krehbiel, for stopping by one day to inspire me, and to Robert O. Thomas, of the Kansas Department of Wildlife and Parks, for sharing materials and information. Thanks, Bob.

PROLOGUE

MADELEINE HERON STARED WITH unfocused eyes at the gleaming gray coffin that held the body of her husband. To her right, behind a sheer curtain, sat most of Sam Craven's family, including his mother and father, who, in a display of contempt, had asked that Madeleine be seated elsewhere. She was given the first pew in front of the coffin, and it was empty but for her. In the rows of pews behind her was a roomful of Sam's friends and former business associates, many of whom looked with angry surprise and spoke in barely concealed whispers when they recognized her.

The weight of the stares and the almost unanimous condemnation in the tiny chapel were more than Madeleine could bear. Her mouth was drier than dry and her pulse raced as she fought to shut everyone out and concentrate on the words of the soft-voiced minister. Her mind resisted his sorrowful droning and attached itself instead to the casket, left open in spite of Madeleine's wish to have it closed.

The stitches in Sam's temple were clearly visible, made raw and ugly by the knowledge of what they covered. The bullet had gone through and through, according to the death certificate; death itself had been instantaneous as a result of a self-inflicted wound.

To Madeleine's distress the drama replayed itself continuously as she sat through the service. The wretched final moments, the screaming, the terrible culmination of two years' worth of daily strife.

The beginning had been much different. Sam had been different, confident and carefree, always flirting with her, ceaseless in his teasing, and endlessly happy. It was good to be around someone who was always happy. Happiness was infectious, and it was especially so with Sam, who lived spontaneously and did crazy, wonderful things just because it made him feel good to do them. He was irresistible.

Then Sam lost his job. At first Madeleine hadn't worried; he was bright and ambitious and they would get by temporarily on her earnings as a college professor. But Sam surprised her by refusing to accept any employment but his previous position as an aeronautical engineer, regardless of the job market. Madeleine tried to be understanding as long as she possibly could, but as the months passed and their savings dwindled she began to urge him to take on other work. Sam was steadfast in his resistance, claiming he would be rehired any day. Soon the savings were gone entirely, and each month it was a nail-biting struggle to make the mortgage payment. Madeleine suggested selling the house in town and finding something smaller, but Sam refused. He grew angry at Madeleine for wearing a diaphragm again, telling her their plans for a family shouldn't change because he was temporarily out of work. Madeleine wore it anyway.

Months passed with no notice for Sam to return to work, and he grew increasingly morose and self-absorbed. Madeleine found herself reluctant to go home to him; she knew she would find him in a drunken stupor before his computer, watching the screen with glazed, unblinking eyes.

The night she asked him to get help he stunned her by flying into a rage and swinging a fist at her. He blackened her eye and savagely threw her out of the house. The next day at school was one of the worst in Madeleine's career. Most of her students knew about her husband, since many of their parents were employed in the aviation industry too—or had been. Madeleine lied in fending off queries about her appearance and dealt with pupils both pitying and scornful, causing her to ask herself why she was still teaching. She missed field work. She missed it desperately. She had achieved her degrees in anthropology to do research and writing, not to spend her days in a college being grilled and examined as if she were on a sleazy talk show.

A student named Alpha was the worst. Alpha was an acne-scarred twenty-year-old with an idea that no female other than Ayn Rand could teach him anything. He made Madeleine miserable in class, forever interrupting, forever asking intentionally insipid questions, and after class that day he waited till the room was empty before approaching and standing beside her desk until she looked at him.

"Yes?" she said finally.

His lips parted in a smile. "You had it coming, didn't you?"

Madeleine blinked and stared at his pitted face.

"Excuse me?"

"What he did to you. You don't kick a man when he's down, and you must have kicked hard. Hard enough to make him fight back. Why don't you help him instead of trying to make him feel worthless?"

Her mouth fell open as she continued to stare, and Madeleine knew she looked as shocked as she felt.

"Everybody knows," said Alpha. "It's not like you have a big secret or anything."

"It's none of your business," Madeleine managed at last.

"Hey, I don't care. I'm just telling you, help the guy out instead of stepping on his balls. Act like a real woman instead of this highbrow intellectual bullshit that nobody ever bought from you anyway."

"Are you finished?" Madeleine asked.

Alpha only snorted and swaggered out of the classroom.

Madeleine went home that evening and told Sam she wanted a divorce. He responded by showing her a notice from his former employer that he had failed a second drug test and would not be accepted for rehire. His voice rose to a scream as he asked her what the hell she wanted from him. When he came after her with blazing red eyes it was her turn to scream and run out of the house. A neighbor saw her and came to her aid, and all was quiet for several minutes as Madeleine shakily asked if she could borrow a phone to call her sister, Jacqueline, who worked at a nearby hospital. Through the picture window of the house Madeleine could see Sam on the phone, and though she wondered who he was calling, she wasn't going back inside to find out.

In the next five minutes the entire neighborhood was stilled by the sound of a gunshot.

Now Madeleine sat by herself and stared at the casket. Her guilt over Sam's suicide was compounded by the discovery that he had cashed in his insurance policy months ago and recently borrowed money from the bank, using the equity on the house. Unable to pay for her husband's funeral, Madeleine was forced to ask his parents for help. Sam's last phone call had been to his mother. He told her Madeleine was divorcing him because he couldn't find work. Madeleine attempted to tell her side, but no one listened, and no one but the police took note of the failed drug tests. Madeleine herself wondered why she had never suspected. She had lived with the man for six years.

The minister cleared his throat suddenly and Madeleine's daze was interrupted by movement to her left. She looked up to see her sister, Jacqueline, and her busy neurologist husband, Manuel, moving to sit beside her in the pew. Madeleine smiled gratefully and clasped Jacqueline's hand when she offered it. In the last few years, friendships had been impossible to maintain, but Jacqueline and Manuel had always been there for her, and it was to their home Madeleine would go after the funeral. She had made immediate arrangements to sell her own home and hired a woman to hold an estate sale the following week. Madeleine had had no choice; she needed money more than she needed china and antique furniture.

THE DAYS AFTER THE funeral passed quickly, with the sale and packing and the handling of finals during the last weeks of school. The house sold within the month, enabling Madeleine to cover all debts, but leaving her homeless, virtually penniless, and forcing her to throw herself indefinitely on the mercy of Jacqueline and her frequently absent husband. Jacqueline swore that Madeleine was no problem, saying she could stay as long as she liked, but Madeleine had no intention of sponging forever. When classes were over she would find a summer job and a cheap apartment while testing the prospects of obtaining a grant and going back into the field.

"You mean you won't be teaching anymore?" Jacqueline asked when Madeleine told her.

Madeleine shook her head and remembered the hateful expression of the student named Alpha when she returned to class after the funeral. The dull red animosity in his acne-pitted face was unnerving.

"No," she said finally. "No more teaching."

Jacqueline watched her. "You haven't cried yet, have you? Not even once."

"What good would that do?" Madeleine snapped in irritation. Then she softened. "I'm sorry. I know you think I'm strange. I'm just . . . numb. I can't feel anything. I don't think I want to."

Jacqueline went on considering her blonde older sister, whose skin was every bit as fair as the freckled, auburn-haired Jacqueline's, but was unmarked. Thinking about it gave Jacqueline a sudden idea.

"We just bought a cabin on the lake, did I tell you?"

Madeleine looked at her. "A cabin?"

"At Green Lake. We went there nearly every weekend last summer. Manny has a boat and he loves to fish. I don't do much but read paperbacks and get sunburned, but it's a great place to relax and unwind. Manny loved it so much he offered to buy the place from the owner, and he finally accepted, so it's ours. What would you think about going there after you wrap up at school?"

"For a vacation?"

"No, to live. For the summer, I mean. Until you get a grant."

"*If* I get a grant," said Madeleine. "I haven't done any worthwhile research in years."

"Okay, *if* you get a grant. What about it?"

"Is it secluded?"

"Not really. There are other people near. Manny and I would come up on weekends, but the rest of the week you'd have the place to yourself. I'm not trying to get rid of you, of course, but I know how you hate feeling like a third wheel."

Madeleine looked at her sister and wondered suddenly if Manuel had said something to Jacqueline. She wouldn't blame him if he had. It must have looked to him as if she had moved in to stay.

"Rent-free," Jacqueline dangled. "We put in our own septic system, a phone, and a miniature satellite dish. A cozy little home away from home, just ninety minutes from the city."

Madeleine moved her head in a small nod finally and gave her sister a grateful smile. "It sounds great, Jac. Really. Thank you for being so kind to me."

"Trust me," said Jacqueline. "You're going to love it."

CHAPTER ONE

THE RANDOM OBJECTS MADELEINE noticed on the drive east to
Green Lake did little to inspire any enthusiasm. The trees beside
the highway were gnarled, desperate-looking things, greedy for
whatever water they received. An occasional length of rubber
from some long blown-out tire littered the side of the road. A big
gray heron flew low over the horizon, and when Madeleine
glanced away from its awkward-looking flight, she saw a red cow
with its tail kinked up, loosing a stream of urine onto the side of
another, smaller red cow in front of a barn.

"Isn't it beautiful out here?" Jacqueline was draped elegantly
across the front seat of her husband's Jeep Cherokee. "Just look
at those gorgeous, rolling hills."

Madeleine stared at her from the seat in back. She saw nothing
but rocks, urinating cows, and more rocks.

"I think I've been in the city too long."

"The cabin and the lake will charm you, Madeleine, as it has
charmed the two of us," said Manuel in his thick accent.

She looked back to the highway in time to see a dead, bloated
black and white cow being lifted out of the road by a tow truck.
Beyond the truck were two large black tires stuck on fence posts,
the words KEEP OUT written on the sides in big white letters.

Madeleine closed her eyes and decided to sleep the rest of the way. Five years ago she would have looked at the land and its inhabitants with different eyes. She would have been curious, interested in the geological aspects, and full of wondering about the humans who might have wandered the area centuries ago. Now she felt nothing but a mild case of carsickness from riding in the back seat.

"Almost there now," said Manuel, cheerful but tired.

He had been called in for emergency surgery at the last minute, delaying their start by several hours. It would be dark soon, so Madeleine wouldn't be able to see much that day. Jacqueline assured her they would explore the lake together the next morning. The two of them had gone shopping for food that afternoon and brought along a month's worth of supplies with them. Fresh items could be bought in the tiny town of Green Lake, just four miles away from the reservoir, or in Fayville, a larger town a dozen miles away. Anything else she required she could tell Jacqueline, who would bring it with her from the city.

"You should feel safe at the cabin," Manuel informed her. "Your nearest neighbor is a conservation officer."

"A what?"

"A game protector," said Jacqueline. "They were known as game wardens before, but they're called conservation officers now. We met him last year. His name is Eris Renard."

"French?" asked Madeleine.

"No," said Jacqueline. "He's an Indian. Tall, and ugly as sin, but nice."

"Oh," said Madeleine, suddenly uncomfortable.

"Did he ever say what kind?" Jacqueline asked Manuel.

"What kind?" Manuel echoed, and his wife waved a hand.

"Madeleine should be able to tell us. That kind of thing is her specialty."

Madeleine glanced at her. "What makes you think I'll be able to tell what nation he's from just by looking at him?"

"Not looking. Hearing. I thought dialects were your thing."

"Linguistics, Jacqueline. Languages."

"Sorry, I keep forgetting."

"So do I," Madeleine said under her breath.

"There's another conservation officer that comes around in the summer," Jacqueline went on. "He stays mostly on the water, checking out the boats and such, but this one is a real looker. He won't say much to you, but then neither does Renard. They're polite and all, but they keep pretty much to themselves."

"This Renard lives in a cabin?" asked Madeleine, and Manuel nodded.

"There are several year-round residents. He's one of them. You will meet him soon, since his is the nearest cabin. Most of the other cabins are down the hill, in Briar's Cove. Ours is near the cemetery—"

"A cemetery?"

"A really old one," said Jacqueline. "Most of the stones are so weathered you can't even read them. It's a shame, really. You won't be able to see it tonight, but I'll show it to you in the morning."

Madeleine nodded and was silent for the rest of the drive. The Jeep wound up one dirt road and down another, on and on until she felt she would lose the contents of her stomach to the floorboard. She was glad Manuel had talked her out of driving her car. The mud and rocks would have made short work of her small Audi. Finally they came to a sliding halt, and in the glow of the mud-splattered headlights she could see a small log cabin with a large porch and many windows, most of which had ornate security bars over the glass. To the side, she could see a stone fireplace. A double garage stood detached from the cabin.

"Do you put your boat in the garage?" she asked.

"I do, yes. The pickup I told you about is inside at the moment."

"Okay. Great." She had driven trucks before, though she much preferred smaller, more efficient cars. "Does it have any gas?"

"I'll fill the tank tomorrow."

"Thank you, Manuel. And thank you, Jacqueline. The place looks lovely."

"Wait'll you see inside," said Jacqueline.

INSIDE WAS LOVELY, TOO. The furniture was comfortably overstuffed, the wood stacked up neatly beside the fireplace, waiting to be used. The top of the kitchen bar gleamed. The rugs on the floors appeared to have been recently beaten. Jacqueline took her into the bedroom meant for her and Madeleine found a large queen-sized bed and two dressers. The mirror over one dresser revealed the haggardness of her face, and she excused herself to visit the bathroom and splash some cool water on her cheeks. Inside the bathroom was a free-standing tub with a fancy shower implement hanging over the top. The cabin was wonderful, and once again she told herself how lucky she was to have it offered to her. At the moment, all she wanted to do was lean over the wooden seat on the toilet and throw up.

Jacqueline's voice called her away from the attempt.

"Are you all right?" her sister asked when she emerged.

"I'm fine, Jac. Just really tired."

"I'll put everything away," Jacqueline volunteered. "Why don't you go and lie down?"

Madeleine nodded and left her sister and brother-in-law to put away the groceries and supplies. She went into the bedroom Jacqueline had given her and shook her hair out of its bun before stripping down to her panties and rummaging in her bags for a T-shirt. Only when she stood up straight to wonder which case her T-shirt could be in did she think about the lamp being on and the curtains on the window being open. Quickly she turned off the lamp and hurried across the room to drop the curtains that were tied back.

Later, when she was in bed, she heard the door to the cabin open and listened as Manuel greeted someone. She heard a strange voice, deep and hesitant, and guessed the neighbor had seen the lights and stopped by to say hello. Madeleine dozed off while listening to the sound of their voices.

The next morning Manuel came out of the room he shared with Jacqueline and smiled when he found Madeleine eating a bowl of flakes. He said, "Eris Renard came by last evening. He asked me to please caution you about undressing in front of windows. It may feel as if you are isolated here, but you are not."

Madeleine stopped chewing. Her face colored. "I'm sorry, Manuel. I was so tired last night I didn't realize what I was doing."

"Don't apologize," said Manuel. "How did you sleep?"

"Much better than I thought I would."

"Good. Jacqueline always sleeps well here at the cabin."

"Obviously," said Madeleine. "Is she awake?"

"Not yet. I'm going to look at the lake. Would you like to come?"

Madeleine was already off her stool. "Let's go. Shall we leave a note?"

"No need. Jacqueline will know where I am."

Madeleine followed him out to the Jeep and climbed inside the passenger seat. As he backed out of the drive she eyed the cabin closest to the log home. It was small and white, with a bed of colorful coleus in front. It reminded Madeleine of her grandmother's house.

"That's Renard's place?" she asked.

Manuel looked and nodded. "Yes."

They ambled down the road toward Briar's Cove, and Madeleine frowned as she spied a man in a yellow fishing hat standing in back of a cabin and digging furiously with a shovel.

"What's he doing?" she asked, and Manuel laughed.

"That's Sherman Tanner. We call him the earthworm. The man isn't happy unless he's digging and burying something. He'll plant a species of flower one week and rip them out the next. Always digging. His wife is the same. They're always rearranging the mounds they make and shifting them from one side of the yard to the other. It's the funniest thing."

"Earthworm?" said Madeleine.

"Yes. I should warn you," said Manuel. "There are some strange people here. Quirky, if you like, with some very odd habits. Jacqueline and I have great fun observing them."

"What do you mean by strange?" asked Madeleine.

"You'll see," said Manuel, and as they drove past the tiny band of mismatched cabins that made up Briar's Cove, Madeleine frowned.

"Some of them collect junk," she said.

"Disgusting, isn't it?"

"Others look very nice and well kept. Why do they put up with the junkers? Shouldn't there be some community covenant?"

"There should be, but there is not. Jacqueline and I are lucky to live up the hill, away from the others. Like Renard, we keep to ourselves."

He stopped the vehicle at a point that overlooked the lake and smiled. "Look at that water. So beautiful and still. I love to come here in the morning, before the boaters and skiers arrive."

"It's pretty," Madeleine agreed, looking at the glassy surface of the lake. "Where do you fish?"

"I have my favorite little coves. You must always be careful, though. Some of these people are very private, and do not enjoy intrusion."

"For example?"

Manuel shrugged. "One man has a private dock and frequently swims nude, as do his many guests. I think nothing of it, but Jacqueline says he is an orgymeister."

Madeleine cleared her throat. "Is there a public swimming area?"

"I will show you, although I will caution you about this also, as last summer a young woman reported an attack."

"On the swimming beach?"

"One evening around dusk," said Manuel as he guided the Jeep down to the designated area.

When he stopped, Madeleine gazed around herself with dismay. There was no beach, only a small sandbar that appeared to be getting smaller with each lap of the lake's waves.

"Do many people swim here?" she asked.

"Oh yes. More of them later in the summer, as you can guess. The water is still cold in May."

Madeleine opened her door and stepped out onto the ground. Manuel got out, as well, but he stayed near the Jeep while Madeleine walked down onto the sandbar. She slipped off one sandal and dipped her toes into the water.

It was ice cold.

When she looked at Manuel, she saw another vehicle appear behind his, an official-looking truck with a logo of some kind on the side. She squinted as she saw the driver get out, and she knew immediately it was Eris Renard.

He was tall, dressed in a khaki shirt and olive trousers. A long black ponytail hung beneath his hat.

He spoke to Manuel and handed him something before looking at Madeleine from behind dark sunglasses. Madeleine's cheeks heated and her first impulse was to ignore Manuel's beckoning wave. Grudgingly she made her way up to them and stood biting the insides of her cheeks as Manuel introduced her.

"Miss Heron," Renard said and touched his hat.

Madeleine said nothing to him. Up close she saw the pits in his cheeks and her lip began to curl as she was reminded of another pitted face. Renard's face wasn't as bad as Alpha's, being brown in color, but the distaste had already set in Madeleine's mouth, and she was helpless to disguise her reaction.

Manuel cleared his throat in embarrassment, but Renard had already turned and walked back to his truck.

When he was gone, Madeleine turned to her angry brother-in-law. "I apologize, Manuel. I'm sorry if I was rude."

Manuel refused to look at her. He climbed behind the wheel and waited for her to get in the passenger seat. Madeleine got in and placed her hands in her lap.

"It was not as if he intentionally ogled you last night," said Manuel in a tight voice.

"That wasn't—" Madeleine began, but then she stopped. She wouldn't tell him she had been rude not because the man had seen her nearly naked, but because his face was pitted and he was an Indian and she'd had her fill of pitted faces and had her own face literally shoved in the dirt by more than one white-hating Indian.

"Madeleine, the man is going to be your neighbor. You cannot practice such rudeness."

"Yes, Manuel, I know. I've said I'm sorry. I will apologize to Mr. Renard at the first opportunity. Please don't tell Jacqueline."

"I don't understand you," said Manuel, shaking his head. "Jacqueline does not understand you, either. You have changed."

"I know," said Madeleine.

"You know?"

"Yes, I do."

"Well?"

"Well, what, Manuel?"

He threw up a hand. "You should fit in very well here I think, Madeleine."

Madeleine flared her nostrils at the apparent insult, but she said nothing. There was nothing to say.

CHAPTER TWO

NO ONE WAS MORE surprised than Eris Renard to find the small, blonde Madeleine Heron on his step at lunchtime that day. He put down his sandwich and went to push open the screen door. As the sunlight caught the side of her face he saw that she was older than he had at first believed. And prettier.

Her look once again fastened on the scars in his cheeks. Irritated, Eris removed his sunglasses and said, "May I help you?"

Her gaze shifted and she met his eyes. Eris lifted both black brows as she went on to stare at the gun on his hip. "Miss?"

"I've come to apologize for my earlier behavior with you," she said. "I realize how it must have seemed, but it was nothing personal, believe me. We got off on a bad foot and I'd like to start over, since I'm going to be your neighbor for a while."

Eris nodded. "No apology is necessary. Have a nice stay, Miss Heron."

He had turned away when he heard her say, "I'm a bit old to be called 'miss.' Please call me Madeleine."

"All right, Madeleine. If you'll excuse me, I just stopped in to grab a sandwich."

She backed immediately away. "Of course. Forgive the intrusion."

Eris closed the screen door and went back to the kitchen and his sandwich. He picked it up and took it out to the truck with him. Out of the corner of his eye he saw her walking back up to the log cabin, her spine stiff.

His mouth twitched as he thought of the way she had unabashedly stripped in front of the window the night before. Then he thought of her first glimpse of him, and the way her lip had curled.

He shoved the sandwich into his mouth and pushed his key into the ignition. Pretty girls had looked that way at him for as long as he could remember. It was nothing new.

He guided the truck out of his driveway and onto the road, turning when he reached the road that led to the dam. When he reached the bridge he slowed down to look around. He thought he had spied some oil on the road before, possibly spilled from a boat or some leaking old engine pulling a boat. He saw nothing now, so he guessed it had been his imagination. Oil patches were particularly dangerous on bridges, and would be nothing less than lethal on this one.

A horn tooted behind him and he looked in his rearview mirror to see Madeleine Heron behind the wheel of the old blue Chevy pickup that sat in the cabin's garage. The Ortiz couple were in the cab with her. Eris stuck an arm out the window and waved her around him. She ground the gears and jerked out past his truck. No power steering. Shift on the column. She was going to have her hands full.

Eris sat and watched the truck until it was out of sight; then he went over the dam and down the road to where men fished beneath the dam. Out of the dozen or so fishing there, several would not have permits, or the permits they did have would be expired. Campers without permits, boaters without the proper equipment and/or permits, pyromaniacs shooting off fireworks, drunks on skis and off—all of these things he had to look forward to over the next few busy months. And much more.

It was the middle of his second year as a conservation officer. He had attended college and covered the areas of wildlife biology and fisheries science; he had completed certification as a law enforcement officer and learned how to speak in front of large groups of people. He knew how to operate every piece of required equipment and was expert at catching and trapping wild animals. His colleagues were envious of his marksmanship abilities, but few ever bothered to learn his name. He was always simply "the Indian."

People at the lake were the same. It was never, "here comes the game warden" (which people persisted in calling conservation officers despite the title change), but always "here comes that Indian," or "here comes trouble."

Eris was used to instant animosity. Standing six feet four and having a face like his, people tended toward instant dislike. The uniform enhanced the effect rather than diminished it. Now people not only disliked him on sight, but most stepped back with a glimmer of anxiety and mistrust in their eyes.

Another man might have felt a certain amount of power under such circumstances, having such sway over people, but Eris felt nothing more than irritation. When he spoke to small civic groups or other interested parties he did his best to appear polite and civil and not at all menacing, but still he heard whispers, received numerous distasteful looks and was asked to answer very few questions. His frustration was evident to his superior, but communication with the public was a part of what he did, and Eris had to handle it. He solaced himself with the fact that public relations made up only 15 percent or so of his job requirements.

The majority of his activities involved enforcing laws and regulations by patrolling his assigned area, which included all of Greenwood County. Help would arrive during the summer, when another CO came to take over the task of patrolling the area lakes. Dale Russell had been hired at the same time as Eris, but Russell spent half of his time performing the duties of an administrative assistant and lobbying in Topeka trying to convince lawmakers to give conservation officers more police power.

Eris had made no less than four drug arrests the summer before, and he had testified in all the cases and saw all the defendants convicted; but if a person was speeding through the park, doing thirty miles over the speed limit, Eris was virtually powerless to do anything other than stop the driver—if possible— and issue a warning.

He saw a Camaro speed by on the bridge above just as he left the truck and approached the men fishing below the dam. Eris shook his head and continued walking. The owner of the Camaro was a spoiled, rich little miss whose parents owned a large pontoon boat used mainly for fishing and parties. He had stopped the girl twice last year to ask her to slow down while in the park area and she'd shaken and trembled and pretended penitence, looking under her lashes at her friends the whole while and garnering giggles for her performance. The last time he stopped her she had winked and licked her lips suggestively, still smiling at her friends. Eris wanted to shake her.

The men fishing below the dam were ready for him when he approached, and Eris spent the next half-hour checking licenses and making small talk. When he left the area he passed the old blue pickup on its way back to the cabin and lifted a finger in acknowledgment of Manuel Ortiz's wave.

Manuel Ortiz was cordial and respectful, and when he asked Eris for the latest boating guide summary the evening before, Eris had been only too happy to comply. He chalked up Ortiz's manners to being foreign born and gave him another five years before learning to demand rather than ask, like most Americans. One of the worst was Sherman Tanner, a year-round denizen who liked to stop Eris every chance he got and demand that an end be put to this and a stop be put to that and why didn't he do something since he was supposed to be some sort of law who carried a gun and everything.

Eris tried to tell him he wasn't that kind of law, not a community constable or a personal-security officer placed on the hill for the protection of Sherman and Gudrun Tanner from loud kids and obnoxious boaters. If he didn't like dealing with lakeside activity, then he shouldn't live by a lake. The digging fool.

The rest of Eris's day was spent in patrolling, putting miles on the truck and making occasional stops to talk to people. A new farmer had a problem with his pond; all the fish he had stocked the year before were now dead and floating on the surface. Eris took samples of the water for analysis and told him to keep the cows out. By the time he made it back to the reservoir it was nine-thirty and he was hungry and tired.

He put the truck in his own detached garage and stepped up to his back door to insert his key in the lock. He paused when he heard music. Not the music that frequently came from Briar's Cove or the bay area, but soft classical music.

Manuel Ortiz, he thought, and he opened his back door and let himself in the house. In the kitchen he opened a window so he could still hear the music while he fixed himself something to eat. He glanced up toward the cabin while he made himself another sandwich and through the open curtains in the cabin's living room saw Manuel and his wife, Jacqueline, slow dancing across the floor. Madeleine Heron sat on the front porch of the cabin, and in the light from the living room Eris saw her head in her hands.

Desolation came from her in waves, and Eris stood motionless while he watched, wondering why the impulse to go up there was so strong when he knew he would face nothing but rejection. Some kind of human response mechanism, he guessed.

He had to wonder about her. She obviously possessed no desire to be here, and yet she was here for the summer, Ortiz had said.

A broken marriage? he wondered. A tragic loss?

It was somewhat unusual, he figured, for a woman like her to be sequestered away in a cabin alone for the summer.

He wondered if she had any children.

Her head came up as he watched and she looked directly at his cabin. Eris knew she saw him standing in his kitchen in the dim glow of his fluorescent bulb. He made no move to turn away or to do anything but finish eating his sandwich over the sink, where he usually did his eating.

She watched him steadily for several minutes; then she surprised him by stepping off the porch and walking down the path toward his cabin.

Eris's first impulse was to turn off the light and refuse to open the door.

When no knock came, he was both relieved and curious. He walked into his darkened living room to look out the window and see where she had gone. When his eyes adjusted he saw her walking down the path to Briar's Cove and Vista Bay.

She was foolish to be out walking alone. The water was nearly a half-mile away; anything could happen during a nocturnal stroll in these parts. He would have to speak to Ortiz again and ask him to warn her about the strange people in the area.

Eris sat by the window for over an hour, waiting and watching for her to come back again. When he finally saw her top the hill, he sighed and began to unbutton his shirt. He had to get to bed.

CHAPTER
THREE

AN ODD SENSE OF panic set in Sunday night as Madeleine watched her sister and brother-in-law haul their suitcase out to the Jeep.

Don't leave me! she wanted to shout. *I've seen the Earthworm and last night just after dark I stumbled across a fat, middle-aged couple having sex on an air mattress in their front yard while two dogs sat wagging their tails and watching.*

She clamped her lips shut and said nothing. She would seem ungrateful beyond words if she opened her mouth now.

The moment they were gone she would take out her portable word processor and begin a series of letters begging every university in the Mississippi Valley for a grant. She was open and accessible, interested in other areas of anthropology, and she was still relatively young. There were many aspects of Native-American culture she could research without actually living among them again, though in truth she longed to do just that. It was courage she lacked. Her last experience was still fresh in her mind, and though Madeleine knew the only way to conquer her fears was to face them, she still felt she was not quite ready.

The unsightly Eris Renard made her feel even less ready. He reminded her of the worst of everything she had faced in her life, with the possible exception of her husband's suicide, and it didn't help that his black eyes were so still and watchful or that his mouth hardly moved even when he spoke. Madeleine lumped him in with the other people she had been exposed to thus far, and she found she preferred her hip, snotty college students to the population of Green Lake.

When Jacqueline and Manuel were ready to depart, they asked Madeleine for the hundredth time if there was anything she needed before they left. For the hundredth time, she told them she would be fine. There was gas in the old truck and groceries in the cabin. She was all set. She gave them what she hoped was a supremely confident smile and then went into the cabin and banged her head against the door when they left. Before the sound of their engine died away, she had her word processor out on the kitchen bar and was composing her first letter. She wrote three and had stuffed them in envelopes when she realized she had no stamps.

Muttering under her breath, she placed the envelopes in her purse. She had seen a tiny post office in the town of Green Lake. She would go there in the morning to post the letters and buy some stamps. The mailboxes for the cabins were all out on the road, built into a frame that held at least ten mailboxes. Madeleine's and Renard's mailboxes were separate from the others, but on a similar frame and hunched close together so that they resembled some odd squirrel feeder more than a pair of mailboxes.

Thinking of squirrels made Madeleine walk out to the porch to look at the tomato plants she had purchased that day from a woman at Diamond Bay. She enjoyed fresh tomatoes and knew she had to get the plants into the ground soon. She left the porch and walked around the cabin, finding plenty of good sun on the south side. The earth looked all right—not wonderful, but the plants would grow. Madeleine walked back to the garage to look for a spade or a hoe. Minutes later she came out again, shaking her head.

What on earth made her expect to find something as simple as a garden implement in the garage of a cabin by a lake?

Calling on her years of living with people who had to do without, she searched all around the cabin until she found a long, sharp rock suitable for digging. She carried the rock to the south side of the cabin and got down on her hands and knees to start.

She had been digging and turning earth for maybe ten minutes when she felt a pair of eyes on her. Her head came up and jerked toward the road, where she saw Sherman Tanner, the Earthworm, watching her with an expression of incredulity while holding onto the leash of a small multibreed dog.

"Is that a rock?" he asked from the road.

"Yes," said Madeleine.

"What are you doing?"

"Making a bed for my tomato plants. I have no spade."

Tanner's thin eyebrows disappeared beneath his yellow fishing hat. "Why don't you just borrow one? What are you, one of these survivalist nuts?"

Madeleine rose to her feet. "No, I'm not. But I am new here, and people usually aren't willing to loan something to a stranger."

"Well, Renard has one, I'm sure. You should have asked him. You really can't dig in this muck without a good spade or a shovel. Limestone here, clay there, it's a mess."

"Would you have a spade I could borrow?" asked Madeleine. "Or a shovel?"

"I really wouldn't feel good about that," said Tanner. "Ask Renard when he gets home."

Madeleine snorted and put her hands on her hips. "Did I miss something here? Weren't you the one who just suggested I borrow a spade?"

"From Renard, not me. My tools are my babies. I use them every day and don't ever let them out of my sight."

"So I've heard," muttered Madeleine.

"What?"

"You dig a lot," she said louder.

"Who told you that?"

"No one. I saw you myself yesterday."

"Oh, well. I was burying a hand I found in the water, but Renard made me dig it up again this morning and turn it over to him."

Madeleine stopped cold. "A hand? A human hand?"

"It floated right up to me while I was standing near the boat ramp at Vista Bay. I just knew it came from that skier who had a terrible accident last weekend. More than his hand was torn off, you know."

"How . . . did it happen?" Madeleine asked.

"Two boaters didn't see each other, or were too drunk to care. Happens occasionally. Once Gudrun and I found an entire arm in the water. They wouldn't let us keep that either."

"Why did you want to bury it?" asked Madeleine, almost afraid to hear the answer.

Tanner shrugged. "Kind of symbolic, don't you think? A hand or an arm buried in your yard, always pointing."

Madeleine forced herself into a nod. "Well," she said, "I'd better get back to work here, before I lose my light."

Sherman Tanner looked at the fading sun and gave a tug on his dog's leash. "Craziest thing I've ever seen, digging in the ground with a rock."

"No crazier than you," Madeleine murmured as she sank back to the ground.

"What's that?"

"I said have a good day."

Tanner eyed her, then said, "Not much of this one left. Do I take it you'll be staying around here awhile?"

"For a while," Madeleine answered.

"All right, then."

Tanner said nothing further, merely continued walking his dog up to the turnoff where the old cemetery lay. Madeleine felt as if she had just been given permission to exist by the wiry, suspicious-eyed Tanner.

Who did he think he was? she wondered. Keeper of the hill?

By the time he returned with his dog, Madeleine was carrying her tomato plants back to the three holes she had made. She felt Tanner's eyes on her as she placed the plants in the holes and began to fill in around them. When she could take it no more she paused in what she was doing and turned to stare at him. He quickly averted his gaze and pretended to be looking at the other side of the road. Madeleine sniffed and went on filling in with dirt. Nutty old bird. Burying human hands and arms. What was wrong with him?

She had tamped the earth down and was watering each plant when she heard the sound of a pickup truck skid to a halt right in front of the cabin. Madeleine hurried around the side of the cabin in time to see a door of the truck's cab open and somebody toss something into her yard.

"Hey!" Madeleine yelled, and the driver of the truck threw rocks and gravel as he floored the accelerator.

Madeleine squinted in the growing dusk and just barely made out the license plate. Then she walked to see what in the name of Adolph Coors had been thrown in her yard.

She heard them before she saw them. No beer cans these, but three tiny kittens, each one round-eyed and mewling in terror, making their way across the lawn.

"Dammit," said Madeleine as she stared at the small felines. Two were gray-striped and one was black.

Disgusted with the people in the truck, Madeleine gathered the kittens against her shirt and took them up to the porch. There was a large box in the garage that had once held Manuel's small satellite dish, and Madeleine placed the kittens in the box with two towels and a big bowl of milk. Then she went into the kitchen to write down the tag number and pen a note to Eris Renard.

He came home while she was slipping the note inside his screen door, and he looked inquiringly at her as he got out of the truck. He appeared tired, which made him look even more forbidding to Madeleine. She backed away and held up the note.

"Two people in a pickup came and dumped some kittens in my yard. I got the tag number."

"Good," said Renard, and he approached her to take the note. Madeleine had to steel herself not to jump away.

Renard sensed her stiffening. He stopped and held out his hand, palm up. Madeleine dropped the note in his hand and he turned to open his door. She shifted behind him.

"The kittens are on my porch in a box."

He glanced over his shoulder at her but said nothing.

"You can pick them up anytime," said Madeleine.

He looked at her again, and one brow lifted. "Would tomorrow morning suit you, Miss Heron?"

Madeleine noted his irritation and responded coolly, "Tomorrow morning will do just fine, Mr. Renard."

He nodded and pushed open his door. Madeleine ambled up to the cabin and heard the scratching and scrabbling of three tiny pairs of claws trying to climb their way out of the box. She went inside and made herself some supper, and by the time she was ready for bed, the cries of the kittens were driving her crazy. She went out to the porch and scooped them up to bring them inside with her. She used a shoebox and some gravel from Jacqueline's terrarium as a litter box and issued a stern warning to the kittens before she climbed into bed. Their bellies plump with canned tuna, the kittens sat down on the end of the queen-sized bed to clean themselves. The feel of one rough little tongue on her big toe made Madeleine sigh, and for the last time that day she asked herself just what the hell she had gotten into. Dirt diggers, dumped kittens, mean-mouthed neighbors and buried hands always pointing. Pointing at *what*?

CHAPTER FOUR

ERIS STOPPED BY THE log cabin on his way out the next morning and got out of his truck to pick up the box of kittens on the front porch. He paused when he saw nothing inside but a bowl and two towels. He thought of knocking on the door, but it was early yet, so he walked back to his truck and climbed inside. He would stop by during lunch and pick up the kittens.

It was a point in her favor that she got the tag number. Most people wouldn't be so alert. Eris had the piece of paper she had given him in his pocket. As far as he was concerned, the people who dumped the animals were no better than criminals and would be treated as such.

Before he made it down the hill he spotted something on the lake that made him curse and step hard on the truck's accelerator. A boat was on fire, the people inside moving frantically away from the black plumes of smoke that billowed from the engine and rose high in the morning sky. Eris radioed the location of the boat to the nearby lake office of the Department of Wildlife and Parks and learned another crisis was unfolding. A young father had taken his three daughters fishing before dawn and returned with only two of them. The smallest of the girls had wandered off somewhere in the dark and was now missing from the dam-site area.

"How old is she?" Eris asked into the mike.

"Just turned three," came the answer.

Eris exhaled and asked what she was wearing.

"Yellow sweatsuit and a blue windbreaker. Blonde hair and blue eyes. Her name is Kayla Michelle Lyman. Dale Russell showed up this morning and took a boat out. He's over there right now. I'll radio him about the fire and tell him you're on your way."

Eris replaced his mike and pushed the truck forward, wondering what went on in the minds of men who took little three-year-old girls out near a dam site when it was still dark and then took their eyes away for even one second. There was no telling what had happened to her.

Dale looked relieved when Eris arrived at the dam site and got out of his truck.

"Shit's started early this year," Dale muttered in greeting, and the thick-chested, dark-haired officer was only too happy to take his boat out and check on the fire, while Eris was left to deal with the frightened parents and siblings of the missing little girl. The girls began to cry when Eris said hello to them. The mother moved protectively near her children, while the father stuck his hands in his pockets and said, "What're you gonna do?"

"Bring in some more people and begin a search. Where was she the last time you saw her?"

The man pointed. "Right there on the bank with her sisters. They weren't payin' any attention and didn't see her wander off. I was castin' over there toward the dam and wasn't lookin' at her, either. Where you gonna get more people? You talkin' about the State Patrol?"

Eris was thinking more along the lines of the Lions Club group partying at the shelter on Diamond Bay. There were dozens of men in the group, good Samaritans every one, and he could have them here within the hour. He walked back to the truck and radioed his plans to the lake office, then he placed himself behind the wheel and told the family to stay put. He would be right back.

"Keep yelling her name," he suggested as he backed the truck out.

The mother and father exchanged a glance and Eris could see he hadn't given them much hope. He was doing what he could, the same plan the sheriff's deputies would implement once they arrived.

As expected, the Lions Club group was only too happy to come and help search for the little girl. They came out in droves, half of them in boats and several on jet skis and four-wheelers. Eris drew a grid for them and showed where to begin the search. The father joined in and the mother took her two other daughters back to their campsite to wait. Dale Russell returned after towing the burned boat to shore and writing up the owner for not having a fire extinguisher on board. No one was hurt, but the boat was in bad shape.

Russell joined the other boaters in the water to search and Eris coordinated the groups on land. By six o'clock that evening the searchers were tired, hungry, and losing hope fast. The father of the girl finally lost control and sat down on the ground and cried. Several tried to comfort him, but his sobs went on and on, as if a valve had been turned on somewhere inside him and the pain was running as thick and hot as the blood in his veins. When darkness came he was silent and still and watched with dull eyes as the weary volunteers drifted off to their campsites. The sheriff's deputies had arrived to officially begin their search. Divers would be brought in at dawn the next day, as well as a trained dog.

Eris took the father back to his campsite and stayed with him a few minutes. The motor home in use was at least twenty years old, with rust spots and what looked like tar adorning the surface. Wet clothes hung on a makeshift clothesline made out of rope and tied between two trees. The two little girls eyed Eris warily as he approached with their father. The wife, apparently blaming her husband for losing their little girl, refused to speak to her man. She gave Eris an apple and thanked him for doing what he could. He assured her the search was not over, and that dawn would see more teams at work. She thanked him again, her voice small and quiet, and Eris left them to return and go over the continuing activities with the deputies.

"Damned stupid, you ask me," said one of them. "I got a three-year-old, and I ain't even thought about takin' him fishin' yet."

"They have any more kids?" a deputy asked Eris.

"Two girls," he answered.

"Besides the one that's missing?"

"Yeah."

"Well, hell, they still got two, then, don't they? That's something."

We're not talking about sheep or cows here, Eris wanted to say; instead he turned on his heel and walked to his truck. His stomach was growling fiercely, and he reached for the apple the missing little girl's mother had given him. He took a bite and started the truck's engine, wondering if he had anything in the house to eat. He hadn't been to the store in two weeks, and his shelves were as empty as his refrigerator. He had eaten the last of his sandwich meat last night.

At home he had just stepped out of his truck when he heard Sherman Tanner calling to him. He looked over his shoulder and saw the reedy Tanner hurrying up the hill, jerking his little dog along behind him. Eris drew a breath and stood to face his neighbor.

"Did you find her?" Tanner asked.

Eris didn't have to ask how Tanner knew. Tanner always seemed to know. Eris suspected he had a radio tucked away in his cabin somewhere.

"No, we didn't find her."

"Three years old?"

"Yes."

"Tragic," said Tanner with a tsking sound. "Just tragic. How are the parents holding up?"

"As well as can be expected, Mr. Tanner. Please excuse me."

"Going back out again tomorrow?"

"The search will continue, yes. Goodnight, Mr. Tanner."

"All right, then," said Tanner, and he grudgingly turned to make his way down the hill again.

Eris went inside and headed for the kitchen, where he spied a carton of eggs in the back of the refrigerator and found four eggs intact inside.

He ate the eggs scrambled while standing over the stove, and when the skillet was clean he dragged himself into the shower and scrubbed away at the insanity of the day. The warm spray was soothing, but did little to erase the memory of the father's loud, aching sobs or the mother's haunted eyes.

As he turned off the water Eris suddenly froze as what sounded like a cry reached his ears. He waited, holding his breath, trying to hear it again. His long black hair dripped water down his back and over his shoulders as he stood listening. When it came again he snatched up his briefs from the floor and hurriedly stepped into them before jerking open the bathroom door and heading for the living room. He rushed out the front door and promptly fell face first over a box sitting on his porch. He stubbed his toe hard enough to bleed and scraped both knees on the hard concrete edge of his porch before falling off into the grass.

"Shit," he hissed in pain. Then he heard the mewing of the kittens in the box. The cries he had imagined.

"Sorry," said a nearby voice, and Eris jerked as he realized Madeleine Heron was standing to one side of the porch and looking at him.

She didn't sound sorry.

"I thought I'd bring them to you," she said, and the unspoken part was: *since you didn't come and get them.*

Eris got off the ground and tried not to hobble onto the porch. His big toe was covered with blood and his knees stung. "I came by this morning but they weren't in the box," he told her through gritted teeth.

"I had them in the house with me. I'd like to, but I can't keep them. I can't afford to feed them."

"Will you keep them one more day?" Eris asked as he sat down to look at his toe. His wet hair fell across his face and he pushed it back again. "I can't get to them tomorrow. I'll be busy elsewhere."

"The missing little girl?"

Eris looked up from the attempt to examine his toe in the darkness. "How did you hear?"

"I went to the post office at Green Lake today. A woman inside was talking to another woman. They heard about it from the wives of two of the Lions Club members out searching."

Eris made a face as he pulled away a piece of loose flesh. Half his damned toe had been shredded. Wearing a shoe tomorrow was going to be a test in pain tolerance.

"I'll come and get the kittens as soon as I can," he said as he got to his feet once more, and it was only then he realized he was wearing nothing but a pair of briefs. He quickly looked at her, but she appeared undisturbed by his state of undress. He turned to the box with a jerky movement and felt his wet hair cover his face once more. He tossed it back and saw droplets land on her cheeks. She calmly wiped them away and held out her hands for the box.

"If you find something else to do with them before I get to it, feel free," said Eris.

"Like what? Drowning them in the lake? I thought you had somewhere to take them, like a nearby animal shelter, otherwise I would never have bothered you with this."

When he made no immediate reply, she dropped her hands and said, "Well? Do you have somewhere to take them or not?"

Her apparent exasperation angered him, and he chose not to respond to her. Favoring his injured and still bleeding toe, he turned and went inside the house, closing the door firmly behind him.

He heard what sounded like an unladylike snort and a muttered utterance of some sort before she turned to carry the box up to the log cabin.

Like he didn't have enough to worry about without her selfishly dumping kittens on him that had been dumped on her. There was a county animal shelter, but he wouldn't have time to deal with it tomorrow. He had other items on his agenda to worry over, things these people appeared too stupidly cruel to care about. Sherman Tanner was bad enough, but now to have Madeleine Heron looking down her straight white nose at him.

For the first time since his arrival, Eris considered finding another place to live. Somewhere away from other people, like he had dreamed as a youth. He had chosen the job of conservation officer because of the time spent alone. Most days he spent hours by himself, speaking only to those he stopped for a license or permit check. Summer on the lake was different, and as Dale Russell said, the shit had started early this year.

Eris looked down as he made it to the bathroom and he cursed loudly when he realized the blood from his toe was dripping on the floor and making large blots on the rug. He had probably left a trail all the way from the front door.

The thought of a trail yanked his thoughts back to the coming day. He took disinfectant and bandages out of the cabinet and sat down on the toilet lid to doctor the toe, telling himself the pain he was feeling was nothing compared to what a certain mother and father were going through that night.

It couldn't be.

CHAPTER FIVE

RONNIE LYMAN AND HIS wife Sheila sat on lawn chairs and looked at each other. Ronnie was drinking his last beer, so he took his time sipping out of the can and holding the beer in his mouth before he swallowed. When it was gone, Ronnie tossed the can behind his back and wiped his mouth with the rolled-up sleeve of his work shirt. Sheila got up when she heard a whimper from one of her sleeping girls; then she came and sat down again in the lawn chair next to Ronnie.

"You think she's all right?" she asked.

"Yeah, I'm pretty sure."

"I know she's missin' us. You know how she is."

"She'll be okay."

"Your mama doesn't always eat right. I hope she remembers to feed her regular."

"She'll feed her."

"You sure no one saw?"

"Kelsey and Kendra didn't see, did they?"

"No. But I feel bad about scarin' 'em. Don't you?"

"Better'n havin' 'em blow it for us, ain't it?"

"I guess. How come no one came out today?"

" 'Cause the law keeps these things quiet as long as they can, so no nuts'll come out and claim they got her or anything. Somebody'll be out tomorrow, just you wait and see."

Sheila sat and thought about that as the cool night air brought goose pimples to her bare arms. She looked at her husband and wondered about asking him to shave, since they were going to be on TV and everything. Ronnie was looking pretty grungy lately, and she was out of shampoo herself. Last night she had used a bar of ivory soap on the girls' hair, but couldn't get Ronnie to wash his thinning, reddish blond mess.

"Who?" she asked finally. "Who d'you think'll come? Think they'll send the gal from channel twelve?"

"Maybe. Her or that other guy, the one with the hair that sticks out on both sides."

"I don't remember everything you said to say," said Sheila.

"You will," Ronnie told her. "I'll be right there."

"But what if they come while you're out lookin'? You gotta go out and look again, Ronnie. Wouldn't seem right if you didn't."

"Yeah, you're right. Well, if I ain't there, just remember to say that you never thought times could get much worse for us. Say your husband done got laid off, you lost your house 'cause we couldn't make payments, and now we lost our little girl."

"What about our campin' permit? Should I say somethin' about that? About how our twenty-eight days is up tomorrow, and how we just can't leave until we found our little girl?"

"Yeah, you better tell about that. How we been livin' out here and makin' do as long as the park'd let us."

"Should I say how we come here from doin' the same thing at Toronto Lake? And Cheney Lake before that?"

"Nah, better not. It'd make us look bad. We ain't no white trash, we're just tryin' to get by the best we can."

"What if—"

"Sheila, don't start with that again. Ain't no one goin' to find out if you keep your mouth shut. We'll get on TV and tell our story, and maybe somebody'll start a fund for us or somethin'. Next Tuesday or so, maybe Wednesday, Mom'll drop Kayla off at that bait shop up there on the access road, then she'll light out and we'll have our darlin' little baby back. Hell, maybe even more people'll send money once we get her back, you never know. We just gotta make it sound as awful as we can and look like we're hurtin' real bad, make a lot a folks feel sorry for us. Hell, I nearly puked today, cryin' so hard."

Sheila's chest lifted with a troubled sigh. "That Indian already feels sorry for us. The game warden? Made me feel so bad I give him an apple."

"I saw it. We got any more?"

"Two." Sheila was silent a moment, then said, "Ronnie, what if Kayla says somethin'? You know they're gonna wanna talk to her."

"Me and Mom worked it all out. She's tellin' Kayla what to say when people talk to her. She'll say a man took her and then let her go."

"A man?"

"Yeah, you know. A pervert, or somethin'."

"What?"

"Well, who else would take a little girl?"

"Why didn't you just say a couple took her? A couple who couldn't have babies and wanted a little child of their own?"

Ronnie looked at her in exasperation. "Why would they bring her back?"

Sheila tossed her stringy brown hair and raised a hand. "I don't know. Maybe because she still wets the bed and they want one who doesn't."

"That's the stupidest goddamned thing I ever heard," said Ronnie. "Get in the trailer and go to bed before you piss me off. You ain't gonna blow this for me, damn you."

"I ain't gonna blow anything, Ronnie. I'm just scared about doin' somethin' like this. I know you said it ain't really illegal, but it still feels wrong to have all these folks so scared for us."

Ronnie gave his wife a shove. "Go on to bed. We ain't gonna talk about this no more. I told you what to do and you'll do it, you hear?"

"Don't get mad again, Ronnie. I didn't mean anything but that I'm nervous."

"I didn't hit you, I just gave you a little push. Now get in there," Ronnie warned, and from the redness of his eyes, Sheila knew to start moving. She wouldn't mess with him now, not when he was under so much pressure to be something he wasn't.

CHAPTER SIX

MADELEINE LAY IN BED that night thinking of the scars she had seen on Eris Renard's chest, back, and shoulders. She had seen skin like his before. Sometime in adolescence Renard had contracted chicken pox, and the itchy, erupting pustules had scarred the flesh of his face and upper torso. She thought of the pain he must have suffered, the agony of adolescent angst, and felt ashamed of herself for being so hateful to him when he did his best to be polite and civil toward her.

She was in such a state she didn't know what she was doing. Already she was dying of boredom and anxiety and cursing herself for believing a jobless, rent-free summer had been the thing to do. All day she had fought against thinking about Sam, and all day she had failed. Over and over she saw the hole in the wall and the clotted blood that stained the carpet and had to be cut out.

She didn't know why she was thinking about him. The guilt still stung her, and the traumatic memory of finding him dead kept her eyes open on many nights. But more and more she found herself growing angry when she thought about him. Angry at him for his weakness, and his petulant attitude about his lost job. People lost jobs all the time, and most didn't look at it as a personal judgment of their worth as a human being. Sam had been unable to accept the fact that he was no longer wanted as an employee. The rejection was so completely alien to him that it had injured his entire concept of himself, and left Madeleine struggling to hold together the pieces of his shattered ego, all for the sake of a marriage she had been reluctant to enter into in the first place.

"Ouch!" She shot up in bed as one of the kittens began kneading her leg with its claws. She plucked him away and rubbed at the flesh of her thigh. The other two kittens were curled up on the bed at her feet. Madeleine placed the awake kitten with the others and got up to go to the living area and turn on the television. She flipped through channels on the remote for a moment, then put it down and went to look outside. The waxing moon was bright in the cloudless night. She thought she saw movement in the old cemetery and she jumped and squinted, trying to see.

There it was again. Someone was moving around just beyond the gate.

Just as Madeleine was about to go to the phone, she recognized the yellow fishing hat atop the skulker's head.

What on earth was Tanner doing?

She was tempted to go out and see, but common sense told her it was best to steer clear of weirdos in the moonlight.

Besides which, Renard had looked exhausted again that evening and would doubtlessly resent being disturbed for so trivial a reason as Tanner.

Madeleine thought of Renard sitting on the front porch in his briefs, trying to look at his bloody big toe, and had to smile. Renard was on the slender side, and while he was bent over with his wet hair in his face, he had reminded her of a ceremonial dancer, and of the many nearly naked men she had witnessed on numerous occasions while living among various Native-American tribes. It made her feel close to him, and at the same time it irritated her for the other memories he inspired.

The man who had ridden on her back and whipped her with a stick she would never forget. Never.

But thinking about him was almost worse than thinking about Sam, so she turned abruptly from the window and looked at the television again.

Five minutes later she clicked off the TV and went back to bed, stroking each of the kittens before she laid back and closed her eyes.

THE NEXT MORNING SHE awakened to the ringing of the telephone, and she hurried out of bed to snatch up the receiver, afraid the caller would hang up before she could reach it.

"Hello?"

"I'm at the grocery store," said a familiar deep voice. "What kind of cat food do I buy?"

"Renard?"

"I don't have long. I have to get back. What kind do you want?"

Madeleine started to tell him no thanks, she would get her own cat food if she got any at all. Then she thought of the last can of tuna and the three furry babies who kept her company in the big bed and said, "Anything with tuna in it. They love tuna."

"All right. I'll drop it off when I get back."

"Thank you," said Madeleine, but he had already hung up. She made a face at the phone and it rang again almost immediately, causing her to start and stare for half a second. Finally she picked up the receiver, and she was relieved to hear her sister's voice wish her a cheery good morning.

"Jacqueline," she said, pleased to hear from her.

"How's it going so far? Okay?"

"It's fine. I'm fine. Give me a while and I'll tell you more."

"You're not scared, are you? To be by yourself?"

"No. Not really."

"That's good. I was worried you might be after hearing about that missing little girl. I heard it on the radio this morning on the way to work."

"Really?"

"Bad news travels. Is our neighbor out looking for her?"

Madeleine's mouth twisted. "At the moment he's out buying cat food."

"He doesn't have a cat."

"No, but we do. Three kittens, dumped in our yard courtesy of a noisy rumbling pickup and two good ole boys."

"You're kidding."

"I'm not. Is it all right? Can I keep them awhile?"

"Of course. Manny loves cats. Are they cute?"

"Two feisty tiger-striped and one black."

"Company for you," Jacqueline observed. "Why is Renard out buying food for them?"

"It's a long story."

"He's quite the reserved gentleman, isn't he?"

"I suppose he is, yes."

"Uh-oh," said Jacqueline. "I don't like the sound of that. What's happened?"

"Nothing."

"You're sure? You get along all right?"

"The man is always gone, Jacqueline."

"Have you seen the other one yet?"

"The other one?"

"The other conservation officer. The handsome one."

"No, I haven't," admitted Madeleine. "But I haven't been out much. Just to the post office."

"Well, go down to Vista Bay and sit yourself down by the swimming beach. Sooner or later he'll cruise by and you'll get a look at him."

"Jacqueline," Madeleine began in a hesitant voice. "I'm not really interested in looking at anyone right now, if you know what I mean."

"I'm sorry," Jacqueline said quickly. "I didn't realize. I was just gabbing."

"I know. Don't apologize. It's just too soon for me to think in those terms."

"I know it is, Mad. I won't say any more. Have you thought of anything for me to bring this weekend?"

"A gross of paperbacks," said Madeleine, only half joking.

"Can do," Jacqueline said, and then she had to go. "See you Friday night."

" 'Bye," said Madeleine, sorry the conversation was over.

She showered and washed her hair, brushed her teeth and dressed in a white blouse and shorts, and was slipping into her sandals when she saw Eris Renard come to the door with a sack in his hands.

"Good morning," she said, and opened the screen door.

He nodded and handed her the sack. Inside were a dozen tall cans of cat food. Madeleine blinked and looked at him. "You want me to keep them, I guess."

"They were on sale," said Renard, and he turned away from her to step off the porch.

"How's the toe this morning?" asked Madeleine, determined to be cordial.

"Sore," he said, and kept walking.

"Thanks for the cat food," she said, and he tipped his hat without looking at her.

Madeleine muttered something under her breath about his surliness and allowed the screen door to slam shut.

Eris Renard didn't notice. He climbed in his truck and took off down the road again, his eyes straight ahead.

Gone to join the search again, Madeleine told herself, and for a moment she imagined the terror a young child might feel, or the child's mother, under such circumstances. The sense was too much like the horror she had found with Sam, and Madeleine forced her thoughts away from such morbidity.

The kittens gobbled up half a can of cat food from a paper plate, and when they were finished, Madeleine put them outside in the yard in hopes they would relieve themselves outdoors rather than in the shoebox, which was already beginning to stink. She needed to get into town and find a litter box, she decided as she herded the kittens into the grass.

Sherman Tanner was walking by with his dog at the time, and Madeleine saw the small canine leap and nearly strangle himself at the end of his leash to get at the tiny kittens. Tanner, his lip curled, picked up his little dog and went on his way.

Madeleine made a face at his retreating figure and thought once more about his moonlight trip to the cemetery. She really should have told Renard, but she had the feeling he was now lumping her in with all the other residents in Briar's Cove and labeling her a nuisance right along with Sherman Tanner.

Curious to see if the man was going back to the cemetery, Madeleine looked up to the road again. She saw no sign of Tanner. The next moment she was up and walking in that direction, telling herself a little investigating was in order.

The cemetery was indeed old, and most of the stones were unreadable. Many looked as if there had never been any writing on them at all, and Madeleine wondered suddenly if she was standing in some sort of potter's field, where the sinners, misfits, and outcasts were buried. She walked slowly across the grassy plots, looking for signs of recently overturned earth. She couldn't imagine what else the Earthworm would be doing in a graveyard at night.

A trip around the entire cemetery turned up no evidence of digging, and Madeleine puckered her brow as she scoured the surrounding area. Nothing. Just a cemetery full of very old bones and lots of weathered stones.

"But what a strange place to find a cemetery," she said aloud as she looked in the direction of the lake. From what she understood, the lake had been constructed sometime in the mid to late forties. Most every readable stone was much older, so all of the people buried in the ground beneath her had probably lived, farmed and died on land now covered by the waters of the lake.

She heaved a sigh and then sucked in her stomach to slip through the gate again. At the cabin she gathered up the kittens and put them inside before reaching for the keys to the truck and her purse.

As she drove by the dam site she saw what looked like a hundred people milling around the area. She and her truck were scrutinized by several sheriff's deputies, which caused Madeleine to blink and hurry on. She saw Renard's truck, but he was nowhere in sight. There were television remote vans from every local affiliate squeezed into the area, and people walked around trailing wires and fighting the sudden breeze that had kicked up earlier. The place was a circus.

She drove down the road to Green Lake and was disgusted to find no litter boxes and no cat litter at either of the two small grocers' establishments. She was cheerfully given directions to Fayville, and told to try Rob's IGA. Madeleine made the drive to Fayville and took advantage of the larger store to buy a thick paperback and a newspaper, which she missed reading. She wondered if Renard had access to one and decided to ask him the next time she saw him. It would be no trouble for him to bring it home with him. He could leave it on his porch for her.

She poked through the store as long as she could, and then left to poke through the town, larger than Green Lake, but still no bigger than a pothole in the road. She stopped at a place that called itself a crafts shop and got out to look at what other bored, lonely women did with their time. She was awed by the time-consuming work that had obviously gone into each item: needle-point, crocheted doilies, quilts, afghans, teddy bears, bunnies, wood projects, silk and dried flower arrangements; and she shook her head knowing she could never do anything similar.

Little had changed really, since the Victorian era, she found herself thinking. Women still concerned themselves with beau-tifying their surroundings, while men concerned themselves with staying unconcerned.

She left the crafts shop and climbed into her truck to return to the reservoir. The circus at the dam site was still in progress, with dozens of onlookers come now to stand around and talk about what the television people looked like in person. How much taller this one was, or how much thinner, and how bad their skin looked up close without all that makeup.

Renard's truck was gone, with an official-looking Bronco in its place. Madeleine kept her foot firmly on the accelerator as she passed, and found herself hoping the little girl was all right. The odds were not good, she knew, and the more time that passed, the worse the odds became.

She closed her eyes briefly and felt her stomach roll at the sudden image of Sherman Tanner, standing on a dock some-where and eagerly scanning the lake's surface for a small, float-ing body.

Ugh.

To punctuate the thought, the truck she was driving suddenly sputtered and died, leaving her staring incredulously at the dash and fighting to get the thing over to the side of the bridge. She tried the starter again and again, looking at the gas gauge, the oil light, and temperature gauge, but still the truck wouldn't start.

"Dammit," she swore as she threw open the door and slammed her way out of the truck. She walked to the front and raised the hood, not knowing what she was doing, but thinking someone would stop once they saw it.

Someone did stop.

There were three of them in the Blazer, and all of them got out when the driver pulled up behind Madeleine's truck. They were young, dressed in baggy jeans and dirty T-shirts, and two of them wore beards and cowboy hats, while the third wore a baseball cap pulled down low over his eyes.

"Engine trouble, ma'am?" said the man in the baseball cap.

"Yes," she said and stood away as the three of them came up to crowd around the raised hood. None of them were looking at the engine, she noticed.

"You want us to check it out for you?"

"If you would, please," she said; then, "Are you part of the search party for the missing little girl?"

She hoped to take their attention off her bare legs.

"Yes, ma'am, we were for a while, but we give it up when they found that windbreaker in the water. They ain't gonna find her. Not till she washes up somewhere. Me and the boys was on our way back to the boat. Figure to get some skiing in before the day's over."

He leaned over the engine and began touching things, starting with the carburetor. The others watched, and one of them snickered and said something about a new transmission. Madeleine's brow dipped. She was beginning to feel uncomfortable.

"Been out here long?" one of the bearded men asked.

"No. It happened just before you arrived."

"Your lucky day," said the other bearded man. "Or ours."

"Ma'am," said the one in the baseball cap, and he gestured for her to come and stand beside him. Madeleine forced herself to move as naturally as possible. When she was beside him, he slipped an arm across her shoulder and said, "Look here, you see this valve here?"

Madeleine attempted to shrug off his arm. "Yes, I see it."

He tightened his grip. "And this float thing here?"

"Yes," she said through clenched teeth. Her nostrils wanted to pinch shut at the smell of alcohol coming from him.

"You gotta whack the shit out of it ev'ry once in a while, 'cause gas'll get it cruddy and make the float stick and really fuck up everything. Now, I ain't sure that's what's happened here right now, but I'm just telling you so you'll know, okay?"

"Please let go of me," said Madeleine, and at the sound of her voice, the two bearded men moved closer, both of them grinning.

"Let go? Shit, I was just gonna ask if you wanted to come partying with me and the boys on our boat. What do you say? Come with us now and we'll pick up the truck later."

"Let go," Madeleine repeated. "I'm not going anywhere with you."

She attempted to wrench herself away from him, and he laughed and snatched her by the arm.

"Hey, now don't get upset. The last time I fucked anything like you I was twelve and she was paid. We just thought you might like to come and party with us."

"*Let go of me!*" Madeleine shouted right in his face, and he lifted an arm as if to smack her, but she ducked and threw herself away from him, right into the path of an oncoming truck.

Renard hit the brakes and Dale Russell was out of the passenger door before Eris could throw the truck into park. Russell picked Madeleine up out of the road and asked her if she was all right. Her entire body trembled as she pointed at the dead truck.

"I broke down. I thought they were going to help me, but they tried to make me go with them. He wouldn't let go of me when I asked."

Russell placed her beside the CO truck and walked after Renard, who was already towering over the man in the baseball cap.

"We stopped to help her and she came on to us, man."

"That's a lie!" Madeleine yelled.

Renard said something low to the man, something Madeleine couldn't hear, and he took off his sunglasses as he said it, so the man could look at his eyes.

The drunken man smirked, snorted, and began to back away from Renard. Within minutes, the men were in the Blazer and speeding off across the bridge. Russell walked back to Madeleine, while Renard bent over to examine her truck.

"What did he say to them?" she asked.

"Just threatened them with arrest. My name is Dale Russell." He offered his hand to Madeleine and she shook it, thinking this had to be the one her sister kept going on about. He was definitely handsome. Hazel eyes a shade darker than her own, wavy brown hair, a broad chest, and narrow hips.

"Madeleine Heron," she said. "Glad to meet you."

"Likewise, though the circumstances could have been better."

"I was ready to panic," Madeleine confessed. "There was no telling what might have happened if you and Renard hadn't come along."

Russell looked surprised. "You know Renard?"

"He's my neighbor."

"So you're staying in a cabin then?"

"I am. It belongs to my sister and her husband. They come up weekends, but I'm here for the summer."

"Lucky Renard," said Russell, smiling again to show the compliment was an honest one.

Madeleine looked away from him to see Renard glance at them from behind his dark glasses. She left Russell and walked over to him. "Can you see the problem?"

"Yes," he said.

For some reason, Madeleine didn't think he was talking about the truck.

"Well?" she said, when he didn't elaborate. "What's wrong with it?"

"Fuel filter," he said. "I've got one in the truck that should work."

"You carry an extra fuel filter?"

"It comes in handy."

"You can put it on right here?"

"We need to get the truck off the bridge."

"Of course," Madeleine said, and smarted at having been made to feel stupid.

"What did you say to those men?" she asked.

Renard finally turned to look at her. "Go to my truck and pull the seat down. The fuel filter is in a plainly marked box behind the seat. Bring it to me, please."

She returned to the truck and heard Russell talking on the radio to someone. He smiled at her and leaned away when she reached in to get at the seat. Madeleine looked at him and was surprised at herself. A few short months ago she would have been pleased to be smiled at so warmly by such a handsome man. Today she felt as if her answering smile was forced.

"This it?" she said as she returned to Renard.

He looked up and nodded, then took the box from her fingers and placed it beside him while he concentrated on what he was doing.

"Your toe still sore?"

"Yes."

"The kittens enjoyed the food this morning."

"Good."

"Did they really find the little girl's windbreaker today?"

He glanced at her. "In the water."

"Those men told me. They said they were part of the search."

"Maybe," said Renard with a grunt.

"Do you get a daily paper?" she asked.

"In the mail," he said.

"Would you mind sharing it with me? It seems strange not to get a paper."

He nodded and continued with what he was doing. She glanced back over her shoulder and saw Russell still on the radio. He was laughing now.

"You can go back and wait with him if you like," said Renard.

Madeleine looked at him. "I'm fine just watching. About the paper, you could leave it on the porch in the morning if you like, or in the evening, whenever you're finished with it."

Renard breathed out through his nose and looked at her. "Miss Heron, has anyone ever told you how demanding you can be?"

"Demanding?" she said in surprise.

"Put the paper on your porch in the morning?"

"Not *my* porch," she said quickly. "*Your* porch. I can walk down and take it off your porch. I would never ask you to walk up and put the paper on my porch."

"Wouldn't you?"

Madeleine stood back, angry beyond belief. "How much do I owe you for the fuel filter?"

"Two dollars."

This made her even angrier. To think that she had broken down, nearly been assaulted, and gone through all this insult for a two-dollar auto part nearly made her spit. She jerked the door of the truck open and dug in her purse for the two dollars.

He was wiping his hands on a rag when she approached and reached up to stuff the bills in the pocket of his shirt.

"Thank you so much for coming to my aid, Mr. Renard. In the future I promise to be less demanding. You can take your paper and shove it up—"

"Whoa, neighbors," said Russell, walking up in time to interrupt. His smile was broad as he looked at Madeleine and Renard. He clapped a hand on Renard's arm and said, "You're not letting this ugly old Indian get to you, are you?" he said jokingly to Madeleine.

"Not at all," she said.

"Good. You look like the quiet, cultured type. Mind if I ask your situation?"

Madeleine lifted her brows. "My situation?"

"What you do. Why you're here."

"I'm an ex-professor of anthropology," Madeleine answered. "As for why I'm here, well, I've been wondering that myself for the last three days."

She felt Renard look at her when she mentioned being an ex-professor, but he soon busied himself with finishing under the hood and getting in behind the wheel to try and start the truck.

"An anthropologist," said Russell with undisguised admiration. "I spotted that gleam of intelligence the moment I saw you."

"Lying in the middle of the road and screaming my head off?"

"The next moment then," said Russell, smiling his broad smile again.

Beside them, the truck's engine started and began to idle. Madeleine thanked Russell for his help and heard him say he looked forward to seeing her again, perhaps at the dance the following Thursday at Diamond Bay.

"A dance?" said Madeleine.

"A band comes in and sets up among the RV hookups. People get a chance to know each other and have some fun. You should come over."

"I'll consider it," said Madeleine.

"Good."

She turned away from him to find Renard holding the door of the truck open for her. She couldn't read his eyes behind the dark glasses, and she kept hers purposely expressionless.

Demanding, he had said.

"Thank you again for your assistance," she said, and watched as he did nothing to acknowledge her thanks. Not even a tip of the hat.

When she was on the seat and had her seatbelt on, he closed the door of the truck and walked away, back to his own truck. Russell gave her a final wave, and Madeleine nodded to him as she put the truck in gear and pulled away from the bridge.

On the way home she found herself thinking of the way Renard's mouth had twitched when Russell called him an "ugly old Indian." Madeleine didn't think he was necessarily ugly. It was the pits and scars that made his face appear so frightful. And neither was he old. It was difficult to tell, but she thought he was still under thirty.

Perhaps compared to Dale Russell, Eris Renard was ugly, but his better features were fated to be forever obscured by the proliferation of scars. Frequent exposure to him revealed a nice mouth with a perfect shape, though she had never seen him smile. His eyes, too, were striking, with long, thick lashes and curved black brows.

Madeleine experienced a strange spark when she saw his mouth twitch, and the urge to berate the handsome Dale Russell for his remark was strong. But she would only have embarrassed Renard by opening her mouth, and so she let it and all the anger she felt toward him pass.

Back at the cabin she fed the kittens another half can of food and watched as they snorted and sneezed and waded around on the plate. When they were finished, she got up and prepared their litterbox, placing it in the corner of what Jacqueline called the mudroom, where a miniature washer and dryer sat. One by one she showed each kitten the position of the litter box and placed them inside to sniff and scratch around. When she was satisfied they knew where to find it, she went into the kitchen to wash her hands and see about something to eat for herself.

She had left a chicken out to thaw earlier and was busy preparing it when she realized that up to now she had been joking and kidding with herself about being lonely, but suddenly it was no longer a joke. After only a few days on her own with no sister and no students and only a surly neighbor to talk to, she was ready to cry her eyes out.

"It's got to get better," she whispered to herself as she marinated the chicken in Italian dressing.

She thought of the dance next Thursday and wondered what her chances were of running into the three idiots who had accosted her that day. Or worse, of running into any of the neighbors she had met thus far.

She put the chicken in the oven and stuck some potatoes in the microwave to bake. She made a salad, some rolls, a steamer full of broccoli, and took out a cheesecake to thaw. In the back of her mind she knew she wasn't going to eat all of it herself, and when she saw Renard's truck pull in that evening she had the plate all ready. She carried the food down to his cabin and knocked on his door. His expression was one of irritated disbelief when he opened the door and saw her standing there. She could tell it was a struggle for him to resist shutting the door in her face.

"Is there a problem?"

She held up the plate. "In return for sharing your newspaper, I've brought you some supper."

He only looked at the plate before excusing himself. A moment later he returned and opened the door to hand a paper to her. He made no move to relieve her of the plate.

"I told you I would share the paper."

"Yes, and I'm sorry you mistook my meaning about how we would go about it."

There was no response, and as the silence lengthened Madeleine began to feel ridiculously stupid standing there with a complete chicken dinner in her hand and having it rejected by a man who was probably salivating at the sight of the tin foil.

"Take the food, Eris. Can't you see I'm trying to repay you for your kindnesses to me?"

His lids blinked at her use of his name. Still he said nothing, and still he made no move to take the plate.

She wanted to throw it at him, but instead she put it down at her feet and turned wordlessly away, clenching her teeth all the while and silently calling him every vile name she could think of. He wasn't about to make anything easy for her. He was probably still punishing her for their first meeting, and her initial response to him.

Fine. She could handle it. She had dealt with any number of mute, recalcitrant males in her time, and she could deal with this one. It might actually prepare her in a way for going back into the field. She needed all the help she could get for that.

CHAPTER SEVEN

ERIS SAT IN HIS recliner eating the meal Madeleine Heron had given him and had to fight to keep from wolfing it down. Everything tasted so good he was nearly drowning in the juices from his mouth and stomach. She had stacked the plate high with two of everything, and by the time he was finished he had to unfasten the top of his trousers.

He lay back in the recliner and let the food settle in his stomach while he tried to recall when last he had eaten so well. It had been a long time.

The plate sat on the porch about thirty seconds before the smell got to him. He was starving, as usual, and had been about to stick a frozen dinner into the microwave when she knocked on his door. The temptation to shut it in her face had been great, but that would mean she was getting to him, and if Sherman Tanner, the slimy Earthworm, didn't get to him, then no blonde-haired, aristocratic ex-professor of anthropology was going to get to him.

He thought of how large and dark her eyes had looked as she stood there on his porch. How small the wrists were that held the plate. She wasn't very big, but she could certainly be imposing. Her soft feminine features could go hard as rock in an instant, something the three jerks who had stopped for her that day found out. Eris had seen them around, had seen them out on their boat, and knew the way they liked to party. He despised manhandlers of women, and his threat to the three had reflected that fact. It wasn't what he said, particularly, but the way he used his size and his face to emphasize the point.

What happened afterward surprised him: her coming to the truck and attempting to chat with him instead of staying to talk with Dale Russell. Either she didn't care, or it was good strategy on her part. Eris had seen women do anything short of a back flip to get Dale Russell's attention. The younger girls were more his style, however, so Eris had been further surprised at his mention of the dance to Madeleine.

Not that he could blame Russell. Even while he tried to avoid her Eris found himself thinking about her flawless skin and unusual brown-green eyes. When he stood beside her he felt very tall and awkward and yes, ugly, though a part of him hated Russell for saying so. It was the same part that was envious.

Eris had had a girlfriend in college; she had graduated first in her class and was now an astrophysicist. He thought of her sometimes, mostly when he missed having someone to be with. The romance hadn't exactly been hot, but it had made both of them comfortable. Since then he had dated once or twice, but either he wasn't interested or she wasn't interested, and nothing had ever meshed. He thought he might one day again find someone to feel comfortable with, but he wasn't out there looking. When and if it happened, it would have to happen on its own.

He rubbed his eyes and left the recliner to go and take a shower. He took the band off his hair and let the water run over his scalp as he thought of Madeleine again. He had seen more of her in the last three days than he had seen of anyone in weeks. She was lonely, he guessed, and probably unused to being by herself. Things would be better for her on the weekend, when her sister came. She would leave Eris alone then and he could get back to worrying about drunken boaters, horny skiers, and missing, presumed-drowned little girls.

The next morning he took her plate and another newspaper up and left it on her front porch. He didn't see her that day, or that evening, but the next morning when he drove up and tossed his paper in her yard, he saw his mailbox hanging open. He looked in and found a brown paper sack with a sandwich, a banana, and a bag of peanut butter crackers inside.

For putting it on the porch anyway, the note in the sack read. Eris shook his head and put the sack beside him in the seat.

"It's in the yard now," he said as he drove away. He had some unsavory business to attend to that day. The parents of the missing little girl had used up every extension they were allowed, and the rules said they had to take their motor home and leave the park. Eris argued for special consideration and was denied. Rules were rules, and several goodwill shelters offered to take in the family since their plight aired on local television. Eris had to tell them to pick up and move along.

The Lymans did not take the news well. Ronnie Lyman's eyes reddened and his wife Sheila sat down and stared at the ground. The two little girls stopped playing and looked at Eris with round, fearful eyes, as if he were about to pounce on them.

"Your permit could be extended for three days only," said Eris. "I asked for longer, but they turned me down."

"We appreciate it," mumbled Sheila.

"Yeah," said Ronnie.

"You'll have to get your gear together and leave the park today."

Ronnie began to shake his head. "They don't understand. How can they make us leave when we don't know what happened to our little girl yet?"

"It's been several days, Mr. Lyman. People are still looking, but not as intensively as before. There is nothing you can do here. I understand that several shelters have offered space to you, and I suggest you take advantage. Wherever you go, you will know immediately the moment there is any news. You have my sympathies."

"It ain't right," said Ronnie. "It just ain't right, you kickin' us out like this. I'm goin' on TV again and tell 'em all about how the Department of Parks and Wildlife is kickin' us out of the park where our little girl got lost."

"You're free to do as you wish, Mr. Lyman," said Eris. "But take your family and leave the park today."

"Or what?" said Ronnie, his lower lip quivering with anger.

"Or I will arrest you and take your family to a shelter myself."

Ronnie could see Eris meant it. Ronnie struck a pose and whined, "I thought you were on our side, man."

Eris only looked at him.

Sheila swallowed and said, "we'd better start gettin' our stuff, Ronnie."

Ronnie snorted. "You start gettin' our stuff. I'm goin' to find a phone." He looked at Eris and said, "That all right with you, Tonto?"

Eris's mouth twitched. He nodded and then turned and walked back to his truck. "I'll be back after lunch. Be gone by then."

As he drove past them on his way out, Sheila Lyman's eyes lowered and refused to look at him, while Ronnie Lyman glared.

The glare made it easier to get over the feeling that what he was doing was wrong, even if it was his job. He drove far away from the reservoir that day to check out areas he had missed for a while. One stop was the farm pond where the fish had died. He talked with the owner about the alkalinity of the water, gave him some guidelines and other printed material and then left.

On Highway 99 he came across an elderly man who had struck a deer with his truck and banged his head hard on the steering wheel. Eris took the dizzy, befuddled, bone-thin old man to the nearest clinic and then returned to dress the doe and haul it to a meat locker, where he impulsively paid for the preparation of the deer, then gave the name and address of the old man and told them to call him when it was done. The deer hadn't meant to get hit and the old man hadn't meant to hit it, but at least he would eat well while nursing the stitches in his head.

It was long past noon when he made it back to the Lymans' campsite, where he was relieved to see the motor home and its occupants gone. His relief was short-lived, however, when he drove out to leave the reservoir again and saw the Lymans' motor home parked at the Haven, a tiny bait shop and convenience store just off the access road. Beside the motor home was a mobile unit from a local television station, and as he passed by, Eris could see a mournful Ronnie Lyman, eyes lowered to the ground, responding to questions from the reporter.

Eris thought about sticking around and watching Lyman's next move, but he decided it would make him look like too much of a hardass. If they were still here at the end of the day, Eris would make good on his threat to arrest Lyman. He was already a little disgusted at the way the man was capitalizing on the disappearance of his little girl. He showed not an ounce of pride while on television, complaining long and loud to all about a lost job, a lost home, no more unemployment benefits, and struggle, struggle, struggle, milking every second of air time for all it was worth.

Eris felt for a man who had lost his job and couldn't keep up the payments on his house, but there were other things to do besides living in parks and fishing the days away. Ronnie Lyman needed to get off his lazy ass and find a job or two. Three, if he had to, because idle hands and mind led to loss of self-respect and eventually to self-hatred, something Eris was familiar with in his life. He had watched his adoptive father go from a bright, contented, hard-working man to a sneering, vindictive, cantankerous old bastard. A man's work was his life, and when Jean Renard left his twenty-five-year military career behind and accepted a pension for a permanently disabled back, he gave up on living.

And started picking on Eris, who was only seven at the time and did not understand why the love and affection he had been shown up to that point appeared to have been rescinded by the stranger who now stayed home days instead of going off to work. At first the anger and bitterness had been directed at Eris's adoptive mother, but then it turned upon Eris, the outsider, the interloper, and there was no one to protect him, since even his mother became cold to him to keep from drawing the heat of his father's fire back onto herself.

Eris ran away from his parents at the age of thirteen. He rode a bus all the way to Kansas City, telling himself he was going to find his real parents on the nearby Sauk-Fox reservation. The whites hated him and he didn't want to live with them anymore. He knew he was Fox, because his adoptive parents always laughed and said they wanted a little Fox baby since she had Fox blood in her, and because the name Renard meant fox. They also told him the name Eris was given to him by his natural mother, and they had no idea what it meant, but they kept it because it was unusual and seemed to suit him. Eris had the idea that if he visited the reservation and told people his name, someone might remember something.

An hour after he reached the reservation he knew his task

would be impossible. His plight was not unusual, and few cared to help him even by trying to remember anything. He returned to the bus station and walked inside to sit at the diner. Several people eyed him, but since his hair was cut short and his clothes were clean, he passed inspection. He saw a notice printed on the chalkboard that a dishwasher was needed in the diner, and Eris applied on the spot. He was thirteen, but he was tall enough to pass for sixteen and no one ever asked him any questions. He was paid cash and he slept on a bench in the bus station at night, until he could afford to rent a room.

He worked at the diner a year and a half, until he got on another bus and went to Oklahoma, because he heard there were Sauk-Fox there, too. In Oklahoma he hired on with a construction crew. At fifteen years of age he stood six-one and had good muscle definition, so, again, no one asked for anything but a social security number. He had one, courtesy of the military man who had called himself father. He let his hair grow long, like the other Indians on the crew, and he saved half of every paycheck, turning down invitations of the older men to go out and party with them. His spare time was spent looking for his natural parents.

When he was sixteen he contracted chicken pox and was sick for several weeks. A girl he had dated steadily bid him adieu after the pustules appeared, and only when he was in the worst stage of the disease did he realize what was happening to his previously smooth, brown skin. Afterward he became bitter and stayed in his room nights, refusing to go out or to talk to anyone. The men at work teased him mercilessly about his face and chest and back, until Eris finally lost control and went after one of them with a shovel. The incident saw him fired from his job.

He remained in Oklahoma long enough to receive his general equivalency diploma. At the age of seventeen he picked up his GED and took himself and all his saved money back to Kansas, where he enrolled himself in Kansas State University.

Eris was a good student. He worked hard at his studies and made one or two friends while there. He took another job, this time at an animal shelter, where he was placed in charge of euthanizing the hundreds of strays that went unplaced each month. He vomited nearly every time he performed the task and was later given other work, but he still had problems. Regretfully, the operators of the shelter let him go.

It was in his second year of college that he decided to be a conservation officer. He liked the idea of being outdoors all day, with no one but himself to answer to or be responsible for.

Obtaining his degree took longer than he thought it would, since he kept running out of money. During breaks he worked full time at temporary jobs, and in the summer he hired on with construction crews and saved every penny so he could stay in school.

It was more than pride and stubbornness that made Eris so determined. It was the way he felt about himself, and how he wanted to go on feeling about himself.

He graduated when he was twenty-four, and had numerous interviews with the state, finally going on to the police training academy and becoming certified as a law enforcement officer. A few months later he was assigned an area of his own, and now, two years later, he was dealing with what the other COs called "a year that rains shit," when every minute something was happening, and no sooner did he catch his breath than something else cropped up that needed his attention.

Still, he was all right doing what he was doing. He stayed busy most of the day, every day; he was rarely idle. It was what he wanted.

Next Friday was his twenty-seventh birthday, and he would celebrate it like he celebrated all the others, by himself, with an hour or two of maudlin thinking about his real parents. Then his birthday would be over and it would be the next day again.

That night on television he watched as Ronnie Lyman tearfully complained about the treatment of his family by the Kansas Department of Wildlife and Parks. How they couldn't bear the thought of their little girl possibly finding her way back to the campsite, only to find it deserted.

"Christ," Eris muttered.

The reporter had enough sense to interview Eris's superior, and the reason the Lymans were asked to leave was fully explained. Still, the worry-worn faces of the Lymans had an effect, and Eris was certain the cards, letters, and checks would see an increase. Missing little girls often awakened people's hearts.

He threw a frozen dinner in the microwave and looked out his kitchen window to see Madeleine sitting on the front porch playing with the kittens. Her hair was out of its usual tight bun and flowing freely down her neck and shoulders. It was a nice picture, and Eris stood looking at it long after the timer on his microwave had beeped.

He was about to turn away when he saw Sherman Tanner making his stealthy way up the road. The dog wasn't with him, so Eris figured he was going to the cemetery again, where he liked to rub himself against the stones and jerk off. Eris had caught him at it more than once, but he was too embarrassed by the man's behavior to open his mouth and speak. Tanner had something about buried things, obviously. And burying things.

Eris only hoped Madeleine didn't run out there and catch him at it some night.

He shook his head and was about to walk over to the microwave when he saw Madeleine lift a hand and wave to him. Eris turned his head and moved away from the window, not responding.

CHAPTER EIGHT

MADELEINE BOLSTERED HER COURAGE enough to walk down to the swimming area the next day. Jacqueline and Manuel would be in for dinner, and she wanted them to know she hadn't stayed holed up in the cabin the entire week. Over her one-piece suit she wore shorts and a top, and she carried a paperback in her hand as she made her way down the road. A woman standing in front of a cabin and drinking a huge glass of tomato juice nodded to her as she passed. Madeleine returned the nod and walked on. The cabins seemed to fill up from Thursday till Monday with people like her sister and brother-in-law, who visited the lake and then drove away again, leaving the place to the full-timers.

Down at the swimming beach she started to groan in dismay when she found the place full of kids, but on closer observation she paused and found herself watching.

The children were disadvantaged, most of them appearing to be afflicted with Down's syndrome. One woman on her own was attempting to keep them together and instruct them on the building of sand castles on the tiny sandbar. Madeleine counted twelve children of all colors, shapes, and sizes, only a few of them paying attention to what the woman was saying.

Slowly Madeleine approached the group and gave the faces that turned to see her a cautious smile.

"Hello," she said. "I couldn't help noticing. Could you use some extra hands?"

"How many have you got?" asked the woman with a wide smile.

Madeleine lifted her hands and then offered one to the woman. "My name is Madeleine Heron."

The woman shook her hand. "I'm Denise Lansky. Can you build a sand castle, Madeleine?"

"Give me a bucket and a shovel and I'll do my best."

"Great." Denise turned to the children. "Hey, kids, this is Madeleine, and she's going to help us out. Why don't you count off, and the first six of you go with her to that side, and the other six stay here with me on this side. Okay? Ready, now. One . . . two . . ."

Six children bumped and jumped to their feet to go with Madeleine down the beach a few paces. She caught the bucket and shovel Denise tossed her and received another broad smile from the attractive redhead.

For the next hour she helped build sand castles, wetting the coarse sand and shaping it, helping small fingers poke holes and smiling at their grins of delight. She couldn't believe how relaxed she became, or how quickly the children seemed to take to her. Madeleine had never been around smaller children; though she liked them and enjoyed spending time in their presence, she simply didn't know anyone who had children. She had always believed she would have little patience with them when tested, but she had never been given the opportunity to find out.

"Want a job for the day?" asked Denise when it was time to dole out snacks for the children.

Madeleine looked at her. "I was just wondering if I could hack it."

"I'm serious," said Denise. "I'm supposed to have two assistants, and the only one who showed up went to the hospital last night with colitis. I've called and sent for someone else, but I could sure use your help the rest of the day."

"How long are you here with them?"

"For the week. It's a camping adventure we do every year. I thought I'd have to take them all home early, but my husband agreed to come out and help me with them. What do you say, Madeleine? I'll pay you for a full day."

Madeleine looked at Denise's earnest blue eyes and ginger red hair before giving a brief but firm nod. She didn't exactly have pressing business back at the cabin. "What do we do first?"

"We feed them, apply another dose of sunscreen, and take them on a hike. Later on this afternoon, after lunch, we meet someone from the park who tells them about good camping habits and gives them all stickers; then we go on a short boat ride, courtesy of a friend with a pontoon boat. After that it's supper and a sing-along before bedtime."

"A big day," commented Madeleine.

"I show them a good time," said Denise, "and wear my butt out in the bargain. But it's worth it. Just look at those happy faces."

Madeleine looked and had to agree.

"I need to run back to my cabin and leave a note," she told Denise.

"I'll be right here," Denise told her. "Slathering on the sun block."

"Be right back," Madeleine said, and she jogged up the path that led to the cabins. She dashed off a quick note to Jacqueline and Manuel and then hurried back down to the swimming beach. Others had arrived by this time, some throwing distasteful glances and others indulgent as the children squirmed about on the small sandbar. Denise had three more bodies to apply sunscreen to, and she looked tremendously relieved when she saw Madeleine.

"I had this terrible feeling you weren't coming back. You're either incredibly bored or very naive about kids."

"I'm both," said Madeleine. "Where do we hike?"

"Not far. We're actually camped near Diamond Bay, but there's no swimming beach. The minibus is up in the parking area. I thought we'd go on a little nature walk, look at the trees and rocks and such. Are you ready?"

Madeleine was already panting from her first jaunt, but she could do more. She thought she probably shouldn't have sold her exercise bike and treadmill. A few months of inactivity and already she felt completely out of shape.

She was to feel even more out of shape as the day wore on. After lunch the children were more boisterous than ever, excited about their park visitor, who turned out to be Dale Russell. He said a quiet hello to Madeleine and Denise before turning his attention to the children, who watched in awe as he told them stories about litterbugs and firebugs and gave each one of them an official PARK PROTECTOR sticker when he was finished. Before he left, Dale looked at Madeleine and said, "Thursday?"

She shrugged a shoulder in reply and he gave her one of his heartwarming smiles. Madeleine only lifted a brow in response.

"Did he ask you for a date?" Denise asked in surprise.

"Do you know him?"

"I know he told the daughter of a friend that COs were discouraged from becoming romantically involved with the locals. I didn't know if that was baloney or what."

"He didn't ask for a date," Madeleine clarified. "He simply asked if I was going to the dance next Thursday."

"He's also supposed to be engaged. I was relieved to hear it, since my husband's convinced Dale is gay."

"I've heard some of the best-looking men are," Madeleine said, and at her tone, Denise looked at her.

"You sound curiously uninterested."

"Do I?"

"Yes." Denise and Madeleine grinned at her.

"No. Will you be going to the dance?"

"No. We leave the day before. You should go. I went last year and had a really good time. Are you with anyone?"

"Me? No, I'm staying at my sister's cabin for the summer."

"All the more reason you should go." Denise looked at her watch then. "Time for our boat ride. We need to get to the dock."

The next half-hour was contained madness as they hurried to strap twelve little bodies into twelve personal flotation devices and hustle them aboard the huge pontoon boat owned by Denise's obviously wealthy friend, introduced to Madeleine only as "Bill." She and Denise put on their own life jackets and sat squat-legged on the floor of the boat with the children, while the owner's teenaged daughter flopped into one of the seats and studied all their faces.

"A new assistant, Denise?" she asked, and pointed to Madeleine.

"Just day help," Madeleine answered.

"Ignore her," said Denise under her breath, and then the engine started and no one could hear much of anything for several moments as they pushed away from the dock and headed out onto the lake.

The children clung to each other and to Denise and Madeleine as they moved over the choppy water. Several of the children's mouths never closed, but simply remained open in drooling pleasure.

"You never said whether you were going to the dance with Dale Russell or not," Denise said to her in a loud voice, and before Madeleine could answer, the teenaged girl was leaning over Denise, her nostrils flaring.

"What did you say?"

Denise leaned back. "I wasn't talking to you."

"Did you say Dale Russell asked her to the dance?" She pointed rudely at Madeleine again.

"What if he did?"

The girl straightened. "Sonofabitch."

"Hey," said Denise. "Watch your mouth around these kids."

The girl sneered. "Don't tell me what to do on my own goddamned boat."

Bill heard that one, and he barked at his daughter to shut her mouth. She stomped away, and Denise's lip curled as she watched her go.

Madeleine began to smile, and she started to say, *I think you did that on purpose*, to Denise, but a sudden, sharp scream from one of the children caused her to jerk her head around and look to see what was wrong. Suddenly every child on the boat was screaming, and then Denise, and even Madeleine, screamed when she saw the tiny, limp body caught in the ropes trailing along beside the boat. The girl's blonde hair floated like seaweed in the water above the yellow of her sweatsuit. Her upturned face was bloated and discolored, and Madeleine slammed her eyes shut and turned abruptly away before the image of the little girl's staring, milky eyes could stick in her mind the way that reddish black hole in the side of Sam's head had.

Then she began yanking children back and gathering them to her, trying to cover their heads with her hands and telling them in a shaking but soothing voice not to look, just don't look.

Bill, his face white, had stopped the pontoon boat and was radioing for help.

Help in the form of Eris Renard came nearly a half-hour later.

He was in a boat by himself, and Madeleine saw him give a start to find her there, surrounded by twelve shaken Down's children and a sobbing redhead.

"Great," muttered the teenaged girl. "It's the ugly one."

Eris pulled the boat along the opposite side of the pontoon where the body floated. He climbed onto the pontoon and walked to the opposite edge to look over. Madeleine saw him go very still for a moment; then he abruptly turned and jumped back into his own boat to pick up the radio.

"No hoax," she heard him say. "She's here."

The response was difficult to hear, and Madeleine heard Eris tell whomever he was talking to that a dozen kids were on the pontoon boat. When he turned around again his face was grim, and she clearly heard a voice instruct him to spare the children further trauma and bring in the body himself. The sheriff's department would be waiting on shore.

Eris took a tarpaulin and laid it on the seat beside him, then he guided his boat around the pontoon boat and placed it as close to the body as he dared. Without hesitation he went into the water, and Madeleine watched through slitted eyes as he attempted to untangle the body from the pontoon's rope. His face held no expression, though his long brown fingers worked frantically. When the body was finally free, Eris held onto one sleeve of the yellow sweatsuit and swam with it to the side of his boat before motioning to Bill that he could go on.

As the pontoon pulled away, Madeleine's eyes were glued to Eris's face. She saw him place an arm of the body behind the ladder of the boat to hold it there until he could get on board and get the tarpaulin. She saw him wrap the tarpaulin around the body and slowly lift it over the side of his boat. Then, though they were many yards away by this time, she saw him lean over the side of the boat away from them and hang there for several minutes. Madeleine's heart went out to him as she watched him heave.

Denise had stopped crying by that time, and she was attempting to calm the children, who were full of frightened questions. After listening to her for several minutes, Bill's teenaged daughter shook her head and said, "They've seen enough bodies and dead people on TV by now that I wouldn't be too worried. That pockmarked CO probably scared them worse than the floater."

Madeleine stood and extended a stiff arm to put her finger right in the middle of the girl's chest.

"You *shut* up."

The girl backed away in belligerent surprise. "God, what is your problem? Dad, did you see what she did?"

Bill did, and when they were safely docked again, he came to apologize. "Denise, Miss Heron, I won't make excuses for my daughter, or for what happened out there today, but I will say I'm sorry."

Denise nodded to him and touched his shoulder. "Do you think . . . I mean where do you . . . how do you think we got her?"

He rubbed at a temple and said, "The only thing I can figure is that we snagged her right here at the dock just after Shelly took care of the lines. She never does it the way she's supposed to, which is probably how we wound up carrying the body along with us, with the line trailing along with her under the boat. Then, when we slowed down, she had time to bob up from underneath us."

"Under the boat?" said Denise, looking sick. "She was underneath the boat the whole time?"

"I'm sorry," Bill said again, and he left them alone with the children.

Supper was a somber affair, with more questions, questions, questions, and much interest and curiosity in the dozens of sheriff's department cruisers now parked around Diamond Bay. As they were ready to begin their evening sing-along, Denise's husband, Tim, arrived. After staying for one or two songs, Madeleine bid everyone goodbye and slipped away, refusing payment for the day or a ride back to her cabin. She had seen Eris's truck parked at the dock, and she figured to ride back with him. It was late, nearing dusk, and he would be going home soon.

She found the truck and opened the passenger door to climb inside. There were people milling around on the dock, uniforms of all sorts, deputies, morgue assistants, people from the coroner. She couldn't see Eris.

Madeleine settled herself against the seat and looked around the interior of the truck. It was clean, like his house. The dashboard was free of dust and had a freshly washed look to it.

No wonder he eats over the sink, she thought. *He doesn't want to get anything dirty.*

She opened his glove compartment and was stunned to find his wallet inside.

How careless, Madeleine thought, leaving his wallet inside an unlocked truck at a busy dock.

But it was an official truck, and Eris had probably been in a hurry to get out on the water, which explained why his wallet was there. He didn't want it to get wet.

Hating herself for doing it, but eaten with curiosity, Madeleine opened the wallet. Inside she found fifty-nine dollars and a ticket stub from a music theatre presentation of *Man of La Mancha*. There were no pictures of anyone in his wallet. He had a driver's license, an insurance card, a social security card, a library card, various official-looking permits and things . . . and that was it. She looked at the driver's license again to find his birth date. After doing some quick figuring in her head, she realized he was going to turn twenty-seven the following Friday.

She did some more figuring and began to frown. Madeleine was exactly eight years and two months older than him. Sighing, she put his wallet back into the glove compartment and closed it up tight. She leaned back against the seat and allowed her lids to drift shut while she waited.

In the next moment she jerked awake as the overhead light in the cab came on and Eris stood with his hand on the door, looking in at her.

"If you're going home, I need a ride," she said, and after a pause he got in the cab.

Madeleine buckled in as he turned the ignition. She eyed his profile and found his eyes straying to the glove compartment.

It's still there, she wanted to tell him, but she didn't. He looked more tired than she had ever seen him, and she wondered what kind of man he was to enjoy working himself to exhaustion day after day.

"You're sunburned," he commented as he drove the truck up and away from the dock.

She glanced at the pink tops of her thighs and felt the tenderness of her arms. "I don't tan. I never have."

They rode quietly along, and on impulse she reached across the seat to gently touch his arm. She felt him flinch, but went on. "You did a good job today, Eris. I want you to know that. I don't know anyone who could have handled the situation as well as you did today."

For several moments he was silent. Then he asked, "You saw her?"

"I did, yes. I won't forget it any time soon."

There was silence between them again, until he looked at her suddenly and asked in a rough voice if she had a specialty in anthropology.

Madeleine looked at him in surprise, then understood by the swift change of subject that he was trying to guide his thoughts away from the day's events and his part in them.

"Native-American languages," she answered. "And some music."

Eris turned full face to look at her, his own surprise apparent by the action.

"Are you Lakota?" she asked.

"Fox," he said, turning back to the road again.

"Minnesota? Canada?"

"The white people who adopted me said I was born here in Kansas."

That explained why his wallet held no pictures, she told herself. Partially, anyway.

"Where are they now?" she asked. "Do they live around here?"

"I haven't seen them in years," he said. "When I left, they were in New Mexico."

"My parents live in Santa Fe," said Madeleine.

She expected him to say something else, like what part of New Mexico his adoptive parents were in, or why he hadn't seen them in so long, but he said nothing further, only stared out the windshield and drove. When they reached the log cabin she saw Manuel's Jeep Cherokee in the drive and lights burning in the windows.

Eris stopped the truck in the road and waited for her to get out. Madeleine unbuckled herself and said, "Thanks for the ride."

He nodded. She hesitated, looking at him. He looked back at her, still and silent.

"Would you like to come in and have a beer?" she asked.

"No, thanks."

"Eris . . ."

"Tell Mr. and Mrs. Ortiz I said hello."

She was dismissed. Madeleine got out and slammed the door behind her. She marched across the lawn and up the steps without once looking over her shoulder. She heard his truck pass on toward his cabin.

That's what she got for being concerned about him, for trying to be nice again. He didn't know what nice was. Madeleine herself was going to be having more than one drink that night. She had no more of the sleeping pills her doctor had given her, and she knew she was going to need something to help her blot out the memory of that floating blonde hair and sodden yellow sweatsuit. If Eris Renard didn't need something to help him, or someone to talk to, then he was made of unfeeling stone.

CHAPTER NINE

Eris HELD UP THE bottle of Jack Daniel's and swallowed three times before he put it down again. He rarely drank, but it was an effective painkiller.

Madeleine Heron had no idea how much he had wanted to take her up on all the sympathy her eyes offered. When she touched him on the arm he wanted to stop the truck in the middle of the road and wrap himself around her, crush her to him, so he could know the feel of a warm, breathing, living being in his arms, instead of the memory of a cold and dead one.

He took another long drink and put the lid back on the bottle. He had contacted the Lymans, as promised, and was forced to listen to Ronnie Lyman call him a liar, over and over. "She ain't dead, y'hear? I'm tellin' you my little girl ain't dead. She can't be."

Eris had to tell him it was in fact his daughter. He had taken her out of the water himself and requested that Ronnie come and identify her. Ronnie said that by God he would, and the lying goddamned bastard would see it was not his little girl.

When Ronnie arrived and saw Eris was telling the truth, that his little girl had drowned, he fell into a dead faint on the ground and cracked open his head, requiring twelve stitches to sew it back up again. Reporters descended upon the scene then, and questions were fired nonstop at park officials, only a few meriting an answer. When Eris was asked by someone whether he still considered the park safe, he nearly lost his temper.

The girl was three, he wanted to shout. *You don't leave a three-year-old girl in the dark by a dam.*

His superior had stepped up in time to save Eris and keep his face off TV.

Eris walked away to help Dale Russell keep the numerous nosy boaters and curious onlookers out of the way. Russell had been away from his radio when the call came for someone to go out on the water and check out the pontoon boat. Eris had been forced to drive twenty fast miles to get back to the reservoir and get in a boat.

He closed his eyes and unscrewed the lid on the bottle again as he thought of his first glimpse of her.

Bad.

Don't think about it, he immediately told himself. *Think about anything else. Think about Madeleine, and the way she's starting to look at you.*

Truth be told, he didn't know what to think about that. She acted as if she were actually interested in him, and after learning what he had that evening, he began to wonder if maybe he wasn't some new and different kind of case study for her. Her interests lay in Native Americans, and he was as native and as American as they came, so maybe she was actually following her educational leanings when she tried to talk to him.

Whatever she was doing, she was making him think more about her, and he knew he was only setting himself up for disappointment in doing that. She would be packing up and leaving at the end of the summer, making all considerations moot. He would rather she go back to being haughty and demanding than feeding him and touching him and saying nice things to him. She didn't know how long it had been for him, how the weeks had blended into months and the months into years and how he was usually so utterly exhausted when he came home that he was too tired even to touch himself and masturbate away the pressures inside his body.

She had a way of making the tiredness seem less. When he found her sitting in his truck that evening his adrenaline went to work all over again, and when she spoke, talked about his doing a good job, he experienced an odd flushing sensation under his skin, more pleasure than pride. Still he didn't know how to take her. She was different from anyone he had ever been exposed to, even in school. He had never had a teacher who looked like Madeleine Heron. He might not have graduated if he had.

He took one last drink of Jack Daniel's before putting the bottle away in the cabinet. His senses were practically reeling now, unused as he was to the effects of alcohol. He moved to the kitchen window and looked up to the log cabin. The curtains were closed, but he saw a light in Madeleine's bedroom, the same bedroom where he had seen her take off her clothes on the first night.

Eris thought about what he had seen that night, the generous, rosy-tipped breasts, and the slender, curved stomach above rounded white hips, and he went to lie down on his bed.

Before he could lower a hand to touch himself, the image of little Kayla Michelle Lyman intruded, her silky blonde hair wrapping itself around his wrist while he struggled to free her from the pontoon boat's rope.

Eris rolled off the bed and stumbled to the bathroom, hanging his head over the toilet and vomiting until the water was brown with undigested whiskey and even his eyeballs hurt with the effort to vomit more.

THE NEXT MORNING HE showered, toweled himself, and brushed his teeth, all without managing to meet his own eyes in the mirror. He felt like shit, and he wasn't going to get into the reasons with himself. He took a Diet Coke out of the refrigerator for breakfast and downed four aspirin before leaving the house.

He called the lake office by radio later that morning to see if anyone had heard whether the autopsy on the little girl had been completed. It had, but the voice on the other end said he had been instructed not to talk about the results over the radio. Eris stopped at the first phone he came to and called his superior.

"She had semen in her stomach," he was told. "Some bruising around her ears and jaws."

Eris swallowed and felt his own stomach deliver a threatening rumble. "Did she drown?"

"Yes. You might stay close to the lake today. When people hear some sick bastard is out there getting his rocks off killing kids, there could be a mass exodus."

Eris disagreed. People would keep a closer watch on their children certainly, but the idea of such deranged activity would see most hanging around, looking with suspicion at strangers and talking in shocked, hushed tones to their neighbors. People were funny that way, and they weren't going to change any time soon. The park would go on as before, with a little more tension than usual, and a little less friendliness.

Sometime that afternoon the news leaked out, and Eris was stopped no less than a dozen times by people wanting to know if it was true. Eris said there had been no official word yet. Technically, he was not lying. There had been no official news release.

Around three o'clock he spotted Manuel Ortiz edging around a tiny cove. Ortiz called to him and docked his Ranger bass boat at a private dock so he could lope up and talk to Eris. Eris watched him approach and prepared himself to answer the same questions he had been answering all day.

"You know the people who own that dock?" Eris asked when Manuel reached the truck.

"No," said Manuel, grinning. "Are you going to arrest me?"

"Not today," Eris answered. "How are you?"

"Very well, thank you. Madeleine has mentioned your kindnesses to her in the last week, and Jacqueline and I thought to repay you by inviting you to dine with us this evening."

Eris opened his mouth, and Manuel held up a hand.

"Before you say no, let me tell you about the juicy porterhouse steak that awaits you if you say yes. I will begin cooking at seven, and it would please me very much if you agree to join us. Madeleine's life of late has not been easy, and we appreciate anyone who makes the effort that you have. She can be a difficult woman, and she has admitted to being difficult with you."

This surprised Eris. He couldn't see her admitting to being difficult. The part about her life of late not being easy intrigued him, but he wouldn't ask.

He wondered what else she had said to them about him. He didn't want to spend the evening talking about the dead little girl, or his part in yesterday's nightmare.

"Thank you," he said, "but I'll pass."

Manuel was disappointed. "She can be quite charming when she chooses. She is not so . . . hard . . . always."

"I've got things to do at home. Thank you for the invitation, and good luck with your fishing."

Manuel stepped away from the truck, and Eris drove on before he could say anything further to persuade him. He liked the idea of sitting down and eating a good steak with nice people, but none of them really knew each other, and Eris felt awkward and ill at ease in such situations. There were always those preliminary questions, covering everything everybody did, and where everybody went to school, and if they knew anyone in common. He wasn't any good at just sitting and chatting with people. Maybe if he drank more he would be better at it, but he didn't enjoy drinking and didn't trust himself when he did drink. It surprised him that anyone did. He was still paying for the desperation of the previous night.

As he drove on he thought about the Lymans and wondered how they were holding up. He felt suddenly bad for thinking ill of them and their grandstanding on television. They couldn't help what they were anymore than he could help what he was. It was just the way things turned out.

RONNIE'S WIFE WAS SICK. She had been sick ever since Ronnie called her yesterday and told her that her baby was dead. She couldn't eat anything, and even when she drank something she threw it right up. The people at the Trinity Shelter in Augusta were worried about her, and they couldn't understand why she was so angry at her husband, whose poor head was shaved half bald where it had been stitched, and who looked as if someone had gut-kicked him and left him fighting for air.

The reason for Sheila's anger was clear to Ronnie. She thought he had done it. She thought he had killed their baby girl to get more money coming in. Not enough money was coming in, so she thought he had killed Kayla to get more sympathy and more begging time on TV.

He *had* called his mom and told her to bring Kayla to the Haven a day or two early. He had to, because they were kicked out of the park, and he was going for really high drama by having his little girl show up looking for them just one day after they had been kicked out.

But someone else had snatched her from in front of the Haven after his mother drove away. Someone bad had taken her and done dirty things to her before killing her, and it was killing Ronnie because he couldn't get his wife to believe that it wasn't him who had done it.

What kind of wife would believe something like that about her own husband? Ronnie asked himself as he received yet another evil glare from the pasty-faced Sheila. She was sick, all right. She was sick in the head, thinking such things about him. She was making everyone in the shelter stare at him and whisper. Last night he had wanted to hit her so bad he nearly bit his lower lip in two trying to prevent it. If word got out that Ronnie Lyman slugged his wife, then those little five- and ten-dollar checks that were dribbling in out of sympathy for them would stop quicker than a mouse pissing.

They might, anyway, if he couldn't get her to be nice to him again. Goddammit, they were going to bury their little girl to-morrow and she shouldn't be treating him as if she hated him. She even had Kelsey and Kendra looking at him like he was some bad old half-bald bogeyman.

He threw himself onto his bunk and closed his eyes, tired of it.

Sheila watched him, hating every freckle, every little hair in his eyebrows. The lazy, greedy, worthless bastard. She knew she should have left him the first time he hit her. She knew it. But by then she already had Kelsey, and no way to get a job without a high-school diploma. Her mom couldn't keep Kelsey because she worked, and there was no way Sheila could go back to high school with a baby. It was stupid to go on and have another baby, and even more stupid to have a third one. But Sheila loved her babies so much. They took all the love she had to give and gave it all back to her, something Ronnie would never come close to experiencing, let alone understanding. He was incapable of feeling love for anything. All he wanted out of life was food, shelter, free money, and someone to hit.

That someone wasn't going to be her anymore, Sheila told herself. The filthy, disgusting animal wasn't going to get near her or her two other little girls. Let him go back to live with his mother and knock *her* around again. She was used to putting up with it. She had put up with it from Ronnie's dad, and then from Ronnie's older brother, and then from Ronnie. She did everything she was told and never argued. If anyone asked, she thought her boys were the most wonderful men ever to walk the earth. There were none better.

They were all sick, Sheila told herself.

All of them but her. After the funeral tomorrow, she was getting away. She was leaving and going to one of the other shelters who had offered help. Maybe they would help her get a GED so she could try and get a job somewhere. She could live in low-income housing and take a bus to work. She and the girls would get on all right without Ronnie. They might even do better, looking at the way things had gone for them so far. Sheila had never felt right about taking things from other folks. Her own mother was dumb as dirt and twice as poor, but she never took nothing from no one. She waitressed and carhopped and worked from the time she was fifteen, and there were plenty of times she could have applied for welfare and gotten it, but she never did.

Sheila wasn't going to apply for it if she didn't have to, but she would wait and see how things worked out. The people in the shelter were really understanding and helpful and easy to talk to about such things. They understood when women feared the men they lived with, but feared going it alone even worse. But this thing with Kayla, this thing with her poor, dead baby was all she needed to get her mind made up. She had to get away from him. He was bad and he always had been bad and he wasn't going to be getting better anytime soon. All she needed for tomorrow was to line up some transportation for herself and the girls. Then she would be gone, and Ronnie and all his lying, scheming, and cheating people by crying on television would be behind her.

CHAPTER
TEN

"HE DECLINED," SAID MANUEL in answer to his wife's question about whether Eris Renard would be joining them for dinner.

Madeleine had known he would, but still her limbs stiffened.

Jacqueline glanced at her before continuing to mix a blender full of daiquiris.

"I forgot to mention it earlier, Madeleine, but your in-laws called me Thursday evening. They wanted to know where you were and how you're getting along. I said you were at our cabin, but I didn't say where. They wanted to know if you needed any money."

Her head lifted sharply, and Madeleine stared at her sister. "What?"

"His mother admitted how insensitive they were after Sam's suicide. They blame it on shock. Now they realize everything you said was true, and they want to try to make it up to you."

"Bullshit," said Madeleine, and Manuel frowned at her in disapproval.

Jacqueline's look was patient. "I told them I would speak to you. If you wanted to contact them, you would."

"I don't want to."

"I thought as much."

"Can you blame me?" Madeleine asked, her temper flaring.

"They practically accused me of murdering their son. How do you expect me to feel?"

"Just as you do," Jacqueline soothed. "Forget I mentioned it." She turned to Manuel then said, "Madeleine took me over to meet her new friends today."

"The children you mentioned last night?"

"Yes," said Madeleine, relaxing somewhat. "We had a good afternoon."

"I got to call bingo," said Jacqueline, pretending to preen. "And I was very good."

Manuel smiled at her and reached down to hand a scrap of the fat he was trimming off the steaks to the kittens at his feet.

He did like cats. He played with them and talked to them and lovingly scratched their arched little backs.

"Hey," Jacqueline said. "Don't feed them on the floor. Find a plate if you're going to give them scraps."

Manuel swatted her on the bottom and she swatted playfully back, until he caught her and brought her to him for a kiss.

Madeleine noiselessly excused herself and went out to the front porch, feeling embarrassed and a little envious of her sister and her luck in finding someone who suited her so perfectly.

Sam and Madeleine had not been nearly so compatible, and she often thought she had married him simply because of the horrible experience she had had in her last year in the field and because she was nearing thirty and wasn't married yet. The day she married him she knew in her heart she did not love him in the romantic sense of the word, but he was funny and witty, handsome and athletic, and she loved being with him.

Until he lost his job.

Damn his parents for even daring to offer money after the way they had treated her at the funeral. Their cold stares and their refusal to ride in the limo with her or even sit near her during the service. How they had the gall to call up Jacqueline and—

"Hello," said a nearby voice, and Madeleine jumped to see Sherman Tanner strolling toward her with his little dog.

"Hello, Mr. Tanner. How are you?"

He ignored the question. The eyes in his thin face were practically glowing.

"Did you hear what they found during the autopsy on the lost little girl?"

Madeleine's mouth tightened in discomfort. "No."

"Semen," Tanner said in a delicious, sibilant whisper, as if he were savoring the word. He waited until he saw Madeleine's eyes grow round before he added the words: *"In her stomach."*

A shudder passed through Madeleine, and she carefully lowered herself to sit on the porch step. "She was murdered?"

"It would appear so, wouldn't it?" Tanner answered.

A flash of the little girl's face and body appeared in Madeleine's mind and she squeezed her eyelids shut and attempted to push the image away.

"Horrible, isn't it?" said Tanner, still speaking in a whisper.

Madeleine could only nod.

"I heard Renard was the one who found her," Tanner said.

"A pontoon boat with twelve frightened children found her, Mr. Tanner. Renard took her to shore."

"Says who?" said Tanner.

"Says me. I was on the pontoon boat."

Tanner's eyes opened wide. "You were? You were on the boat with the kids? How did you find her? What did she look like?"

Madeleine stood up in disgust, and she was about to open her mouth and tell Tanner how sick she thought he was when Jacqueline opened the door and said the steaks were almost ready.

"Hello, Mr. Tanner," she said upon seeing the neighbor. "How are you?"

"All right, then," said Tanner, and he took his little dog and walked across the yard to the road.

Inside the house Jacqueline imitated his walk and brought a smile to Madeleine's face, but she had lost all desire to eat supper.

"Are you all right?" Jacqueline asked in concern.

"I'm fine, really. Just not as hungry as I thought I was."

She wouldn't tell them why. She had no wish to destroy their appetites by spreading Tanner's news.

She poured herself a daiquiri and went outside again. She walked around the cabin to check on her tomato plants, and then she found herself wandering over the grass in the direction of Renard's house. He wasn't home, and she didn't quite know what she was doing, but once she was on his porch she somehow felt better.

When he came home it was dark, and his headlights picked her out on the porch. He put his truck in the garage and came around.

"What is it?"

"Nothing," she said, and sipped at her daiquiri. "Why didn't you come to dinner?"

"I didn't want to."

"How's your toe? I never did see you limp."

"Better."

She stood and used one hand to wipe off the seat of her shorts before stepping down. She moved to stand next to him and look up into his face.

"I came because I needed to be with someone who saw what I saw, not necessarily to talk about it. The image of the little girl is still fresh in my mind, and it became even fresher about an hour ago, courtesy of Mr. Tanner. I couldn't eat when I heard, and I couldn't tell Manny and Jac about it, so now two expensive steaks are going uneaten."

Eris exhaled and fingered the keys in his hand. "Just don't think about it, Madeleine."

"I'm trying," she said, aware that his expulsion of breath had fluttered the top of her hair. "Would you talk with me?"

"About what? Linguistics of the central Algonquian tribes?"

She stared at him. "Have you been reading up, or was that a joke?"

"Both." He hesitated, then asked if she wanted to come in.

Madeleine blinked in surprise. "Yes," she answered, "I want to come in."

Eris moved past her to unlock the door and push it open. He extended a hand, indicating that she precede him, and she stepped inside. She stopped immediately, since the house was dark and she didn't know what was in front of her. Eris bumped into the back of her and she heard him apologize as he grasped her by the arms and moved her forward a step. He fumbled at the wall and flicked a switch that turned on a light in the ceiling of the living room. Madeleine looked around herself and frowned. He had a recliner, an end table on one side of the recliner, and a small TV sitting on top of a cabinet. The rest of the room was empty. She could feel him looking at her.

"I'm not here much," he said.

"I know."

"You can sit in the chair."

Madeleine sat. It was a nice chair, roomy and comfortable. She dropped her sandals on the floor and pulled up her feet.

He seemed unsure of what to do for a tense moment or two. Finally he sat down on the floor in front of her and said, "Tell me about your field work."

"Are you interested?"

"Yes," he said.

"How much do you know of your heritage?"

"Very little. I was raised white."

"Do you want to learn?" Madeleine asked. "I can help you if you like." She couldn't help noticing the band on his hair was loose; the silky black strands that fell over his shoulder made him look somehow wild. The dim light in the living room softened the scars on his face and made his eyes appear jet black as they roved over her features.

"Learn about my heritage from a white woman?" he said with the ghost of a smile.

Madeleine's heart did a strange flop. "Take what you can get."

"Tell me about your field work," he said again, and then he asked her if she wanted a Diet Coke. When she said no he retrieved one for himself and settled his long length in front of her again, this time removing his boots. Madeleine looked at his white-stockinged feet and said, "I haven't talked with anyone about this in a long time. My last year was a nightmare."

"Where were you?" he asked. "On a reservation?"

"Yes. I was studying the evolution of the Sioux languages over the last hundred and fifty years. I became familiar with nearly all the adults, but the children were told never to bother me, and the younger people would have nothing to do with me. I was surprised because everywhere else it was the other way around, with the old ones being mistrustful and ignoring me. Here it was different."

"By younger you mean teenagers?" Eris asked.

"On up to early twenties," Madeleine answered. "They behaved as if I were a nonentity. I didn't exist."

"Must've been difficult for you," said Eris, and Madeleine looked at him.

"What's that supposed to mean?"

"Nothing. What happened?"

She was silent for a moment, studying him, and then she said, "They abducted me from my bed in the middle of the night, painted my body white, spit on me, kicked me in the face, rode on my back while I crawled on all fours and beat me until I bled. When they were finished doing that, they inserted hot peppers in my lower orifices. Then they left me naked in the middle of a deserted highway, where I wasn't discovered for a day and a half. I was burned, dehydrated, and I gave up field work immediately upon my recovery. I had no way to fight that kind of white hatred."

Eris was silent for some time, his dark eyes leaving her and then coming back again. Finally, he said, "You didn't press charges?"

"No, I didn't."

"You started teaching when you came back?"

"Yes."

"And now you've given up teaching and want to go back in the field?"

"I don't know which was worse," said Madeleine, "the peppers or the snotty students."

Abrupt laughter escaped Eris, and Madeleine found herself watching him.

"You have a nice smile," she told him, and his face slowly sobered.

"What about it?" she said after a long moment of silence between them. "Do you want to learn about the Sauk-Fox?"

"What are you going to learn?" he asked in his deep, quiet voice.

Madeleine only looked at him.

In the next second she heard Jacqueline's voice calling her name. Madeleine left the chair, slipped on her sandals and walked to the door.

"Come and see me next week," she said, and didn't wait for a response from him.

She left his tiny, barren house and walked back up to the log cabin. She didn't know if he would come or not. With Eris Renard, it was impossible to tell.

*   *   *

ERIS LAY ON THE floor of his living room after Madeleine was gone and cursed himself for asking her in to begin with. He took long breaths to still the heart that had begun racing the minute she stepped in the door; it had continued to pound the entire time she was there, causing Eris to sit as still as he could and fight to make his voice sound normal.

She didn't know. She didn't know what he went through when she moved so close to him and stood looking up into his face.

He was driving himself crazy wondering if she was teasing him or not, playing with him the way some women liked to play with ugly men.

He thought of what the young Sioux had done to her and knew why she flinched the first few times she was around him. He could only wonder what happened afterward in her life. The difficulty Manuel spoke of earlier.

Eris sighed and covered his face with his hands. He thought he was past all this. He believed he would never put himself through such pangs once he was a grown man, with a grown man's responsibilities. He had no idea what to do about it, other than to stay away from her. But he couldn't see himself staying away from home the entire summer. He guessed maybe he should begin looking for another place to live.

He wondered suddenly what would happen if he turned the tables and came on to her. What she would do. Eris snorted then and sprang up from the floor.

Like he was capable.

He shook his hair loose from its band and went into the bedroom to get out of his uniform. He took a long, warm shower and let the water beat against his head and shoulders until his flesh felt numb.

He had a funeral to go to tomorrow. His superior had asked him to go and represent the department. Eris told him the Lymans were bitter toward him, but in the end it meant nothing. He probably wouldn't even see them, his boss had said. Maybe so, but *they* might see *him*, Eris knew, and the prospect made him uncomfortable.

His sleep that night was fitful. He experienced dream after confusing dream, and when finally he rose from damp sheets to slake a sudden thirst with a glass of water, he saw a light in Madeleine's bedroom. His microwave clock read half-past two.

Eris looked at the cabin again and was surprised to see the silhouette of a truck parked on the side of the road just above the cabin. He strained to see if anyone was inside, but the darkness thwarted him. Just as he was ready to go and put on his pants, the truck eased away. Eris put his glass in the sink and went to bed.

When he awakened in the morning he knew immediately what was ahead of him. He showered again, brushed his teeth and combed and tightly banded his hair. He put on a fresh uniform and knew he needed to make a trip to the dry cleaners in Fayville to take care of his others. He shined his boots and dusted off his hat and glanced at his reflection in the mirror. He would need his dark glasses. They hid some of the scars and kept people from looking at him too long since they couldn't tell if he was looking at them or not.

He put a load of socks, T-shirts, and underwear in the washer and gathered up his dirty uniforms to dump them on the chair while he stood over the sink and ate a bowl of flakes for breakfast. There was no activity at the log cabin. Manuel's Jeep was gone, and Madeleine would probably be sleeping in after her late night.

When he was finished with his cereal he went back to the bathroom to run his toothbrush over his teeth again, and then he checked on the washer. Five more minutes to go. He returned to his bedroom and straightened the bed, telling himself Madeleine would have seen more furniture if she had come back here. He had a king-sized bed—the only size bed his feet didn't hang over——a night stand with a lamp, a dresser with a mirror, and a bookcase full of books. Eris didn't spend money on things he didn't need. He spent very little money at all, saving most of it and only occasionally giving himself an evening out. He didn't go often because his appearance usually drew people to look at him and he didn't like it. He sometimes thought if he weren't so tall he would blend right in with everyone else.

Which only made him wonder about his mother and father, how tall they were, what they looked like, and whether he looked like either of them. He knew he didn't want his father to be one of the numerous drunks he had encountered, and he didn't want his mother to be one of the women on the reservation who looked as if life had kicked her in the face. The inner strength and resilience he took pride in had to have come from somewhere, he told himself. His deep, heartfelt sense of right and wrong and the duty he felt to himself and others . . . he didn't think he had acquired those values from the Renards.

Eris did want to learn about his heritage, if only to try to find something else to feel good about. He didn't have much, but he was proud of his abilities and of the inner man he had become, even if the outer man made small children cry and women's lips curl.

Before he left the house he transferred his clothes from the washer to the dryer and picked up the load of dry cleaning to take to Fayville. The funeral was at the Dunsford Funeral Home in Augusta at ten o'clock. Eris had never been there, but he would have no trouble finding the place. Augusta wasn't a large city.

He arrived at nine-fifty and found only a handful of people inside the small chapel. He entered through the back entrance and sat in the last pew, hoping the people sitting in the front pew would not turn around. Ronnie Lyman's shaved head was lowered. His wife stared straight ahead at the tiny white casket surrounded by long white lilies.

Eris's nostrils quivered as he thought of what lay inside the casket.

He hated this. He hated the whole idea of funerals.

A couple came through the door and sat down in the pew in front of him. Eris recognized two reporters sitting near the front of the chapel, pens in hand, writing down the details.

"Wonder who's paying for it?" whispered the man in front of Eris. His wife gave him a sharp look and shushed him. Eris, too, wondered who was paying. That pearl-white casket was not exactly a cheaper model.

The sound of an organ began then, and one or two long, drawn-out songs were played by an unseen organist, who warbled along with the music. Eris sat fingering his hat and wondering who the people in the chapel could be. One woman beside Ronnie had to be his mother. She had the same color hair and the same washed-out eyes. Another woman on the other side of Sheila and the girls was probably Sheila's mother. She had a look of resignation that suggested this was only one of many funerals she had attended in her life.

A minister stepped up beside the casket as the music ended

and led them all in a prayer before he began to speak about the
innocence and sacredness of children. Eris listened for a time,
and then he stopped listening, because he heard his adoptive
mother's Baptist teachings and he grew irritated by the memories it inspired. When the minister stopped speaking, attendants
came to usher the group in the chapel past the open casket. Eris
slipped out the back door again. One of the reporters saw him
and beckoned, but Eris shook his head and got in his truck. He
had decided against going to the cemetery, but something he saw
as he sat in his truck with his hand on the ignition changed his
mind for him.

Ronnie and his mother were the first family members to
emerge. Ronnie was sobbing and his mother was trying to comfort him. Ronnie shoved his mother violently away from him and
reached for Sheila as she came shakily out the door. Sheila stood
like a statue while Ronnie threw his arms around her and cried.
Sheila's mother put the two girls in the limousine and climbed
in after them. Ronnie's mother crept over to join them. Sheila,
meanwhile, had not moved a muscle, and Ronnie finally lifted
his head to look at her.

Eris could read her lips from where he sat. She said, "Get away
from me."

Ronnie dropped his arms and his fists clenched. His jaw
worked furiously as he looked around himself, and in that moment Eris knew Ronnie Lyman was into physical abuse. Every
muscle in his body was tensed and ready to erupt into aggression;
only the circumstances and the curious onlookers prevented it.

Sheila walked stiffly to the limousine and, after taking a deep
breath, Ronnie followed her.

The funeral procession was a short one, with only six or seven
cars following the hearse and limousine to Elmwood Cemetery.
Eris was last in line, and he decided to stay in the truck for the
graveside service and simply observe.

The wind had come up, whipping women's dresses and flapping men's jackets open and messing up carefully done hair. The
tent belonging to the funeral home tossed and pitched and looked
several times like it was going to blow over. When the service
concluded, most people stayed for only a brief show of respect
before walking back to their cars. Eris saw Sheila pick up a white
lily and toss it into the open grave before blowing a last kiss to

her baby girl. Ronnie put his hand on her shoulder and tried to lead her away from the grave, but Sheila shook him off. She took one little girl in each hand and walked to meet a woman who was standing by a van and obviously waiting for them.

Ronnie shouted at Sheila, and, even with the wind, Eris could hear him ask what the hell she thought she was doing.

Sheila turned back and said something Eris couldn't hear, but it was something that made Ronnie stop dead in his tracks and stare. Then he charged.

Eris threw open the door of the truck and hit the ground running. By the time he reached them, Ronnie had shoved his wife against the side of the van and was holding her by the throat with one hand and pointing in her face with an angry index finger, telling her she wasn't going anywhere. Sheila's face was turning purple as she gasped for air, and she gestured desperately for someone to take away her two screaming little girls.

Shocked eyes all around fell on Eris as he grabbed Lyman by the shoulder and attempted to spin him around.

Ronnie held on to Sheila's neck for all he was worth, not even looking to see who was trying to peel him away.

Eris growled between his teeth and punched Lyman hard in the right kidney. "Let go, dammit."

The hold was broken, and Ronnie buckled and fell to his knees, gasping in pain. When he looked up and saw Eris, his eyes rounded. Sheila was gagging and coughing, her face still purple, and when Eris looked to see if she was all right, her husband sprang up from the ground and hit Eris in the face as hard as he could, knocking off his glasses and sending him back into Sheila and the van and splitting one side of his mouth open. Before Eris could react, Lyman swung again, this time laying into Eris's nose and cheek. Eris took the blow, spat blood, and then barreled head first into Lyman, connecting with his solar plexus and knocking him to the ground, where he lay gasping for air while Eris moved up and put a knee on his neck.

"Don't move," Eris warned. He looked around then. "Someone call the police."

"I'll do it," said the woman with the van. "I have a car phone."

"Go ahead," Ronnie grated. "She won't press charges."

Eris hawked blood and looked at Sheila. One hand at her

throat, she hoarsely promised, "This time I will. And I'm gonna tell 'em everything."

Ronnie squirmed violently beneath Eris. "No you won't!" he screamed, his face red and veined. "You won't say shit! You do and I'll kill you, you hear me? I'll come after you and kill your ass!"

Sheila stared at him, her eyes frightened, and Eris pressed down harder with his knee, choking off anymore sounds from Lyman.

"Be sure and add that to your complaint," said the woman with the car phone as she finished her call. "Murder threats are not something the courts take lightly these days."

Eris wiped at the blood running down his face from his nose and his lip and noticed for the first time the number of people standing around and staring. The reporters were scribbling furiously.

"Go home," he said loudly. "Give the police a chance to get in the cemetery."

"You're lucky he didn't go for your gun," someone said, and Eris exhaled a bubble of blood in response.

Slowly, the lingerers began to leave, and soon the police arrived and took over. As Eris walked back to his truck, he saw a reporter hurrying to catch him.

"Your name," she huffed. "I need your name."

Eris kept walking.

CHAPTER ELEVEN

SHERMAN TANNER WAS BUSY digging around Eris Renard's coleus plants when he saw the conservation officer come rolling down the road. Tanner straightened and immediately started to hurry off, but it was too late. The Indian had already seen him. Renard parked his truck beside the house and got out frowning.

"What are you doing?"

Tanner ignored the question. His eyes were glued to the blood on Eris's clothes and the swollen state of his lip and cheek.

"What in God's name happened to you?"

"Nothing," said Eris. "Stay the hell out of my yard, Tanner."

Tanner puffed up his chest. "I was just doing some thinning on your coleus. I didn't realize it would offend you so badly."

"Next time, ask."

Tanner snorted in indignation and carried his spade away from the man and his precious plants. If he was going to be that way, then just let him. Sherman Tanner didn't need anything from his yard. He was curious, was all.

Desperate to spread the news about Renard's condition, Tanner went into his house to tell his wife and give her the plants he had obtained, and then he hopped into his car and hurried down to the swimming beach, where he had seen the two pretty sisters from the log cabin go, flaunting their bare legs and flimsy swimsuit coverups.

He found the blonde on the sandbar with a fat paperback; the redhead was out walking around in the water.

Sherman pretended to be strolling along the beach when he approached Madeleine.

"Why, hello there, neighbor."

"Hello, Mr. Tanner," said Madeleine, clearly not pleased to see him.

"Enjoying the sun, I see."

"Yes."

"It's smart to wear a hat, with skin like yours."

She said nothing, only looked at him.

"Just saw the strangest thing, up at the cabin," he began. "I was taking some of the coleus plants Renard said I could have when I saw him come driving up. Now, it's past lunch, and he doesn't usually come home around this time, but, anyway, the man was covered with blood. Both his shirt and pants were splattered with it, and his face looks a mess. Not that it's so attractive to begin with, but—"

Tanner stopped when she got up and put on her sandals, and he stared in surprise as she began to run up to the path.

"Madeleine?" her sister called from the water, but the blonde didn't stop.

Sherman was only too happy to approach the redhead and tell his juicy bit of news all over again. He loved being the first to tell people things.

MADELEINE WAS BREATHING HARD when she reached Eris's door. It was open and she walked right in, calling out as she moved through his house. He came from a room at the end of the hall and stared at her in her swimsuit.

She moved closer as her eyes adjusted. He was barechested and barefooted, wearing nothing but a pair of faded blue jeans.

"Are you all right?" she asked, and then she made a face as she spied his lip. "Ouch."

Eris shook his head and went back into his bathroom.

Madeleine followed and saw him lift a washcloth to the cut to clean the dried blood away.

"Let me do that," she offered.

"I can do it," he said, his voice irritated.

"Oh, shut up and sit down." She placed her hands on his back and eased him to the toilet, where she put the lid down and pushed him to sit on it. She glanced at his hardened brown nipples and took the washcloth from his hands to dab gently at the split and swollen lip.

"I doubt he was bigger than you," she said, "but I still have to ask the outcome."

Eris mumbled something she couldn't understand, and she took the washcloth away.

"Come again?"

"I said he's in jail right now."

"Oh. Good. Do you have any kind of ointment? It'll be easier on the lip when it starts to heal."

"There's some Mycitracin in the cabinet."

"Okay. I'll get it in a minute." She placed a hand under his chin and tilted his head up so she could get the last of the dried blood off his face. She found herself studying the scars on his skin and unconsciously smoothing them with a finger. When she glanced at his eyes she saw him look quickly away from her, as if he had been studying her while she studied him. She smiled and lightly tweaked him on the nose, only to see him grimace in pain.

"Oops, sorry."

She opened the cabinet and found the ointment inside. Putting some on the tip of her finger, she placed herself in front of him again, standing between his open thighs. She saw his eyes light on her breasts a fraction of a second before moving up her chest to her neck. Madeleine grasped him by the chin once more and gently applied the ointment to the cut, smoothing it over the lip and accidentally getting some on his teeth. He was very still, she noticed; it was almost as if he had stopped breathing.

"Hurt?" she said.

"Nnnh."

"Your cheek is going to bruise," she said. "Not much you can do about it, unless you've got an herbal poultice handy. That might be one advantage to learning about your ancestors."

He looked at her and said, "I want to."

"Do you?" she said, pleasantly surprised. "When?"

"Whenever."

"Meaning whenever you get around to it? I've checked, Eris, and I've found that most conservation officers are married with families. None of them are so devoted to the job that they keep the same hours as you do. They have their beepers if anyone needs them, and you have your beeper if anyone needs you."

"You called the office?"

"I did. The man I spoke with told me it was impossible to be on call twenty-four hours a day every day. You should take some time for yourself this summer."

"And provide diversion for a bored anthropologist?"

Madeleine searched his dark brown eyes and felt her spine stiffen.

"Just when I was starting to like you," she muttered, and she stepped from between his legs and tossed the tube of ointment in the sink.

"That's the part that's bothering me," Eris said before she could leave the room. "I think we'll both agree that a woman who looks like you usually has little to do with a man who looks like me."

"Is that how you judge your self-worth?" Madeleine turned to ask, her voice sharp.

"It's nothing but a fact, Madeleine. I don't know what you're after, and I can't help thinking I'm slated to become some kind of summer project for you."

Madeleine stood listening to him and in her annoyance she grew suddenly confused. *She* no longer knew her reasons for wanting to be around him or the impetus behind her actions, so how could he?

She met his gaze and said, "I have no explanation to offer, other than the fact that I think you're a good man, Eris."

He stood and moved to look down at her. "Manuel told me you've had a bad time of it lately. I didn't ask what, and I don't want to know. All I ask is that you not fool yourself into believing I'm going to be your buddy, or that you'll be a little less lonely if you stroll down and chat with old Eris once in a while. I don't want to be part of your recovery."

Madeleine looked into his earnest, swollen face and regretted the obvious discomfort she had caused him thus far. He thought she was using him, teasing him, playing with him, all to build up her own battered and bruised ego.

Maybe she was.

And maybe she wasn't. Maybe somewhere in all the sniping and foot stomping she had genuinely begun to like the silent Eris Renard. She knew she did, otherwise she would never have run all the way here from the swimming beach to see if he needed help.

But there was no way to prove it to him. She had no choice but to back off and let him be, show him she wasn't vain and stupid and desperate to be wanted by someone.

"I have been lonely, yes," she said slowly, "but it's been a long time since I've lived alone. I don't think I'm using you, but I don't really know. I haven't asked myself why I'm drawn to you. Maybe I should do that. And if you're right, if the reason has something to do with what drove me here, then I will apologize to you with all my heart."

They stood just inches apart, Madeleine acutely aware of the scent of his warm, bare skin, and Eris looking at her face with an expression that made the breath catch in her throat.

Madeleine forced herself to turn away and walk out of his house.

CHAPTER TWELVE

IT WAS DAYS BEFORE Eris saw her again. He did his best not to look, but his eyes went to the log cabin anyway, and to the garage, to see if he could see the truck inside. He couldn't tell if it was inside or not, and she never left the door of the cabin open anymore, so he had no way of knowing if she was home or if she had gone somewhere.

On Monday he reported to his superior about what had occurred at the funeral. He was surprised to learn Sheila Lyman had in fact pressed charges against her husband, and that Ronnie had fought with another inmate at the jail and had the holy shit beaten out of him. Eris's swollen mouth twitched when he heard the news.

Tensions at the lake intensified since the day Kayla Lyman's body was discovered. Everyone was on the lookout for a child-molesting killer, and parents frightened their children at night by telling them about the poor little dead girl found floating in the water.

Tuesday night Eris had another run-in with the twenty-something in the baseball cap and his two good-old-boy buddies. They were tearing through the park in a four-wheel-drive Blazer and smashed into a trash receptacle overflowing with garbage. When Eris came upon them they were dazed and trying to pry the receptacle from the grill of the Blazer. He asked to see the license of the driver, and found out the baseball cap's name was Bruce Beckworth. He was twenty-five and he lived in Fayville. His attitude toward Eris was belligerent, and Eris wrote him up for destroying park property.

Beckworth was smart enough not to foul-mouth Eris while in hearing distance, but he did flip him the bird once they were back in the Blazer and speeding away again. Asshole. If there was anyone Eris wanted to beat the holy shit out of, it was Bruce Beckworth.

On Thursday night, Eris drove over to the dance. He wasn't actually on duty, but it couldn't hurt to check on things. He couldn't admit to himself that he went more to see if Madeleine was there than anything else. There were so many people crowded into the campground that he couldn't see from his truck, so he got out and walked around the perimeter, stepping over the wires and hookups used by the band playing in the center of the crowd. He saw Dale Russell talking to the snooty teenager from the pontoon boat, but there was no sign of Madeleine. He walked around again, unable to tell if he was more relieved or disturbed. He guessed he was relieved.

As he was leaving the dance he saw Bruce Beckworth and his cronies arrive. Eris was tempted to stay and monitor their activity, but he decided to let Dale Russell handle whatever problems arose.

He drove home, eyeing Madeleine's cabin as he passed by. There was a light on in the living room, but otherwise the place was dark. Eris put the truck in his garage and was letting himself in the house when he saw a lone figure come walking up the path from the cove. At first he thought it was Sherman Tanner, but this person was smaller and more fluid in movement. It was Madeleine.

Eris walked across his yard and out to the road to meet her. He couldn't see her face very well, but he detected a nod. "Eris. How are you?"

"It's not safe to be out walking alone after dark," he said to her. "It's not safe in the city, and it's not safe here."

She took something out of a pocket to show to him. "I have my pepper spray. Just wanted to get out of the house for a while."

Eris watched her put the tiny canister back in her pocket. He wanted to tell her the spray wouldn't do much good; instead he said, "Did you forget about the dance?"

"No. I don't really know anyone. I'd feel awkward. What about you?"

He shook his head.

"Right. Well, I'll go on now. Thanks for the warning."

She started away from him and Eris could only stand and watch her go. Suddenly she turned back and said, "I almost forgot. Happy birthday tomorrow." He lifted both brows, and before he could ask, she added, "The night I was in your truck I looked through your wallet. I'm sorry. It was there, so was I. Have a good birthday, Eris."

He stood there and nearly strangled with all the words that wanted to come out of his mouth, but nothing made it past his lips.

No one had wished him a happy birthday since he was twelve years old.

CHAPTER
THIRTEEN

DALE RUSSELL WATCHED THE crowded dance and wished Renard hadn't left. He wouldn't admit it to anyone in a thousand years, but Dale felt better when the tall Renard was around. Things seemed easier to handle when he knew the other CO was there to back him up.

The day the little girl had been found in the water Dale ignored the radio call and later told everyone he was in the shitter when it came and hadn't heard. He heard, but he didn't want to go. Let Renard do it.

He didn't actually mind watching the dance, but it was bigger than last year, and the crowd was a little more unruly, mostly due to a jerk in a baseball cap trying to pick fights. Dale had to keep walking away from the women he was talking to and tell the man to either settle down and have a good time or get the hell out. While he was saying this he made sure he was touching the gun at his hip.

Dale hadn't expected public relations to make up such a large part of his job. He was good at it, certainly, but he had envisioned a more authoritative position, with less exposure to and contact with the lowlife lake element.

But then visibility was the name of the game when it came to dealing with boaters and jet skiers and everyone else who wanted to have a good time out on the water. One glimpse of Dale and they hid their beers and drove a little more cautiously. That was the part that felt good.

Still, Dale envied Renard his much wider area of responsibility. Renard put miles and miles on his truck every day, ranging over entire counties, while Dale was stuck at the reservoir, checking boat registrations and playing Mr. Friendly Park Ranger to whatever group wanted to come along for the show. It was his own fault, he supposed, for talking so long and so loudly about his aunt, the governor.

She had called him yesterday after hearing the business about the little Lyman girl. She wanted to know the ugly details, and what had been done. Dale gave himself a much larger role in the drama than he had actually played, but his aunt would never learn otherwise. He even claimed to have been there to help Renard subdue the wife-beating Lyman at the funeral, but he had asked the reporters to keep his name out of the paper. His aunt, the governor, praised Dale until he began to feel embarrassed for lying.

The embarrassment didn't last long. Dale had learned long ago his looks would carry him only so far. If he made it anywhere in life it would be through sheer improvisation.

He looked at his watch at eleven o'clock and realized suddenly that Madeleine Heron had not come to the dance. Not that Dale was starving for female company that night, but he had specifically mentioned the dance to her, and came to find out her hard-to-get act was not an act at all.

Dale didn't date, and he had lied about being engaged. He talked to women all the time, loved their flirting and thrived on their attention, but there was no one he wanted.

The little Lyman girl was the first time he'd slipped up in years.

He had driven up to the Haven that day for a can of Dr. Pepper and a candy bar when he saw her sitting outside. Suddenly he saw himself at fourteen again, luring a little girl away from her sandbox to come and look at the tadpoles in the ditch with him.

"Are you lost?" he had gently asked the blonde tot in front of the Haven.

She nodded.

"Want me to help you find your mommy?"

She nodded again.

"What's your name? Can you tell me?"

"Kayla."

"Okay, Kayla. You come with me. We'll get in my truck and we'll go find your mommy."

She came without argument, without fuss, following him into the seat of his truck.

That was when Dale realized no one had seen them. The Haven was deserted but for someone talking loudly on a phone in the back. His nostrils had opened and begun to quiver as he stared down at the little girl in the cab of his truck. The memory of the long-ago girl at the ditch toyed with him, caused the hair on his arms to raise as he remembered the sensations, the incredible paroxysm of pleasure he had experienced that day, not to be repeated since.

His hands had shook as he reached over to smooth her silky blonde hair.

"We're going to have some fun first," he told her in a voice wavering with a mixture of fear and anticipation. "Would you like to have fun?"

She shook her head no and told him she wanted to go to her mommy.

"It'll be really fun," Dale promised as he started the truck's engine and drove away from the Haven.

No one will ever know, he repeated constantly to himself.

He hadn't actually been caught at fourteen, but the little girl told on him when she recovered from her broken jaw, and Dale was sent to a boys' ranch before his aunt intervened and had him taken to a psychiatric hospital, where he stayed only six months before she intervened again and had him released. Not only was his aunt a savvy politician, she was an ace lawyer.

Dale had been a good boy ever since, buying reams of kiddie porn and forcing himself to be satisfied with paper images.

But temptation had finally called in the form of Kayla Michelle Lyman, handed to him like a present from Satan himself, and before Dale ever touched her he knew he would never let her go. It was the only way to make sure no one ever knew.

There had been a moment of terror when his aunt called, because Dale knew she remembered what he had done at fourteen; but that had been well over a dozen years ago, and he had been in no trouble since, so he was not surprised, although still relieved, to hear no trace of suspicion in her voice. He was so grateful he felt confident saying, "Whoever it is, he needs the same kind of help I got all those years ago. I don't know where I'd be now if you hadn't stepped in to help me."

His aunt praised him all over again, and Dale hung up feeling pretty good about himself.

The feeling had waned, of course, with the memory of actually killing the little girl. Drowning her had taken much longer than he believed it would, certainly much longer than when someone drowned on television. She clawed and bit and kicked with every ounce of strength in her body, and Dale was virtually exhausted when the bubbles stopped coming up and her body went still.

When he realized he had taken a life, that he had actually robbed a child of a future and ended all things for her forevermore, he started to cry. With his orgasm had gone the desire to be slick and sneaky and remain undetected in his role as pedophile. He wanted only to be away from the body and the evidence of what he had done. Killing her didn't turn him on in the least, but it was the only way to hide what he had done so no one would ever know.

Dale cried the whole time he waded through the water with her. He took her to a dock at Diamond Bay and stuck her underneath, wedging her with a board so she would stay.

He wouldn't do it again, he promised himself. Never. Not if he was presented with ten lost little girls and no one looking.

It was time to act like a normal man and copulate with something over the age of twelve.

As he looked around himself at the dance, he realized he could have his pick of at least three.

But he wasn't even remotely interested. If they wanted it, he didn't. He had to feel like he was taking something forbidden, like what he was doing was wrong in some way. It seemed to be the only thing that aroused him, shoving it in where he knew it wasn't wanted and seeing an agonized expression before him as he did it.

Dale didn't think he was necessarily bad for feeling this way. Lots of people had perverted streaks, he told himself. People who worked in banks, discount stores, factories. Even people who held office.

He had slipped, but it would never happen again. He made a solemn promise to himself, and he had made a promise to the Lymans the day Renard brought the girl's body back to shore. But it wasn't as if the couple was left completely childless. They still had two other little girls.

CHAPTER FOURTEEN

MANUEL TOOK JACQUELINE AND Madeleine on the fishing boat Saturday and instructed both women to pray for a good-sized bass for supper. The girls rubbed in sunscreen and took out a deck of cards. They were playing War and laughing when Dale Russell motored up to them in his boat and called out to Madeleine.

"I missed you at the dance Thursday night."

"I didn't go," she responded.

"Must be why I missed you. What are you doing tonight?"

"I have plans for the weekend," she said, cutting off the possibility of doing anything the next night. She could feel Jacqueline's eyes on her.

"Keep a night open for me next week?" Dale asked, and Madeleine smiled and waved him on.

He smiled back, provoking a sigh from Jacqueline, and then he motored away again, the waves from his wake rocking them in the fishing boat.

"He is not so handsome," said Manuel.

Jacqueline winked at her husband. "I wouldn't kick him out of bed."

"Be careful, Jacqueline," her husband warned. "You know my jealous temper."

"Your turn," Jacqueline said to Madeleine, getting back to the game.

"Thank you," said Madeleine.

"For what?"

"For not bugging me about going out with him."

Jacqueline brushed a strand of hair out of her sister's eyes. "Only when you're ready."

Madeleine shook her head. "I lied to you about that. It's not really a matter of being ready, because it wasn't as if I loved Sam at the end."

Jacqueline looked up. "Yes, I know. You felt a lot of anger."

"Apathy, Jacqueline. There was no feeling for him. No caring. In those last two years he killed everything I ever felt for him."

Jacqueline's voice lowered. "Then it must be the guilt you feel over his death that prevents you from looking at anyone else."

But I have been looking, Madeleine wanted to say. *Just not at who you'd think.*

She shuffled the cards and continued the game.

SUNDAY EVENING AFTER JACQUELINE and Manuel left, Madeleine's stomach began to rumble. She blinked in surprise at the discomfort and thought immediately of the supposedly fresh shrimp they had purchased from a truck at Diamond Bay. A minute later she was up and running to the bathroom, her bowels cramping.

The diarrhea was terrible, leaving her weak and unsteady as she left the bathroom. Five minutes later she lunged for the kitchen sink, where she threw up the contents of her stomach and held onto the counter with all her strength to keep from sagging down to the floor.

When she could stand without nausea she returned to the bathroom and opened the cabinets in a desperate search for something to stem the sickness. There was nothing.

Before she left the bathroom she had to heave again, and she sank to the floor and hung on with both arms while fluid gushed from her body.

When it was over she could do nothing but sit down by the bathtub and hang her head over the edge. She nodded off, only to be awakened again minutes later by another insistent urge from her bowels. While she was sitting on the toilet she felt herself momentarily black out and go sliding off to the floor. When she regained control she was on her hands and knees, ready to retch.

After the heaving ended, Madeleine felt so weak she began to cry.

Two of the kittens came in to look at her, and one of them sniffed at the mess on the floor while the other gave her toe a tentative lick.

She spent the night in the bathroom being sick, and never had she felt more alone, having no one to help her and no one to call. She would not bother Jacqueline and Manuel at such a distance. Nor would she allow herself to call Renard, whom she would most definitely be using, and whom she had no wish to see in her present condition.

She took sips of water from the tap when she could, and then watched it gush out of her again.

By morning she was able to crawl to the kitchen, where she opened the refrigerator and took out one of Manuel's Diet Sprites. The first taste felt like heaven. The second was dangerous, and the third caused instant rumbling. Madeleine put the can back in the refrigerator and heard the three kittens crying noisily to be fed. She wished she could help them, but she couldn't seem to stand, and her arms felt exhausted simply from lifting the can to her mouth.

She took the Diet Sprite from the refrigerator again and crawled back to the bathroom, where within the hour she gave up the lemon-lime liquid to the toilet.

During the night she crawled out of her clothes and left them in a smelly pile in the corner of the bathroom. She left her bra and panties on and promptly began to shiver with the fever that burned in her.

She hugged herself and closed her eyes.

Sometime the next day she heard heavy knocking on her door, but all Madeleine could do was moan. The fever had her in its grip and she was curled into a ball on the floor of the bathroom, her mouth caked with vomit and her undergarments soiled. The knocking stopped after a while and the person went away, leaving Madeleine to her fitful, feverish sleep.

Later she awakened to tiny claws digging trenches in the

tender skin of her thigh, but she was too disoriented to do anything about it. The chills were worse and all she could hear was
the sound of her teeth chattering in her head. Her throat was
parched, and in her delirium she believed she was back on that
deserted highway, painted white, bleeding, and burning, burning, burning.

The pounding she heard was the slow steady thud of her own
heart that went on and on and on and would not let her rest it
was so loud. Sam added to the noise, whining how he could use
a little understanding, and Madeleine pointed one white arm and
told him he hadn't stopped the burning or the bleeding, and to
please get her someone who could.

Suddenly she felt herself being lifted up, high into the air, and
when she opened her eyes she saw a scarred brown cheek and a
straight nose. The mouth she recognized. She said his name.

He looked down at her with dark, worried eyes, and she heard
herself ask in a croaking voice for a drink of water.

He put her down on a mattress with cool sheets and covered
her up.

She drifted in and out, opening her eyes to find him washing
her face and arms with a warm, damp washcloth, and opening
her mouth to take whatever liquids he poured in. Once she heard
him on the phone in the kitchen, and another time she woke up
to find him sitting on the bed beside her, reading the back of a
bottle of medicine.

It was morning again before she was able to open her eyes and
keep them open. She looked around herself and saw him lying
asleep beside her, his feet hanging over the end of the bed. He
came awake while she was staring at him, and he instantly left
the mattress and came around to look at her.

"Do you want something to drink?" he asked. His hair was half
out of its band and hanging over his shoulder.

"Yes," she said, and he disappeared. She could hear him in the
kitchen, and then he was back again, carrying a glass of fruit
juice. He put the glass down on the night stand and picked up
the pillow he had been using to put it behind her head and prop
her up.

"You need to take as much as you can," he told her.

Madeleine nodded and picked up the glass to sip. "Did I hear
you on the phone with someone? Who did you call?"

"Ortiz. Your sister wanted to come, but she's been ill herself. She said to tell you it was the shrimp."

"How long have you been here?"

"I came at noon yesterday when I noticed you hadn't picked up the papers. I knocked, and there was no answer. I tried again last night and heard you yelling. I came in and found you on the floor in the bathroom."

"I was yelling?"

"Fever," said Eris, and saying the word, he touched her forehead with the inside of his arm. "Still warm."

Madeleine closed her eyes. "I don't think I've ever been so sick." Then her lids came up and she looked at him in dismay. "I'm sorry I keep being a nuisance. You can go on to work now, Eris. I'll be all right."

He pointed to his belt and his beeper on top of her dresser. "I told your sister I'd take care of you."

"That was nice, but you don't have to. I'll get up and get some broth later."

"I don't think you can," he said in a patient voice. "You're weak, Madeleine, and if you try to get up you'll be dizzy."

"I'll be fine. Really. I will ask you to feed the kittens before you go."

"I already did."

"Thanks."

He went on looking at her, concern still apparent in his features, and finally he asked, "Why didn't you call someone?"

"I should have," she said, her lids closing again. "It was awful being so sick and having no one here."

Eris didn't speak, only continued to watch her, and Madeleine suddenly thought to lift the sheets and look at herself.

"Ugh," she said. She was still wearing the soiled things. Eris had stopped washing at her waist, apparently.

"I need a bath," she said.

"I'll get you a washcloth and a pan of water."

"No, I want to get in the tub. Can you run the water and bring me a towel?"

"Don't you want to eat something first?"

"No. I've got to get out of these things." She gestured weakly at the bra she wore.

Eris drew a breath and disappeared. Madeleine heard the

sound of the taps being turned, then running water. He came back into the bedroom with a large towel and handed it to her.

"Thank you. Can you go out for a minute? I'll call when I'm ready."

He went out and she removed her bra and panties and wrapped the towel around her as best she could before telling him to come in again. He came and stood beside the bed while she gingerly put her legs over the side. He bent over to help her stand, and after only two steps she was sagging against him and losing the towel, her vision gone black and her equilibrium lost. She heard herself moan and she felt his hands come under her legs to swing her up into his arms. The towel came away completely and he kicked it away with his foot as he carried her across the hall to the bathroom and lowered her as gently as he could into the warm water of the still filling bathtub.

Madeleine's hands gripped the sides of the tub until her vision cleared, and then she delicately covered herself until he was out of the bathroom and in the hall. Her head was still spinning, and she lowered it, eyes closed, until she felt stable again.

She stayed in the water until it cooled, soaping herself and rinsing over and over again to rid herself of the smell of sickness. He came to the door once and asked if she was ready to get out. She said no, not yet, and thought of how carefully expressionless was his face as he helped her.

When she finally called to him she twisted herself around in the tub until her back was to him as he came in. He put a towel around her shoulders and carefully lifted, helping her up until she could wrap the towel securely around herself.

"Let me try walking again," she said, and he allowed her to lean against him as they entered the hall. She did well, feeling only moderately dizzy as they reached the bed, which she was surprised to discover had fresh sheets.

"Do you have pajamas?" he asked.

"A T-shirt," she said. "In the right-hand drawer."

He took out the T-shirt and laid it on the bed, his eyes moving over her small shivering frame in concern.

"You need to eat something," he said. "I'll get the broth."

She nodded and gestured for him to go and leave her to get dressed. When her T-shirt was over her head and she was under the fresh sheets, he brought in a cup of hot chicken broth and sat down on the edge of the mattress while she tried it. Madeleine drained the whole cup and asked for another. He brought her another and she drained it same as the first. He gave her some crackers then, and watched as she made crumbs on the clean sheets.

"You really can go," she said. "What time is it?"

He looked at his watch. "One-thirty."

"No beeps yet?"

His mouth twisted and he took the empty cup to the kitchen and came back with a glass of water.

"I'm sorry," she said. "I know your job is more than answering calls."

"You should take some aspirin while you're awake, try to keep your fever down. Right beside you on the stand."

"Okay," she said, and as he handed her the glass of water, she looked at him and said, "It was chicken pox, wasn't it?"

Eris went still as the question registered. Then he said, "Yes, it was chicken pox."

"I've seen it before," Madeleine explained. "You were a teen-ager?"

"Sixteen."

"How were you exposed?"

"Sick kids in Oklahoma."

"You traveled there with your parents?"

"No."

She waited for him to go on, and when he didn't, she said, "Am I correct in assuming you left your adoptive parents at a relatively young age?"

"I was thirteen." He took the glass from her after she had swallowed the aspirin and said, "Sam was your husband?"

Madeleine blinked in shocked, uncomfortable surprise, and it was her turn to ask, "How did you know?"

"It was him you were yelling at when I found you. I mentioned it to Manuel, and he told me your husband shot himself several months ago. He said you found him, and that you're still dealing with the trauma, even in your sickness."

Madeleine snorted and looked away.

Eris said, "I'll stop asking about your life if you stop asking about mine."

"Are you ashamed of your life?" she asked, angry at Manuel for painting such a tragic picture of her.

"Not with any part of it," he said. "I just don't need any misplaced sympathy."

"Neither do I. If I'm ashamed of anything it's the fact that Sam Craven is dead and I don't care."

Once the words were out she paused in alarm. She had said it. The first time she had spoken it aloud. Madeleine waited for lightning to strike. She waited for the god of wedding vows to come and punish her for lying on her wedding day. She waited to be chastised and berated for admitting such a thing about a man whose bed she had slept in, whose life she had shared. Another human being.

Eris took a deep breath and said, "I can see why he shot himself."

Madeleine's head came up.

"If you were my wife," he went on in a quiet voice, "it would kill me to know you didn't care."

She stared at him, and her throat thickened. Her eyes grew moist and she withdrew from him, turning her face into the pillow and pulling the sheet over her shoulder. She had never expected to hear Eris Renard say such a thing. Her weakened heart pounded in her chest as she clutched at the sheet.

A moment later she heard him leave the room.

The next time she awakened she rolled over and found a plate with a sandwich on her night stand. A note said Eris would come to check on her in the morning.

Madeleine crumpled the note in her hand and picked up the sandwich. She didn't know why, but she had the feeling he wouldn't be back. Not after what she had admitted, and not after what he had said.

CHAPTER
FIFTEEN

ON THURSDAY MORNING ERIS rose earlier than usual and was brushing his teeth in the bathroom when his phone rang. He spat out toothpaste and wiped his mouth before going to answer. He was surprised to hear Sheila Lyman identify herself.

"What can I do for you?" he asked.

"I ain't sure," she said, her voice low. "I'm only gonna tell this once, and I'm tellin' it to you because you're the only person who ever stuck up for me against Ronnie, and I want you to know the truth if anything should happen to me. I want him to pay for what happened to my baby Kayla."

"Why should he pay?" Eris asked.

"Because he set the whole thing up. He made his drunk old mama take Kayla and then told everyone she disappeared, when she was with his mama at her place."

Eris stood very still. "The disappearance was faked?"

"Ronnie the genius had it all worked out, figurin' to get sympathy and money from people. He told me what to say on television and everything. He had a deal with his mama for her to bring Kayla and drop her off at the Haven, that bait shop up on the access road there. Only he called and had his mama drop her off early, on account of you kickin' us out of the park. He thought folks'd get mad and maybe send more money if our little girl showed up the day after we had to leave."

Eris was holding his breath, his mind whirring. Finally he inhaled and said, "His mother dropped her off at the Haven as scheduled, and that's the last anyone saw of Kayla, is that it?"

"That's it. Ronnie said some crazy got her in front of the store. I ain't so sure it wasn't him, greedy as he is. No tellin' what he thought, that maybe folks'd feel even sorrier if she turned up . . . well, the way she did."

Eris didn't know what to say. Worse, he didn't know what he could do about it, short of adding a few other charges to those Lyman already faced.

"Will you testify to any of this?" Eris asked, already knowing the answer.

"I can't. Ronnie hurt me bad once, and he'll do it again if he has the chance. I just wanted someone to know what he did, and what he made me a part of. I was scared from the start and didn't wanna do it, and look what happened. All I want now is for me and my girls to start over, and I don't know if we're gonna be able to do it here, not while he's still lookin' for us. We may have to go somewhere else."

"They won't be able to do anything to him unless you testify, Mrs. Lyman. You have to tell other people about the hoax."

"I want to, but I can't. You gotta understand that. I gotta go now, this is long distance. 'Bye."

She hung up, and Eris shook his head as he replaced the receiver.

A hoax. The whole thing had been faked. All those man-hours spent searching. All that misery.

All for a few stinking goddamned dollars of sympathy money.

Eris picked up the phone again to call his superior when he realized it was still too early. The man wouldn't be in his office yet.

One thing made him feel only minutely better. It was possible, if Kayla had been taken from in front of the Haven, that it was someone only passing through, and not a member of the lake community at all.

When he saw Dale Russell drive up to Madeleine's cabin a few minutes later he headed out the door and walked up to see what the other man wanted.

"She's been sick," he said, before Russell could knock.

Dale turned, surprised to see him. "Has she?"

"Very."

"You her doctor?" said Russell, grinning.

"The next best thing," said Eris. "You want me to give her a message?"

Russell turned and held up his hands. "Just tell her I came by. You headed out this morning?"

"After I check on her."

"Okay. See you around."

Eris waited until Russell was in his pickup and driving up the road before approaching the cabin. He let himself in with the key Manuel had given him after purchasing the place. Eris had agreed to look after the cabin during the winter.

He was surprised to see Madeleine sitting at the kitchen counter and drinking a cup of tea.

"Hi," she said when she turned, and he thought to himself that she looked surprised to see him. "Did I hear you talking to someone out there?"

"Dale Russell. He was coming by to see you."

Madeleine rolled her eyes, and Eris nearly smiled.

"You look better this morning," he said and moved to stand beside her. "Fever all gone?"

"Seems to be," she said. "And as for looking better, I scared myself when I glanced in the mirror a while ago."

"Your face is thinner," he agreed, and he spied a plate of toast going uneaten in front of her. She followed his eyes and handed him a piece.

"Want some jelly?"

"No." He took a bite. "You need to eat."

"I will." She turned on the stool. "I called Jacqueline a minute ago. She's still sick, so they don't know if they'll be coming up this weekend. I thought I'd ask if you want to go to a movie, or maybe out to dinner somewhere . . . as payment for your excellent nursing services," she quickly added.

"No payment is required," he said, and he saw a flash of disappointment in her eyes. "We'd end up driving half the night," he explained. "There's nothing close."

"Just a thought," she said, her mouth suddenly tight. She got off the stool and muttered something about Dale Russell as she dumped her tea into the sink.

"What?"

She kept her back to him. "Nothing."

"If you can't afford cat food, you can't buy dinner or a movie," he told her.

"You're right," she said, angry now. "It was stupid of me to ask. I don't know what I was thinking."

Eris didn't know why she was so mad; he was only trying to save her money. He finished the toast and was preparing to leave when the beeper on his belt sounded. He moved toward the phone in the kitchen. "May I?"

She lifted a hand. "Of course."

Two minutes later Eris was hearing about a pair of raccoons trapped in a woman's garage thirty miles away. She didn't want to hurt them, but she was afraid they would poop on her father's precious Packard, parked in the garage for years and years. Eris said he would be there shortly and hung up the phone.

He paused at the door, something in him not wanting to leave Madeleine mad at him.

"Teach me this weekend," he said, and saw her head swivel.

"Teach you?"

"If Mr. and Mrs. Ortiz don't come."

They eyed each other a moment, then she nodded.

ERIS USED A CATCH pole on the raccoons and had them out of the woman's garage in less than half an hour. He had to stop and marvel at the Packard a while after that, because the old woman wouldn't let him leave without doing so. He managed to escape soon afterward and he drove directly to the lake office to call his superior and tell him about Sheila Lyman's call early that morning. Jaws audibly dropped as Eris relayed what he had been told, and Ronnie Lyman had more than one employee of the Kansas Department of Wildlife and Parks promising to put a tranquilizer gun up his ass if he ever showed his face in a park again.

Later that afternoon, Eris was stunned to learn Ronnie Lyman had been released from jail. Sheila and her two girls had disappeared that morning, and once Ronnie's attorney learned she was gone, he called a judge. With no one to complain against him in court, Ronnie got off with time served and waltzed out of the crowded jail a free man.

Eris hoped wherever Sheila had gone after talking to him, it was somewhere safe.

He ran across Bruce Beckworth and a friend just after seven, out on a county road, where they were shooting at birds from the window of Beckworth's Blazer. Eris cuffed them, arrested them, and took them to jail, ignoring their pleas to be let off with only a warning.

He went home then and frowned to see Dale Russell's truck parked in the log cabin's drive.

The bastard didn't give up, Eris gave him that, and suddenly all he could think about was Madeleine's muttered comment that he couldn't hear that morning.

A part of him wanted to go up and knock on her door, but he couldn't make himself do it. He didn't know why he was feeling so proprietary suddenly, as if he had a right to question who came to see her.

He relaxed when he saw Russell come out the door a few moments later. Madeleine stood behind him, a forced smile fixed on her mouth, and Eris felt better. She was booting him out.

Here was one woman unmoved by the charms of Dale Russell, and seemingly impressed with Eris Renard. He felt as if a life-long fantasy was about to come true, where the pretty, intelligent woman spurned the charmers with their devastatingly good looks and opted for someone with no looks but lots of character.

He shook his head at himself and went on watching as Dale got in his truck and backed out of the drive. He glanced back to Madeleine and saw her looking down the yard at him in his kitchen window. She lifted a hand to wave.

Eris gave her a nod in response.

THE NEXT DAY WAS relatively quiet, and around six o'clock Eris found himself getting nervous. He would have to go home soon and change his clothes. He wasn't going to wear his uniform over to see her. His uniform was all she ever saw him in.

At home he changed into a white pullover and a faded pair of jeans and put on some Nikes. He checked the window constantly to see if Manuel's Jeep Cherokee had arrived, but when seven o'clock came and it hadn't appeared, he forced himself out the door and up to the log cabin.

She looked pleased when she opened the door and saw him standing there. She wore a pink sun dress that made him think only of what she looked like without it, and before she could read the thought in his eyes, he stepped past her to go inside. He saw several books on the kitchen counter, and she followed his glance.

"I've been to the library. Come in and sit down. We can sit on the couch, it's more comfortable."

He went to the couch and sat, and she brought the books over to put on the cocktail table in front of him.

"Do you want something to drink? I think I have a Diet Coke around somewhere."

"Fine," he said, wondering suddenly if he should consider this a date. He wasn't sure. He wiped his damp palms on the tops of his thighs.

"Okay." She brought him a Diet Coke and plopped down onto the cushion beside him. "You're probably already aware that the Fox are closely related to the Sauk, speaking the same language and having similar cultures. The Fox called themselves *Meshwahki Haki* or were otherwise known as Mesquakie. It means: the Red Earths."

Eris sat with the unopened Diet Coke in his hand, staring at her. She was jumping right into it. A real teacher.

"The Fox and the Sauk were allies for years, and during the colonial period they fought together against the French, not that they were so enamored of the English, but because they were tired of being cheated by French traders. Like many other tribes, they were actually quite passive. In the fall and winter they lived in camps of rush-mat lodges while they hunted and trapped for furs to trade, and in the summer they moved near river bottoms and became farmers of corn, beans, and squash. They—" She paused and smiled at him. "Am I going too fast? Too pedantic? You have an odd expression on your face."

It was sudden discomfort on Eris's part that caused his expression. He tried to ignore it.

"Am I going to be tested on this material?"

"Of course," she said with a smile.

"All right. Thanks for the warning. Did the Fox have enemies among other Indians?"

"Chippewa and Dakota were the most bitter. Sauk-Fox Indian allies included the Potawatomi, Winnebago, and Iowa. Nearly a century after the French were beaten came the Black Hawk War, in 1832, when the Fox and Sauk were defeated by the good old US Army and sent right here to Kansas."

"From the Northeast?"

"Well, from Iowa, which is where they were located by that time. A lot of them left Kansas and went back to Iowa during the 1850s. Many of the Fox in Kansas joined with the Sauk a few years after the Civil War and moved to the Indian Territory."

"Oklahoma," said Eris.

"Yes. If you were born here in Kansas, then it was from one of the few Fox and Sauk families that remained."

"You know all this from memory?" asked Eris, more impressed than he could say, but still uncomfortable.

"I've been refreshing my memory with these books," she said, and pointed to the stack on the cocktail table. "It would be difficult for anyone to know everything about every nation. There are so many."

Eris finally opened his Diet Coke to take a drink, and Madeleine continued, telling him about Sauk-Fox rituals and patrilineal clans, all the things he would have learned if he had ever actually opened a book about the Sauk-Fox and read it. Something had always stopped him short of learning more than the most perfunctory information. An anger, perhaps, that he should be forced to learn from a book, and not from his own blood relatives.

Now he sat, listening to a blonde-haired white woman who stood no taller than his collar bone and was no more Indian than the actors in black and white Westerns, while she told him about his ancestors.

When she paused he sat forward and put his Diet Coke down on the cocktail table.

"I have to go, Madeleine."

Her mouth fell open and she looked at him in surprise. "Why?"

He got up and walked to the door, unable to tell her what he was feeling, unable to make himself seem small or childish to her, for having such problems dealing with his lack of identity and his anger toward people he had never even met. She would not understand.

"Eris?"

The hurt and confusion in her eyes nearly made him stop and go back, fight his way through his feelings just to be near her a while longer.

But then *she* was confusing him even more, making him wonder if she needed to do exactly what she was doing, if he was, after all, someone she wanted to be friendly with because their interests were ostensibly the same, him being an Indian and all her degrees and work having to do with Native Americans.

"I can't learn from you," he said as he opened the door. "And I can't tell you why."

He turned to leave then, and the breath left him in a whoosh a second later as a tremendous force struck him square in the middle of the back. He wheeled in surprise and saw a book lying on the floor behind him. Madeleine was picking up another book to throw at him, and he took one look at her flushed cheeks and trembling mouth and said, "Don't."

Too late. The next book struck him in the face, glancing off his still sore cheekbone and causing his ear to begin ringing. She picked up another book and he hurried to take it away from her before she could wing it at close range. He grabbed her by the wrist and squeezed until she cried out and dropped the book.

"Stop," he said, his tone warning.

"*You* stop," she said fiercely. "Who's using who, Eris? And what are you using me for? As a whipping post for the people who've mistreated you? What do I have to do to get through to you?"

He stared at her, his hand still holding her wrist, and when he spoke, his voice didn't sound like his.

"I don't understand what you want from me."

"I don't either," she said. "How can I? You're not exactly constant in the way you treat me. How am I supposed to understand anything to do with you when you can't make up your mind how to feel about me?"

Eris dropped her wrist and said, "I know exactly how I feel about you."

Madeleine blinked, and the anger in her slowly diminished as she looked into his face. "Don't say that. Don't say you know exactly, when you have to be just as confused as I am. You keep running away from me."

"What I know, Madeleine," said Eris, "is what I want to do with you. What I don't know is how you'll react if I try."

She froze, as if the breath had been knocked out of her, and Eris felt suddenly damned, believing he had gone too far and said too much, scaring her with his confession.

"Are you saying that's all you want?" she asked, her voice breathless.

"No."

Her lashes lowered and she looked at the floor, and Eris found himself thinking this was the part where she explained she wanted to be just friends.

She said, "I know I said I was going to examine why I feel the way I do about you, but I'm no clearer now than I was a week ago. I still think you're a good man."

Eris's heart began pounding. He lifted a hand to touch her on one cheek, causing her to lift her head and look at him. He searched her eyes while she gazed at him, and Madeleine suddenly lifted herself on her tiptoes to place her arms around his neck. She raised herself up and kissed him on the center of his chin, her lips soft and moist. She moved to his cheek, and along his jaw, planting kisses on the scarred skin of his face while he tentatively placed his hands on her waist and fought to breathe.

When she came to his mouth, she placed a light kiss on his lips and looked at him. He sensed her waiting, and he gently picked her up in his arms and lifted her against his chest, bringing her mouth to his.

Eris nearly came to orgasm just parting her lips. When she made a noise into his mouth and touched her tongue to his, his knees threatened to buckle. His limbs began to shake as he held her against him and kissed her, and when he felt her press herself along the length of him he thought he would fall down. He had never tasted anything sweeter, or held anything softer.

While he could still walk he carried her to the sofa and sat down with her, tearing his mouth away from her lips long enough to ask if he could touch her.

Madeleine guided his hand to her breasts and reached behind herself to unzip her dress. His hand covered hers, and once the zipper was down the two of them pushed the dress over her hips until she was free of the garment. Eris touched the silky skin of her breasts and fought for control while she tugged his pullover free of his jeans, kissing his mouth and neck until he pulled the shirt over his head. When his chest was bare she wrapped herself around him, pressing her naked breasts against him and sweetly pushing her face against his neck and the underside of his jaw.

Eris held her that way a moment, their heated flesh melded together, his hands caressing the skin of her back and the curve of her waist and hips, and soon he felt her fingers pulling at his hair band and tangling themselves in his hair. She pulled his head back until they were looking at each other, and then she placed her mouth on his and kissed him so deeply he felt he would lose part of himself to her. Her hands were on his face and she was on her knees on the cushion between his thighs, kissing him as he had never been kissed, and when she lowered a hand to unzip his jeans and reach inside his briefs, Eris abruptly lost control.

Madeleine didn't pause in kissing him, only held on to him while he jerked and went on touching when he stopped.

Eris clutched her to him and then groaned when she left him to pull off his shoes and the rest of his clothes. When she climbed back onto the sofa with him he slid his hands down over her hips to remove her underwear. One hand went back to caress the area uncovered, and he shuddered when his fingers encountered evidence of her arousal. Madeleine moaned and pressed herself against his hand, and the movements of her body soon had Eris erect again and wanting to know the inside of her.

She tangled her fingers in his hair and breathlessly kissed one ear before he lifted himself up. Madeleine shuddered as he gently probed and then began to push himself inside her. She gasped and clutched at his forearms, and Eris saw her lips part and her eyes squeeze shut, and his mouth went dry as he realized she had come to orgasm just by having him inside her.

The knowledge overwhelmed him, and he kissed her as passionately as she had kissed him, only beginning to move when her hands pulled at him and her hips raised to prompt him. After that he wasn't aware of anything but the taste of her lips, the sounds from her throat, and sensation.

When he stopped his breathing was labored, and Madeleine's chest was heaving. They were silent, looking at each other in the dimness, Eris still inside her and Madeleine's arms wrapped around him.

Suddenly the beeper attached to the belt on Eris's jeans shattered the stillness.

Madeleine jumped but Eris didn't move. He went on looking at her face. Madeleine tightened her arms around him until the beeper repeated. He kissed her on the lips and for the second time that evening said, "I have to go."

He slid away from her and Madeleine reluctantly let him go. She sat up and watched as he dressed, and before he left her, he moved to cup her face with his hand. She turned her lips into his palm. Eris drew a ragged breath and walked away.

Someone was out spotlighting deer that night. Several shots had been fired. Eris hung up the phone in the kitchen and thought if he caught the persons responsible he would probably kill them.

CHAPTER
SIXTEEN

MADELEINE LAY AWAKE FOR hours after Eris left, hugging the pillow beside her and reliving every moment he had been with her. She loved his mouth. And his body. The size of him had nearly driven her wild with pleasure. She had never been with anyone like him, never known what it felt like to be filled so completely or kissed with such emotion.

Her own passion had been a surprise. She had known she was attracted, but not until his naked flesh was against hers and her hands were trapped in his hair did she realize how utterly and completely she wanted him, how badly she wanted to hold on and keep holding him, so that whatever barriers he threw up between them would have no place.

Like his problem with her teaching him. Madeleine didn't understand what that was about. She only knew there was a moment when he had looked at her and seen not Madeleine, but a white woman.

Madeleine had faced similar situations before, but never with someone she cared about. It drove her into a frenzy when he simply got up and said he couldn't learn from her and couldn't tell her why.

He wanted to spend his passion on her, but he wouldn't talk to her about himself.

Suddenly Madeleine wondered if she was making a big mistake. If he even cared about her at all, beyond the fact that she was a woman romantically interested in him.

And she still didn't know *why* she was interested. Because he had spurned every overture on her part and piqued her curiosity? Because he was a tall, dark Indian, and she had a point to prove to herself about not being afraid anymore?

Or was it because he gave and gave and never took anything in return. Because he treated everyone alike, from kittens to earthworms, and because he was human enough to get sick after fishing a little girl's body from the lake.

Madeleine had never known anyone so capable, so able to handle any situation, from conducting a search party to babysitting a woman sick with fever. She wondered if there was any situation he couldn't handle, anything he wouldn't face with the same quiet determination. She doubted it. He was as solid as the earth.

She covered her eyes as she lay in bed, wondering what she was going to do when she had to leave him. She couldn't live in the cabin indefinitely. Her funds were running out.

Madeleine hated even to think about leaving. She hated the thought of being where she wouldn't see him every day.

But she had to get back to work. What money she had would be gone completely by summer's end, and there was no more coming in. She couldn't buy or do anything without having to worry about whether the cats would starve.

She was out of cat food, as a matter of fact, and she had hoped Manuel and Jacqueline would bring some. Since they hadn't come, the babies were going to have to make do with table scraps. And maybe she could catch a fish or two, she thought, remembering having seen a cane pole in the garage. Perhaps Sherman Tanner could give her some tips on where to dig for worms.

A chuckle escaped her lips, and Madeleine found herself wondering if any studies had been done on tiny lake communities like the one in which she was now living. An anthropological study, comparing the village communities of America past with present-day counterparts.

Might be something to think about, she told herself. God knew there was a different breed of people out here among the year-round crowd. Maybe it was something she could work on in her spare time, just to keep herself occupied. Go out and talk to the people, see how they lived. She knew how Eris Renard and Sherman Tanner lived, and since both of them were out of the norm she could only imagine what else she might encounter.

A shiver passed through her as she thought of Eris asking if he could touch her. Who would do such a thing but a man unused to touching a woman?

She squeezed her eyes shut and warned herself to tread with caution. She already knew she was in emotional danger, not because she felt vulnerable after Sam, or because her sexuality had been tapped, but because he was Eris, totally unpredictable and unlike anyone she had ever known.

He had not offered to come back when he was finished, or made a promise to see her tomorrow, or said anything at all to her indicating she would see him again soon.

It was typical of him.

Madeleine yawned and wondered if the difference in their ages would ever come into play. As she drifted off it occurred to her that she had not used her diaphragm, and as she fell into slumber a tiny frown creased her brow.

WHEN SHE AWAKENED IT was midmorning and full sun was coming in her windows. Her first thought was of the night before, and she sighed into her mattress before forcing herself out of bed. A sudden, insistent pounding on her door made her shake a leg, and she grabbed a robe out of the closet and threw it on before hurrying to open the door.

Dale Russell smiled at her. "Morning, sleepyhead. Did I get you out of bed?"

Madeleine's shoulders drooped in disappointment.

"What brings you out, Dale?"

"I was in to see Renard this morning and thought I'd stop and see how you're getting along."

"He's home?" Madeleine said in surprise and looked toward his house.

"He left a while ago. Guess he had a late night, out hunting spotlighters. Did you hear about the hoax?"

"What hoax?"

"The missing little girl wasn't missing at all. Her disappearance was faked by her father and his mother. They were after money."

Madeleine was confused. "Then how did she end up in the lake?"

"Seems Lyman's mother left her in front of the Haven, knowing someone would come and find her, probably take her to the authorities. The wrong person found her."

Madeleine shook her head.

"Makes you sick, doesn't it?" said Dale.

"It makes me angry," Madeleine told him.

"Angry?"

"At the man responsible."

"What makes you think it was a man?"

"Last time I checked, women weren't capable of producing semen."

"You know about that, huh?"

"Everyone on the hill knows about that. Sherman Tanner keeps us all informed."

Dale frowned, and she realized he didn't know who she was talking about. It was just as well.

"Shouldn't you be out on the lake?" she asked.

"Trying to get rid of me?" he said with a grin.

"Yes," she said bluntly. "Honestly, Dale, you're very charming, but I'm just not interested."

"Why?" he asked, just as bluntly.

Madeleine decided on the facts as opposed to the truth.

"A few months ago my husband committed suicide. Is that enough for you, or do you want the details?"

Dale backed up slightly. "I'm sorry. I didn't realize."

"Now you do. I'm flattered, Dale, believe me, but that's all I am."

"Okay. Well, wow, I don't know what to say. I'm sorry, I guess." He paused then. "Do you need a friend, Madeleine? Someone to talk to?"

"I'm fine," she said.

"Because sometimes I do," he said, as if he hadn't heard her. "Sometimes I really need someone just to listen while I talk. If you ever need that, think of me. Will you do that?"

Madeleine was groaning inside, wondering what she had created. "Yes, Dale, I will. Thank you. Goodbye now."

"Goodbye, Madeleine." He reached forward and gave her an impulsive hug. She stiffened and did not move until he released her.

When he was gone, Madeleine jerked off the robe and stepped into the shower, thinking perhaps it was because of Sam that handsome men now gave her the creeps.

AT NOON SHE ATE a sandwich and then went outside to dig worms. Eris hadn't come home for lunch, but he wouldn't, since he had gotten such a late start. She came up with six good-sized worms under the railroad ties bordering Eris's coleus. Sherman Tanner came to see what she was doing and to warn her how Renard felt about his plants.

"I'm not hurting anything," said Madeleine.

"Neither was I. I was just doing some thinning."

"You told me he said you could take the plants."

"He did. He said to ask."

"Before or after you took them?"

Sherman gave her a pinched look and walked away, his shoulders straight and his head held high. Madeleine smiled to herself as she watched him go, then went to fetch the cane pole from the garage.

She found a bobber and a stringer, and noted that a tiny lead weight was already attached to the line. She let the kittens out to play and then carried everything down to the lake in a straw bag, looking as she went for the perfect spot to sit and fish. Vista Bay was too crowded, and the swimmers near the swimming area would scare any fish away. She walked awhile longer and finally found a quiet little cove, where the water was still and looked just right for fishing.

A tiny perch hit on her worm the minute she dropped it in the water and Madeleine gleefully jerked it out and removed it from the hook to place on her stringer.

"One little fishy for my kitties," she sang to herself, and stuck another worm on her hook. Fifteen minutes later she had one fish for each worm, not one of them bigger than her hand.

When her fish were on the stringer, Madeleine fixed her pole and prepared to leave. Then she saw Dale Russell come motoring up to her in his boat.

She held up her stringer. "Look what I caught."

He didn't smile. "Do you have a fishing license, ma'am?"

"A license? No, I don't. Do I need one?"

"You do. Put the fish back or pay a fine."

"What?" She couldn't believe he meant it.

He did. "You heard me."

"But, two of them are dead already. Can't I at least take the dead ones?"

"Put the fish back or pay a fine."

"Why are you being like this? Because I hurt your feelings earlier?"

His face remained implacable. "I assume you want the fine?"

"No," she said, angry now. "I don't." She dropped her stringer in the water and released all the fish, even the dead ones. Without looking at him, she took her pole and carried it up the bank, furious with him for being such a jerk. He was paying her back for not responding to him, for leaving him looking as ridiculous as she felt right now.

"Dammit," she swore as she walked back up the hill.

She was a hundred yards from the cabin when she saw something that made her drop everything and start running. Sherman Tanner's little terrier mixture mutt had one of her kittens in its mouth and was tossing it about like a rag doll. Madeleine screamed and charged at the dog, aiming a kick at its side and seeing it dart away from her, the obviously dead kitten still hanging from its mouth.

"Tanner!" she screamed, her voice raw as she looked helplessly about for the other kittens. She found another one dead in the grass just beyond the porch, half its little face torn away. "Tanner!" she screamed again, tears of rage streaming down her face. A mewing sound made her head swerve and she jerked around to find the tiny black kitten in a tree, calling plaintively to her.

The little terrier mixture dog was suddenly nowhere to be seen. Madeleine went to the tree and took the kitten down to put it in the cabin before she went striding down the hill again to stand and pound on Sherman Tanner's door.

A thin woman with close-set eyes and a long nose came to the door, her brows lifted in annoyance.

"What is it?"

Mole woman, thought Madeleine. The Earthworm and Mole Woman lived together.

"Your dog killed two of my kittens," Madeleine said. "He was in my yard just a moment ago with one of them in his mouth. He ran away when I tried to catch him."

Mrs. Tanner was already shaking her head. "Not our dog. He's been right here the whole afternoon." She stood aside and gestured into the living room, where Madeleine saw the dog sitting on Sherman Tanner's lap as he reclined in a chair before a television.

"*That* is the dog," said Madeleine firmly and succinctly. "No two animals could look like . . . that."

"You're mistaken," said Gudrun Tanner. "Go and beat on someone else's door."

Madeleine put a hand out when the woman would have slammed the door.

"I want the other kitten. You're not going to add him to your little boneyard."

Gudrun appeared shocked. "Sherman, call the police. This woman is harassing us."

"Give me the other goddamned kitten!" Madeleine yelled. "I'll call the police myself and get a warrant to search your yard for body parts!"

Sherman Tanner snorted and came to the door.

"Run along, Miss Heron. It's your word against ours."

"Give him back," Madeleine demanded.

Tanner only smiled. "Guess you'll watch what you say and mind your manners a little better now. You still have one kitten left, don't you?"

Madeleine felt her eyes grow round. "You did this on purpose? You turned your dog loose on my kittens because of what I said to you about the goddamned *coleus*?"

Tanner shut the door in her face in response.

My god, Madeleine thought. What was with these people? First Dale Russell, and now Sherman Tanner, both of them exacting revenge and behaving like vicious, spoiled children.

She trudged back up the hill, stopping to search Eris's garage for a spade. She found one hanging on the wall and took it to the cabin with her, where she picked up the dead kitten in the grass and searched for a place to bury it, somewhere Tanner wouldn't find. She could just see him digging up the dead kitten and re-burying it in his own yard.

She picked a spot near some hedges, where she could camou-flage the overturned earth, and wrapped the kitten in a small dishtowel before burying it. The silence of the cemetery across the road beckoned then, and she went to squeeze through the gate and walk among the stones, destressing herself by reading what inscriptions could be read and thinking about the lives bur-ied deep beneath the earth. It was a strangely peaceful place to sit, and she did just that, until the stone's lengthening shadows and her own growling stomach told her it was time to go.

Madeleine carried the spade back to Eris's garage and found his truck inside. She hadn't seen him come down the road. She walked around to the front yard and saw him lifting up the rail-road ties bordering his coleus.

"What are you doing?" she asked, and he looked up with a start to see her. She waited, breathless, for some acknowledgement in his eyes of the intimacy they had shared, but he only nodded to his porch, where a young bird of some kind sat in a cage, its feathers ruffled up around its neck.

"Looking for worms."

"I already got them," she said, and he dropped the railroad tie to face her.

"Did you take my spade?"

She swallowed and nodded, wondering if he was angry with her. "I had to bury one of the kittens. Tanner's dog killed two of them today."

Eris looked beyond her, toward Tanner's house. "Why did you need the worms?"

"I ran out of cat food and needed something to feed the kittens. I found a cane pole in the garage and decided to try and catch a fish for them. I caught six fish, but Dale Russell made me throw them back because I didn't have a license. When I got back here I found Tanner's dog with a kitten in its mouth. One kitten was already dead."

"Where was Tanner?"

"In his house. When I confronted them they swore it wasn't their dog, but I'd know that sick little weaselish-looking hairbag anywhere."

Eris's mouth twitched. "Russell made you throw your fish back?"

"He was mad because I rejected him this morning."

"He came over this morning?"

"Right after he left your house."

"He left before I did."

"Then he came back. I told him I wasn't interested and he seemed all right with it at the time, but when he caught me with the fish later he was an absolute jerk."

"You don't have a license," said Eris. "Can't fish without one."

The matter-of-fact statement caught Madeleine by surprise and she stared at him. "This day hasn't been bad enough, but you have to come home and side with these lake mutants against me."

"I'll get you a license," said Eris.

"Forget it," Madeleine flashed at him. "I only have one kitten left to feed."

She walked away from him, leaving him to hunt worms to feed whatever bird it was he had in the cage. Beside the door at the cabin she found a sack of cat food waiting for her. She looked over her shoulder but couldn't see him. Madeleine sighed and picked up the heavy sack to carry it inside with her.

Later she carried a covered plate of spaghetti, meatballs, and garlic bread with butter down to him. He was still on his porch, trying to feed the bird.

"What kind is it?" she asked as she set the plate down beside him.

"A red-tailed hawk. Found it in the road today."

"How old is it?"

"Not very. Can't find anything it'll eat."

"Try a meatball."

Eris looked at the plate. "Smells good."

"Better eat, before it gets cold."

"Here," he said, and gestured to a dish with what looked like chopped raw meat inside. "You try."

Madeleine made a face, but she stuck her fingers in the dish while Eris went inside for a fork to eat his spaghetti. She picked up a pinch of the meat and put her hand through the bars to hold it temptingly above the baby hawk's head.

The bird's head moved slightly, but its eyes were in a half-closed state and Madeleine didn't think it was even aware of the food. She dipped her hand to touch it lightly on the head, and Eris came out in time to see the baby hawk's beak open. Madeleine dropped the meat in, and then had the top of her finger punctured as the beak made either a swift gobbling or attacking motion. She jerked her hand out and looked at the blood welling up on the finger.

"Must be a woman's touch," she said.

"Come on," said Eris, and he led the way into the bathroom, where he poured stinging disinfectant over the torn flesh and then put on a bandage.

Madeleine applied pressure with another finger so it would stop the bleeding, and she looked up to find Eris's dark eyes on her face.

Her breathing went suddenly shallow and a surge of warmth spread through her at his expression. She took an unconscious step forward and he leaned down to kiss the tip of her nose before turning her and leading her back outside again.

Madeleine was disappointed. Everything inside her was ready and eager to join with him again, and his eyes told her he wanted the same. She didn't understand why he brought her back outside. She looked at him with questioning eyes as he picked up the plate of spaghetti and began to eat.

She doubted it was hunger that kept them apart. When she was close to him she didn't care if she ever ate again.

He picked up a long instrument that looked like tweezers and handed it to her. "Pick up the meat with this and feed it to the bird."

"Oh," she said, feeling incredibly stupid.

While Eris ate, she fed the bird, who had suddenly found its appetite and was greedily choking down every morsel she passed through the cage. When the dish was empty she put it down and saw that Eris had finished as well. He excused himself to go and clean the sauce off his shirt, and after a moment she followed him into the house. She found him in the bathroom sluicing water over his face. Madeleine propped herself in the doorway and stood watching him until he opened his eyes and saw her.

He took a towel from the rack and dried himself. Then he said, "I don't have anything to protect you."

Madeleine said, "I have a diaphragm."

"Were you wearing it last night?"

"No."

He went still, watching her. Then he asked if she was worried.

She shook her head. "Do you want me to go and get it? The diaphragm?"

"If you're asking me if I want to make love to you, the answer is yes. If you're asking me would I like to see you protect yourself from me, the answer is no."

Madeleine's gaze fixed on his. "You just said you didn't have anything to protect me. It sounded like you were concerned about it."

"For your sake, yes. I'm sure you'd rather not leave here pregnant."

"Then you're all right?" Madeleine asked. "The chicken pox didn't—I mean, sometimes sterility can result."

"I've never found out."

He put the towel back in the rack and moved past her to leave the bathroom. Madeleine followed him and walked out of the house and up to the cabin. She put her diaphragm in place and came back to find him sitting in his chair in front of the silent television. She closed the door behind her and approached the chair. Eris hesitated only a moment before he put out a hand and pulled her to him, bringing her to sit on his lap. She slid her arms around his neck and closed her eyes while she pressed her mouth against his cheek and jaw. He turned his head and caught her lips with his, and she emitted a moan as he opened her mouth and deepened the kiss.

His hand moved to the buttons of her blouse while he kissed her, and her fingers were already busy pulling the band from his hair. She unbuttoned his shirt while he unhooked her bra, and soon their hands were free to touch flesh with no hindrances. Eris lifted her slightly to kiss her breasts and lightly tug on her hardened nipples and she buried her face in the dark silkiness of his hair. When his fingers trailed down her stomach to her navel and beyond, she squirmed so he could get at the snap on her shorts.

The shorts soon joined the pile of clothes beside the chair, and Madeleine gasped as his hand went directly between her legs and cupped the center of her, feeling the moisture that soaked the fabric of her underwear and told him of her state of readiness.

He tugged the panties off her and then lifted up while she struggled to pull his trousers and briefs down to free him. He jerked and drew in a sharp breath as Madeleine wrapped her hand around him. He stared into her face, willing control, and nearly came undone at the way she was looking at him. She moved above him, never taking her eyes off his, and slowly lowered herself onto him, taking him all the way into her and then leaning forward to gasp into his mouth as she settled over him. Eris's limbs began shaking again, and he held off not even half a minute, just long enough for Madeleine to move half a dozen times and come to a quivering orgasm, her mouth still attached to his.

They sagged against one another, still breathing hard, and with all urgency dissipated they relaxed and began to take their time touching and kissing and looking. Neither of them spoke, both unwilling to reduce to words what was happening, or to put a name to the feelings they were experiencing.

Madeleine could never get enough of kissing his lips, or of feeling her naked breasts pressed against his chest. She loved it when he put his arms around her and held her so tightly against him she could hardly breathe. He was telling her things with his actions that would never be expressed in words and it touched her more deeply than any trite, often repeated phrases ever would. She held him just as tightly, until desire arose again and their kisses became impassioned rather than sweet, and their touching had more purpose than tender caresses.

Eris put her legs around him and left the chair to carry her to his bedroom, where he placed her on the bed and then removed the rest of his clothing. Madeleine looked at his long, lean form and wondered to herself how any woman could not find him irresistible. He was so beautifully proportioned and had such wonderfully shaped hands and feet. Not to mention other proportions of him that she had grown intimately fond of.

In her enamored state Madeleine no longer saw why anyone would consider him ugly. She was blinded to the pits and scars that marred his skin and saw only his deep brown eyes and the strong white teeth that hid behind his perfect lips. The color and texture of his hair made her squirm with pleasure when she drew her fingers through it. She wanted it down always, framing his head and giving him a look of wildness that she loved.

He came onto the bed with her and she took his face in her hands as he moved over her. He paused, looking at her, and she whispered to him how beautiful he was, and how she loved to look into his eyes. Eris stared, his dark gaze seeking hers in the dimness, until she found his mouth and began to kiss him as passionately as ever, driving away whatever thoughts her murmuring had brought to him. He soon moved above her and she was carried away all over again by the instant ecstasy he brought to her and her inability to find control over her responses. All he had to do was touch her and she was on the brink.

His own control was much better now, and he was happy to be able to exhaust Madeleine before allowing himself the pleasure of release. Afterward they lay gasping together on the bed.

Madeleine made a trip to the bathroom and found her diaphragm ready to fall out. She stared and wondered if Eris had somehow dislodged it. It was entirely possible. She went to get a glass of water and drank it down at the sink before refilling it to take to Eris. Before she turned away, out of the corner of her eye she saw something that made her stop. She looked up at the log cabin and saw Dale Russell's truck backing out of the drive.

What on earth was he up to?

She went back and told Eris, and he sat up. In the darkness she could tell he was frowning.

"The man obviously has a problem with rejection," Madeleine said.

"I doubt it's ever come up before," said Eris.

"I can't believe he came back after the way he treated me today."

"Maybe he came to apologize."

Madeleine handed him the glass of water. "It won't work." She slid onto the mattress and curled up against him. Eris drank down the water and put the glass on the night stand. Then he turned and put his arms around her.

He didn't ask if she was staying the night and she didn't ask if she could. They simply fell asleep.

WHEN MADELEINE AWAKENED SHE heard the shower running. Noiselessly she left the bed and went into the living room to put on her clothes. Then she walked into his kitchen and opened the refrigerator.

Ten minutes later Eris walked into the hall with a towel wrapped around his waist. He looked to see where she was, and then he returned to his bedroom.

He came back fully dressed, and Madeleine handed him a fried egg sandwich with mayonnaise and melted cheese. He thanked her and moved to stand over the sink while he ate.

Madeleine made a similar sandwich for herself and then joined him at the sink.

He looked down at her and she smiled as she took her first bite.

After they finished eating she washed the skillet in the sink and went into the bedroom to see after the bed. The bed was already made. She found Eris on the front porch, looking after his hawk, and she touched him on the arm and lifted herself to brush him on the lips when he turned to her. Then she went home.

CHAPTER SEVENTEEN

ERIS FELT SICK. HE had been sick ever since he touched her for the first time, and the feeling wasn't going away. His stomach felt as if it were lodged in his throat and parts of his body ached when he was away from her. He fought to keep things as normal and routine as possible, but his thoughts never strayed from her for very long, and what used to be a simple job for him was now a daily test in concentration.

At moments he was angry with her for screwing him up so badly, for taking his life into her small white hands and turning it inside out. The rest of the time he didn't care what she did to him, as long as she went on doing it the way she was doing it. For the first time in his life he felt right. A woman finally cared about him and enjoyed being intimate with him. And this was no ordinary woman. This was Madeleine. He had never known anyone like her. No one had ever looked at him the way she did, or made him so aware of himself as a man.

He shifted in his seat as he drove and fought to think of anything else.

It was useless. He kept remembering what it felt like to be inside her. How small she was. How soft her mouth was.

He made a noise of frustration and made himself concentrate on his surroundings, only to think of the quick breakfast she had made for him. If Eris wasn't smitten before, he fell hard when she joined him at the sink to eat that morning. Any other woman might have complained about the absence of a table and chairs. Not Madeleine. She wasn't interested in changing anything about him, only in sharing with him.

The sick feeling in him intensified when he thought of her someday leaving.

Then he forced himself not to think about it. He couldn't, if he wanted to function normally.

He thought he was seeing things when he drove past the Haven and saw Ronnie Lyman stroll in the door.

Eris pulled in and turned off the truck. He took off his glasses and walked inside to find Lyman talking to the man behind the counter.

Lyman turned when he heard Eris's footsteps, and when he saw Eris he backed up and said, "Don't mess with me, okay? I'm just talkin' to the man here about what he saw the day my daughter disappeared."

"I didn't see nothin'," the man said.

Eris advanced on Lyman and grabbed him by the collar to haul him out of the store. Outside he shoved him against a green Grand Prix and said, "We both know your daughter didn't disappear, but *you might* if I ever catch you around here again."

Lyman's eyes widened. "That little bitch," he said incredulously. "When did she talk to you?"

Eris ignored him. "The police have some questions, Ronnie. And a lot of people would like to kick the shit out of you. I'm one of them."

Ronnie struggled to push him away. "Just tell me where she is. Tell me where the bitch went. The whole damned thing was her idea to begin with, not mine. Yeah, I'm sure she made herself sound real innocent, and you bought every word."

The urge to hit him was overpowering, but Eris managed to satisfy himself with slamming Lyman against the car again.

"Don't even think about selling that line of bullshit. You're the one holding all the cash, not her."

"Did she tell you that? She's lying. I don't have a damn dime, I swear."

Eris looked at the car behind him and said, "Wonder where it went."

"Hey, man, I—"

Lyman was slammed against the car again before he could finish, and Eris suggested holding him there so the police could come and ask their questions.

"They know where to find me," Ronnie snarled. "I'm still at the same place. Tell 'em to come on. I'll talk to 'em and tell 'em the truth about what happened."

Eris released him and Ronnie got in his car and started the engine. He put the car in reverse and said, "You can't keep me out of here. I'll see you bastards in court. This is a public park, man, and—"

Eris kicked the driver's door, making a huge dent in the side. "Sue me."

Ronnie Lyman's face grew purple with rage, and he backed the car wildly away from the convenience store, spinning tires and kicking up dust. Eris stood and watched his departure, and once again he found himself hoping Sheila Lyman had gone somewhere very far away.

On impulse Eris went back inside the store to talk to the man behind the counter.

"Well," he said, after Eris asked his question, "I'll tell you what I told that detective from the county who showed up here. I don't really remember much about that day. I remember talkin' to an old boy from Stockton, Missouri, on the phone in the late afternoon, and that's it. Never saw anyone and never sold a thing until six o'clock that day, according to my register receipts."

Eris thanked the man and left, wondering what the hell Lyman thought he was doing by asking questions and bothering people. Was he making it look good for the press in anticipation of Sheila giving away the hoax? Framing his story about it all being his wife's idea, because he was really doing his best to find out who killed his little girl?

The year that rained shit was getting worse all the time.

As far as his job was concerned, anyway.

HE RAN ACROSS DALE Russell at a fishing dock later that afternoon and asked him about the incident with Madeleine. Russell shrugged and grinned.

"I took a license up to her house later, wanted to tell her it was all a joke, but she wasn't home." He shook his head then. "She's a tough one, little Maddie is. Guess she's had some problems, though, since her old man committed suicide."

Eris's mouth twitched. "Did she tell you that?"

"Yeah. Needs someone to talk to pretty bad. I'll do what I can, but I'm no Dear Abby. She ever talk to you?"

"Occasionally," said Eris.

"If you see her, tell her I've got a license for her. And tell her I was just kidding. She walked off before I could tell her I was joking."

Eris waved to him and drove on.

If he had reason to dislike Dale Russell before, it regenerated itself a hundred times over as he gained distance from the other conservation officer. *Needs someone to talk to pretty bad?* Madeleine had been right about Russell having a problem with rejection.

And Eris had a problem with him. He had been tempted to tell the ass Madeleine had been with him the night before. Renard, the ugly old Indian.

But he didn't need to do that, and he wouldn't. It was enough that Eris knew where she was and what she was doing. No one else needed to know.

"I TRIED CALLING UNTIL all hours last night," Jacqueline said on the phone to Madeleine. "Where were you?"

Madeleine drew a breath and said, "I'm sorry. I've been the butt of a prankster this week and I was trying to ignore the phone." She didn't know why she was lying.

"A prankster?"

"Someone has learned I'm here all alone, evidently."

"I was worried about you," said Jacqueline.

"I'm sorry, Jac. Really. How are you?"

"Feeling good. I've lost ten pounds and I look great. Isn't that awful?"

Madeleine laughed. "I know what you mean."

"How are things out there? How are the kitties?"

"Not so good." Madeleine exhaled and told her what had happened with Dale Russell and the Tanners.

Jacqueline was shocked. "I can't believe the man could be such a monster. You think he actually sicced the dog on the kittens?"

"I believe he intentionally let the dog off the leash when he saw the kittens in the yard."

"Manny is going to be upset. He's been buying flea collars and catnip mouses to bring out this weekend."

"We still have the black kitten."

"You know, I have a problem seeing Dale Russell get snippy over a few perch."

"So did I."

"Are you sure he wasn't joking?"

"If you had seen him you'd know."

"Guess you're really making lots of friends out there, Mad. So far you've alienated Renard, Russell, and now the dirt-diggers."

Madeleine sucked in her breath and went still. Her grip on the phone suddenly tightened.

"It was a joke," said Jacqueline.

"I don't think it was," Madeleine said.

"You have to admit you aren't exactly the friendly sort."

Madeleine's nostrils flared. "What does that mean?"

"It means you don't get along with people, Madeleine. But you expect them to get along with you."

"Are you forgetting Denise and Tim Lansky?"

"No. But they were transitory and your effort wasn't a sustained one. I think that's why you failed at teaching, because you've spent your life studying people, but you just don't seem to like them very much. They always let you down, don't they?"

Through clenched teeth, Madeleine said, "You don't know what you're talking about."

"Maybe I do, maybe I don't. You've had a thing about weakness ever since I can remember. Sam Craven was anything but weak, but once he proved human you couldn't help but let your disappointment show. You helped drag him down and you know it."

Madeleine's jaw went hard. "Jacqueline, don't say any more."

"Does it hurt, Madeleine? Good. This conversation has been long overdue. Someone needed to tell you just how hard you are on people. You love invincibility, but no one is invincible, Madeleine. No one."

"I know that."

"You *don't*. Why haven't you spoken to our father in over two years? I know why. Because after his heart attack he kept right on smoking and eating and drinking and doing everything you and the surgeon general told him not to do. You couldn't make him care about his health, and now he disgusts you. He let you down by being human. By being weak."

"I don't have to stand by and watch him kill himself," said Madeleine, and the moment she said it she knew Jacqueline would pounce.

"The way you stood by and watched Sam? We all saw it, Madeleine. We all saw the way you treated him. I was ashamed, but I thought I understood. Now I'm not so sure. If you didn't love Sam Craven, then you've never loved anyone. You may not even be capable."

"You're wrong," said Madeleine. She was capable. She was more than capable.

"I hope so, Madeleine," said Jacqueline. "Otherwise you're destined for a long and lonely life."

Madeleine was silent a moment. Then she swallowed and said, "Now that you've got all this off your chest, should I be looking for alternative living arrangements?"

"No," said Jacqueline. "Don't you dare run away now. I'm your sister and I should be able to say awful truths to you without driving you away from me. You stay right there and get mad at me Friday if you have to, slap me, spit at me or poison my daiquiri, but don't leave. If you go now I'll never hear from you again. I know how you are. I'm sorry if I've hurt you, Madeleine, but I couldn't hold it in anymore. Just promise me you won't take off."

"I can't promise. All the arrows you've flung haven't reached bone yet. I can't say what will happen when they do."

"I'm not hanging up this phone until you promise. I swear it. I'll stay here until midnight if I have to."

"I promise," said Madeleine.

"You're lying," Jacqueline charged. Madeleine rolled her eyes.

"I have no choice but to stay, Jacqueline. You know it, and I know it."

"All right. Speaking along those lines, have you heard word from any of the people you wrote to?"

"Nothing yet, but I haven't given up hope. I'm sure there's something out there just perfect for a selfish, weakness-hating misanthrope like me . . . providing I can fool anyone into thinking I like them long enough to get a job."

Jacqueline snorted. "How did I know that was coming?" When Madeleine said nothing, she sighed. "You know I love you, Madeleine. I know you love me too."

"I thought I wasn't capable?"

"I'm the exception," said Jacqueline. "Right?"

"Yes," Madeleine told her. "And I promise I'm not going anywhere. All right?"

"All right. We'll see you on Friday."

"Okay."

They said goodbye and Madeleine slowly replaced the receiver on the cradle, hurt beyond words by everything her younger sister had said to her. She wasn't the person Jacqueline had described. She wasn't so shallow, or so cruel.

She loved strength in people, yes, but she didn't judge their worth using strength as a basis. She knew people were fallible and prey to all sorts of weaknesses.

And she had been getting along just fine with everyone until Russell decided he couldn't take no for an answer, and until Sherman Tanner decided to put her in her place. It wasn't any of Jacqueline's business to know how she was getting along with Eris Renard. Madeleine didn't know why she felt that way, but she did. She didn't want to share any part of him yet, not even to talk about him with her sister.

Still she had a lot to think about that day, her mind returning again and again to all Jacqueline had said. The business about their father was true. Madeleine became so frustrated with him it was impossible for her to maintain contact. She could not imagine caring so little about life and one's own body, particularly after her father had watched his own mother die of emphysema and stood helplessly by as a stroke left his father completely paralyzed. The old man had been sent to a home for stroke victims, where he eventually succeeded in starving himself to death.

The sympathy she felt for her grandparents was heartfelt. Little knowledge about diet and health had been available to them. The sympathy she felt for her father, who had been bombarded with the consequences of his actions for the last dozen years and knew exactly what he was doing to his body, was nonexistent. If he did not care, she did not care, and yes, she despised him for his weakness and his unwillingness even to try and change, if only for the sake of their mother. If anyone was selfish, Madeleine thought, it was him.

But then Jacqueline had always been Daddy's girl, not Madeleine.

Madeleine was nobody's girl. She usually found herself standing slightly apart from the others, an observer rather than a participant. She begrudged Jacqueline none of the pampering and attention she received, because Madeleine did not want it. She did not require any such attention and found it only too easy to separate herself from the people who had raised her. She did not miss her parents the way Jacqueline did.

She thought she might miss Jacqueline, if she were gone. A sister was different.

And Jacqueline was special, much more open and giving than Madeleine; warmer, more loving and affectionate. She gave and received so easily, causing envy in Madeleine's breast more than once in her life.

But she was still wrong about Sam.

Madeleine had given him every chance. She had taken everything on her own shoulders and waited patiently for him to recover himself, to show an ounce of initiative and the drive she had believed he possessed. How much more had she been expected to give to a man she wasn't certain she loved to begin with?

You may not even be capable.

Madeleine closed her eyes and let her head fall forward onto her hands as she sat at the kitchen counter.

There was a sharp, arcing pain in her middle as she thought of Eris. It intensified when she thought of him smiling at her, or touching her. She had never felt that with Sam. She had never felt anything but mild sexual arousal, nothing like what she experienced when Eris touched her. Nothing in her life even came close, not the anxiety-filled experimentations with a crude high school date, not the hot, hurried fumblings of a college boyfriend, and not the perfect Sam, with his smooth sexual expertise. No one had touched her as deeply as Eris, with his quaking limbs and unpracticed skills as a lover.

Even her natural modesty was overcome when he placed his hands on her. She did not automatically cower under a sheet or hide behind her arms while he looked at her. She wanted him to look at her.

Her breath on the counter was as warm as her thoughts and she lifted her head to get off the stool and get something to drink when the phone rang. She reached over and plucked the receiver from its cradle, expecting to hear Jacqueline again. "Hello?"

"Is this the woman who lives in the log cabin?" asked a muffled male voice.

"Who is this?" Madeleine replied.

"Someone who's watching you. I'd be careful, living up there all alone. Anything could happen."

"Is that you, Russell?" Madeleine demanded.

The caller hung up.

"Damn you." Madeleine slammed the phone down, and then her brows met as she realized her lie to Jacqueline had just become truth. She put on some sandals and stalked down to the swimming beach, determined to wait and see if Dale Russell would come by as Jacqueline had once predicted.

Russell wasn't there, but Bruce Beckworth and two of his friends were on the beach, talking to some teenaged girls. When Beckworth saw Madeleine he hopped over the girls and came to stand before her, forcing her to stop or go around him. She stopped.

"How's that old truck runnin'?" asked Beckworth.

"Just fine, thanks. Do you mind?"

"Do I mind what?"

"Would you please move?"

"Don't think I will. Not for a snotty little bitch like you."

Madeleine turned on her heel and walked in the opposite direction, wondering why nothing in life could be easy. She groaned under her breath when she heard him following her, and she turned and said, "Just leave me alone. Please."

"Don't want to," said Beckworth, grinning at her.

She kept walking, wondering if he was bald under his cap. That might explain some of his young belligerence.

"Guess you live around here, huh?" he said behind her, and she nearly stopped again, wondering if his could possibly have been the voice on the phone.

No. He didn't even know her name, or the names of Jacqueline and Manuel. There was no way he would have the number.

Madeleine hurried her steps, and she heard him laugh and then speed up. When he gripped her by the arm and yanked her around, she was ready for him, landing a solid kick square in his crotch and shoving up on his nose with the heel of her hand. Before she could even look to see how effective she had been she was off and running, tearing up the path and not daring to look behind her.

As she passed Briar's Cove she saw the woman with the glass of tomato juice standing in her yard and watching. Madeleine ran straight to her and asked for help. The woman lifted the glass and took a sip before saying, "Get behind me. Here he comes."

Madeleine glanced over her shoulder and saw the man in the cap, his face purple, coming after her.

"Earl Lee," yelled the woman, her voice unaffected by the man running toward her. "Toss me that twelve gauge by the door."

Beckworth was ten feet away from the women and closing in fast when Earl Lee opened the door and tossed out a shotgun. The woman dropped her tomato juice and had the shotgun in her hands as Beckworth skidded to a halt. Madeleine stayed well behind the woman, her chest heaving from the mad dash up the hill. She saw the woman lift the shotgun on a level with the brim of the baseball cap and heard her say, "You the one who messed with that little girl?"

Beckworth's eyes rounded. "What little girl? I ain't no—"

The shotgun lowered to point at his crotch. Over her shoulder, the woman asked Madeleine, "What do you think he was going to do with you when he caught you?"

"I don't know," Madeleine breathed. "Hurt me."

"Maybe we oughta hurt him."

"Hey, goddammit," said Beckworth. "I wasn't doin' nothin' but talkin' to this bitch when she unloads and kicks me in the balls."

"You know him?" the woman asked Madeleine.

"No," she said. "He accosted me once before and Officer Renard stopped him."

"You know Renard?" she asked, still holding the shotgun on Beckworth.

"Yes, I do."

Beckworth's lip was curling. "So do I. Tell that jerkoff my fine was a big hundred dollars. Paid it out of my pocket and had dinner with the judge at my dad's house later that night."

"Must have a little dick," said the woman to Madeleine, and Beckworth's head jerked up to stare at her. She continued, "Men with little dicks got all kinds of things to prove to people, mainly that a little dick don't matter as long as you can beat up who you want and buy what you want."

Beckworth opened his mouth to say something to the woman, but a look at the shotgun changed his mind. He pointed at Madeleine. "This ain't over yet. Count on it."

He turned around then and walked down the way he had come. The woman with the shotgun started laughing, and she went on laughing even after Beckworth turned and threatened her, too.

Madeleine stared at the stout woman and saw that her amusement was genuine and that she seemed to have thoroughly enjoyed the entire exchange. Madeleine moved to extend her hand and introduce herself.

"My name is Madeleine Heron. Thank you."

"You're welcome, Madeleine. My name is Gloria Birdy. That's my husband, Earl Lee, standing ready at the window in the house there."

"Earl Lee Birdy?" Madeleine said, and Gloria shrugged.

"His mama had rocks in her head. Thought it was funny."

"You . . . handled that rather well," Madeleine had to say.

"Just like old times," said Gloria. "Me and Earl Lee worked as corrections officers for years."

Madeleine lifted her brows in surprise. "You were a prison guard?"

"I worked honor camps, mostly. Earl Lee worked the hot house."

"The hot house?"

"Leavenworth. He did Lansing, too, just before he retired. We're pretty much used to walking trash you could say."

"He didn't frighten you," observed Madeleine.

"Not hardly," said Gloria with a snort. "You see as many damned crybabies behind bars as I have and you tend to rethink the whole male macho thing, if you know what I mean."

Madeleine smiled and Gloria bent to pick up her fallen glass of tomato juice. Half the juice was still in the glass.

"You see his face when I said what I did about his dick? Nailed that one, I could tell. His hands started twitching like they wanted to cover it up." Madeleine laughed out loud, and Gloria laughed with her. "You wanna come in?"

"Yes," said Madeleine, surprising herself. "Thank you."

She followed Gloria inside the house and found herself being introduced to Earl Lee, who was every bit as tall as Eris, but twice as big around. The man took her hand and shook it, his huge hand surprisingly gentle.

"Have yourself some trouble down at the bay today?" he asked, and Madeleine briefly told them both what had transpired before she rushed up the hill. While she was still thinking about it, she mentioned the disturbing phone call and saw both Gloria and Earl Lee shake their heads.

"Bad business going on at the lake this year," said Gloria, and the conversation took off from there, with Madeleine contributing what she knew and then trading gossip back and forth about the various lake residents—chief among them, Sherman Tanner.

Gloria made a face of disgust. "Have you caught him in the graveyard yet?"

"I've seen him out there," said Madeleine. "I wasn't sure what he was doing. I went to look the next day, but I couldn't find any overturned earth."

"Did you find any sticky stuff decorating the markers?" asked Gloria, and Earl Lee groaned and turned away.

"Sticky stuff?" asked Madeleine, and Gloria made an obscene gesture with her hand over her crotch. Madeleine blinked. Her stomach turned.

"You're kidding."

"Nope."

"The man is sick. How disgusting."

Gloria grinned. "Maybe you'll help me, Madeleine. I'm always threatening to go out there with a camera and catch him at it. Next time you see him up there, call me. I've got the right equipment. We'll get a frontal shot and post copies of it all over the park."

It was past dark before Madeleine got up to leave, and she assured both the worried Birdys that she would run all the way home and scream at the top of her lungs if anyone threatened her.

At home she found not Eris waiting for her, but Dale Russell, and she marched onto her porch and asked him just what the hell he thought he was doing.

He got up from the step and smiled. "Whoa. I guess you haven't seen Renard. I told him to tell you I was just kidding around with you about the fish. I got a license for you and everything."

"You weren't kidding and both of us know it. Why the sudden turnaround, Dale? What are you up to?"

He held up a hand and looked slightly annoyed. "Hey, I'm just trying to be nice here. I was doing my job, for one thing, but for the record, I *was* joking. Come on, Madeleine, give me a break."

"Did you call me today?" she asked. "Was that another joke?"

He stared at her. "Call you? No. What happened?"

"Nothing."

"Don't tell me that. What did they say?"

"He said I should be careful, living up here all alone."

"It was a man?"

"Yes. He had something over the phone to disguise his voice."

Russell looked around himself. "Has to be somebody who knows you."

"He said he's been watching me."

"Maybe it's Renard," said Dale with a smile. "Ugly fool's probably got a thing for you. It happens, you know."

Madeleine said nothing. Her mouth tightened.

"Can I come in?" asked Dale.

"No."

"Why not?"

"I told you, I'm not interested. And I happen to be very tired right now and in no mood for conversation."

She wouldn't tell him about the idiot in the ball cap. She would tell Eris, but not Dale Russell.

"What is it, Madeleine?" he complained. "What the hell have you got against me?"

Madeleine turned on him, wondering what it was going to take to be rid of him. "I get it," she said. "You're one of these men who wants only what he can't have. Because I've rejected you, I'm fair game in the forest, is that it?"

"What else is worth wanting?" said Dale with a sudden smile. "I hate it when things come too easily. I like to be told no on occasion. It's good for me."

"Glad I could be of help," she said, and she opened the door and slipped inside before slamming it shut behind her. For good measure she turned the deadbolt and waited, breathless, until she heard him leave.

Hormones raged among the lake mutant men, she found herself thinking. They were all insane.

With one exception.

She had looked in his garage when she came home but saw no truck inside. She cooked dinner and ate while keeping an eye out for either Eris or Sherman Tanner. She saw Tanner come up the road just after nine-thirty, minus the dog. He was headed for the cemetery. Her hand was on the phone to call Gloria Birdy when she saw Eris's truck stop at his mailbox. She ran to the bathroom to put in her diaphragm before skipping out of the house. She caught Eris just as he stepped onto his porch and she threw herself against him, wrapping her arms around his neck and her legs around his middle. She heard what sounded like a chuckle out of him as he reached awkwardly around her to open his door and carry her inside. She kissed his face and neck and told him how much she had missed him and how happy she was to see him. Then she smelled the blood on him. She leaned away and saw it staining the front of his shirt and the tops of his trousers. She slowly slid out of his arms.

"Are you all right?"

"Fine," he said. "A semi hit some cows."

She made a face and looked at her own clothes. They were still clean.

Eris dropped his mail into the chair and Madeleine suggested he clean up while she fixed something to eat. He nodded and moved tiredly down the hall to the bathroom while Madeleine went to forage in his kitchen.

Twenty minutes later she had a tuna salad sandwich, tomato, pickles, and hard-boiled eggs to eat. Eris came out with wet hair and wearing nothing but a pair of old jeans to sit down in his chair. Madeleine carried a plate in to him and found him staring at an envelope in his hand, his expression strange.

She put the plate down on the table beside the chair and moved behind him to look at the envelope. It was from an adoption agency.

"Open it," she said softly.

"I don't want to," he said. "Not right now."

"Not in front of me?" she asked. "When did you write them?"

"Almost a year ago."

"You've written others?"

"Yes."

"You're looking for your natural parents?" she asked, then shook her head. "Obviously you are. I'm sorry if I sound dumb. I wish you would open it."

He put down the envelope and picked up the sandwich.

Madeleine bit her lip and moved to sit down on the floor in front of him, facing the television. After a moment he picked up the remote and turned it on. She sat and watched a program she couldn't name while he finished eating. When he put the plate on the table beside him and made no move to pick up the letter, she said, "Do you want me to go?"

He said nothing, only sat in his chair.

Madeleine got up and left. On the way to her cabin she saw Tanner coming back. She kept her head down and went inside, unable to face anyone at the moment.

In the bathroom she removed her diaphragm and then went into her bedroom to put on her T-shirt. She was in bed with the covers pulled over her head when she heard a knock at her door. She left the bed and went into the living room, half expecting to see Dale Russell outside. She peered past the curtain on the window and sighed in relief.

She unlocked the door and opened it. Eris stepped inside and wordlessly took her in his arms. He was still shirtless and the scarred skin of his back felt slightly cool from the night air. Madeleine held him and closed her eyes, wanting to ask why he closed himself off from her, why he turned away from her and hurt her so badly.

She said nothing, only sought his mouth when he pulled back to look at her. There was as much desperation in his kiss as in hers, and she could only wonder what the letter had said to make him hold her so fiercely and kiss her so deeply, until she had to tear her mouth away and gasp for breath.

Eris shoved the door shut and pulled her into the hall. As he led her into the bedroom she thought of nothing but the sharp, sweet, arcing pains in her middle and what would help assuage them. There was nothing else.

CHAPTER EIGHTEEN

DALE RUSSELL RAN ACROSS Shelly Bigelow sometime after midnight. He was still brooding over Madeleine Heron and how she had managed to make him feel like shit from a Chihuahua when he saw the drunken girl staggering back to the bay where her father's pontoon boat was docked. Without thinking, he cut the lights on his truck and eased off the accelerator to quietly follow her. He thought about busting her for some offense or another, but Dale knew her father would have her out and about again in no time. They lived near Emporia, where the old man had a huge spread, lots of acreage and cattle, and he spent most of the summer on the pontoon boat on the lake while his wife ran the ranch. Dale had never actually seen the wife. He knew only the old man and his daughter, Shelly, mainly because Shelly had made a point of making herself known to Dale last year.

She used every opportunity to run up and blab, or to touch him in some suggestive way, until the night of the most recent dance, when he finally told her to get lost. The uppity little snot had laughed and said it was fine with her. Everyone on the lake knew what a joke Russell was, how his job wasn't a real job, and how the Department of Wildlife and Parks just wanted him out of the way somewhere safe, where he couldn't get into too much trouble, so his aunt, the governor, would stay happy.

Dale let it go because he had no choice. People were listening, looking, and whispering. How she knew what she did was what pissed him off, and he couldn't help but wonder who had been doing all the talking.

Had to be somebody from the lake office. Somebody who knew the Bigelows.

His job wasn't a real job? Just because he patrolled the water in a boat didn't mean he wasn't working. He got sick of it. He hated staying at the lakes all day every day while Renard got to drive all over and screw around for the whole day if he wanted. Just one day Dale wanted to follow Renard and see exactly what he did. No one was that dedicated to a job, particularly when unsupervised.

Of course Dale realized what a plum assignment he had pulled the last two years. There was not a great deal of nefarious industry at Green Lake; Renard had arrested only four people in connection with drug-related activity last year. The lake traffic wasn't too much. The place was clean and he enjoyed the water. Or at least he had before Kayla Lyman came along and ruined it for him.

But he wouldn't mind a little more responsibility, say having his own area the way Renard did, and actually being able to draw his gun once in a while.

Renard had been shot at twice, both times when he was out trying to catch spotlighters. Dale wasn't too crazy about that, but there were ways to avoid being shot at.

Not that he was a coward. He wasn't. A coward could not have done what he did. He killed a little girl to cover up a terrible, unfortunate mistake. Her death had been an act of desperation on his part, something he was training himself to forget.

And it was working. The memory of her death struggles was already fading. It was the part before, the good part, that he remembered.

Dale's nostrils flared as he thought of the mess concerning the Lymans. The wife had confessed to Renard and Renard told everyone else and brought the cops back to the lake again to ask questions and make everyone feel as if they were guilty of something when all they had done was help look for a missing little girl who wasn't missing at all. People didn't know when to leave well enough alone. They didn't know when to keep their mouths shut.

Like snotty Shelly, spouting off in front of everyone at the dance. Dale had smiled and laughed, all the while wanting to slam his fist into that flapping mouth of hers.

His foot pressed ever so slightly on the accelerator as she turned on the road leading down to where the pontoon was docked. She held out her arms as if for balance, and Dale's gaze locked onto her spine as his foot pressed down even harder on the accelerator. Almost before he knew what he was doing, before his unconscious spoke to his conscious mind, she was turning in the darkness to see the approaching vehicle. Dale mashed even harder with his foot, and when he saw the sunglasses on the dumbshit's face he jerked on his headlights so the glare would be all she could see.

The truck slammed into her doing thirty-five miles an hour and she was thrown nearly twenty feet down the road, landing only a few yards from her daddy's precious pontoon boat.

Dale's anger fled him at the sound of the squishy, sickening thud at the front of the truck and was replaced by panic. He looked frantically around him and floored the accelerator again to escape before anyone chanced a look out a window. He thanked God it was so dark around the lake at night and realized in just seconds he had broken into a full sweat, soaking the collar of his shirt and the area around his armpits.

Nervous laughter erupted from his throat, quickly followed by several choking sobs of terror. The sound of intractable metal and plastic impacting with fragile flesh, bone, and tissue replayed itself in his mind over and over as he sped away.

Then, slowly, he began to calm himself. No one had seen him. Just like with the little girl at the Haven, no one had been around and no one saw what he did. He was on the road all alone. She was the only one out walking. The place was pitch black and stayed that way thanks to the drunken assholes who liked to shoot out the lights around the bay areas.

A sudden thought struck him then, and he drove as quickly as he could to an area he knew was lighted so he could get out and look at the front of his pickup.

It was fine. Later model trucks were equipped with resilient grills that held up against just about anything a person ran into: dogs, deers, or drunken teenaged sluts.

He took a flashlight and went over the front of the truck inch by inch, looking for hairs or flesh or specks of blood, and wiped with a towel every little spot he found.

Then he began to think about Shelly lying down there on the road and wondered how long it would be before anyone found her.

He wondered if he had killed her, or if she was possibly still alive, struggling in her drunken stupor to hold on.

God, what a mess, he told himself, suddenly remorseful. Poor, dumb little bitch. What was she doing out so late? Why was she alone? If only someone had been with her, he would never have done what he did.

After thinking about it for an hour, Dale drove to Fayville and made an anonymous phone call to the police.

Half an hour later his beeper went off, and when he called in he was told by a grumpy, grousing voice that Renard wasn't answering his beeper and someone had to go down to Diamond Bay, where a hit-and-run accident had occurred.

"Who was the victim?" Dale asked.

"A young girl."

"Is she dead?"

"Close to it. She was able to make enough noise for someone to find her, but she's unconscious now. Go on down there and see what you can do for the police. And if you see Renard, tell him to call in."

Dale didn't think he would see Renard, and he was overjoyed to be called into service in his stead. He wondered briefly what was wrong with Renard's beeper, but all thoughts of the tall Indian were dismissed from his mind as he put the truck in gear and drove as quickly as he could to Diamond Bay and the scene of the accident.

CHAPTER NINETEEN

WHILE MADELEINE SLEPT IN his arms, Eris stared into the darkness of her bedroom and wondered what he would do when he met his mother. He knew he would call the number the adoption agency had given him. It seemed to have taken him forever to realize that it was in fact a telephone number, one of great significance, and it was actually printed on a piece of paper he was holding before his eyes.

A letter he wrote on a whim after reading a newspaper article on adoption records had come through for him. His own records had finally been unsealed and his mother was now available to him; after all these years she was suddenly just a phone call away. She had made herself available, the letter claimed, in case he came looking for her. Her name was Sara Bent Horn, and according to the woman at the adoption agency his mother was a nationally acclaimed artist.

Eris was still reeling from the initial shock of finding he actually had a mother and hadn't hatched from some egg under a rock after all.

He didn't know what to think. Just looking at her name felt so strange to him, knowing he had come from her, had been born of this person whose name he had only just learned.

The chaos of his emotions sent him up the hill to Madeleine, whom he knew he had hurt and wanted only to make it better between them, because first he had been given her and now he had been given a mother and a name and a new point of reference and he didn't know what he had done to deserve any of it but he was suddenly deathly, terribly afraid of losing what he had gained so far.

His desperation was evident in his lovemaking and she held him tightly long after it was over, stroking his hair and kissing his face until his pounding heart finally began to slow and the anxiety in him lessened. She was waiting for him to tell her, he knew. But he couldn't. He couldn't put it into words because it meant too much to him still, and he didn't want to lose control of his emotions in front of her. *She* meant too much to him.

Madeleine needed someone strong, as strong if not stronger than she was, and Eris instinctively knew she would be disappointed to see him falter. He felt the same about her. It was her strength that made her so appealing, and he did not know how he would react should she suddenly turn into someone full of need.

They were alike in many other areas; he knew this from listening to her and watching her. She had read many of the books in his bedroom, and she went over the newspaper in the same manner as he did, reading every single story on the front page to completion before moving on to other sections. They liked the same foods and were unconcerned with matters of etiquette. They listened to the same music on the radio and watched some of the same programs on TV.

She didn't feel the need to talk just to fill up silence, and she didn't seem to mind silence from him. It pleased him just to be with her, and he knew she felt the same. They were, in fact, very much alike.

The areas in which they were not alike neither of them could do anything about.

He touched her face as she slept and thought of the things he wished he could say to her, how inadequate with words he felt, and how he wished he could think of some way to ask her to stay.

Suddenly her lids opened, and she looked up into his face. For the longest time she said nothing, only gazed at him. Then she whispered his name, and Eris pressed his lips against hers before she could speak further.

"Sleep."

She closed her eyes and tightened her arms around him, and soon both slept.

HE WAS SITTING AT the kitchen counter eating cantaloupe for breakfast when he realized he had forgotten to bring his beeper the night before. It was back in his bedroom with the belt he had neglected to put on. He left the stool and bent to kiss Madeleine, who was seated next to him. She smiled and touched his bare side with a hand while he leaned over her. He wore the same faded jeans and nothing else. His hair was still loose, falling down his back. He enjoyed the look in her eyes as she gazed at him; it made him feel more than what he was. Much more.

He kissed her again and let himself out. At home he picked up the letter with his mother's number on it and tucked it into his wallet for safekeeping. He showered and was dressing when he turned on the radio and heard a local news report, including the story of a hit-and-run accident at Diamond Bay, Green Lake Reservoir.

An hour later Eris was in the lake office listening to a lengthy phone lecture by his superior. He was never, never to leave his beeper behind him again, no matter what the circumstances. Excuses were for worthless nephews of worthless governors. Since Eris's record had been exemplary thus far, the incident would be overlooked, but it was not to happen again.

The man behind the desk smiled as Eris hung up and handed the phone back to him.

"Hope she was worth it."

Eris surprised himself by returning the man's smile. Outside the office he met a yawning Dale Russell, who asked if he had called the boss yet.

"Just now," said Eris. "You check on the girl this morning?"

"What? No, I just got in. I can do it now. I guess it should be me, since I was the one who handled everything last night."

Eris ignored the dig and got in his truck. "After you find out her condition, radio me."

"Why?" asked Russell.

"I want to know," said Eris, and he started the engine of the truck.

"Where were you last night?" Russell asked loudly.

"Out." Eris shifted into reverse and backed up. The look on Russell's face was the first hint ever given of how he felt about his fellow officer.

Eris's mouth twitched as he drove away. *It's mutual.*

He drove to Diamond Bay and got out to look around. Blood still stained the location where Shelly's body was found, and he went back up the road on foot to see if he could find any skid marks or other evidence left by someone trying to come to a stop.

The road was clear.

It was possible the driver hadn't even seen her, he told himself. Maybe whoever it was thought it was a deer that had been struck and just kept going.

Or the driver, too, was drunk and swerved when he or she should have braked.

Eris regretted that he had forgotten his beeper, but there was nothing he could have done any differently than Russell. There was little to do but coordinate facts with the police. The conservation officers were there mostly as a courtesy, to lend a hand where they could. They knew the area and were familiar with the residents, and if such knowledge was useful it would be passed on in whatever way was helpful.

While Eris was standing in the road, Bill Bigelow came to talk to him. The man was obviously shaken by what had happened to his daughter; his skin was gray, his eyes sunken. He shook his head a half-dozen times while looking at the pontoon boat and finally announced that he intended to sell the thing and get her away from the lake once and for all.

"The boat?" said Eris.

"Shelly," said Bigelow. "She wasn't nearly so wild and crazy until we started coming out here. It was the crowd she fell in with, those wild kids who party every night and drink beer all day long. They don't even ski, or fish; they just come out here to get drunk and pass the hours."

Bruce Beckworth, thought Eris. But Bigelow couldn't blame the kids entirely. He did a fair share of partying on the pontoon boat, pouring martinis and playing host to all sorts, many of them girls only a few years older than his daughter, and most of them fond of swimming nude at night.

"Have you contacted the hospital this morning?" asked Eris.

Bigelow nodded. "I just spoke to her mother. She's still critical, but the doctors are optimistic. Many bones broken, hip, leg, arm, collarbone, ribs, severe lacerations and abrasions, and the loss of a kidney, but thank God the internal bleeding has stopped."

Eris nodded uncomfortably. He didn't like Shelly Bigelow, but he hated to see anyone suffer such a fate.

"She'll hang in there, I'm sure," he said to her father. Then he excused himself and returned to his truck.

He stopped on the dam bridge to look and see who was down below, and while he was out walking around he saw Madeleine coming toward him in the old truck from her garage. He walked out to the road and she slowed to a halt beside him.

"I'm going shopping in Fayville," she told him. "Any requests for dinner?"

"Shrimp?" said Eris.

She made a face and reached out as if to cuff him. He leaned away from her arm and gave her a smile that made her sigh. She looked at his mouth and said, "I love it when you do that."

Eris leaned into the cab of the truck and kissed her. When he lifted his head he said, "I can cook tonight if you want."

"No," she said. "I like to cook for you."

"Let me give you some money."

"Only if you want steak. I was thinking more along the lines of meatloaf."

"Meatloaf is fine, but I still want to give you some money." He reached in his pocket and took out his wallet. When he opened the wallet, the folded letter from the adoption agency fell out. He bent to pick it up and saw her eyes following his hands. She blinked, but her lips went firmly shut. She would not allow herself to ask him, he saw. He handed her fifty dollars, and her eyes searched his as he replaced his wallet. He smiled again.

"Buy some ketchup for that meatloaf?"

"Oui, Monsieur Renard. Au revoir."

He tipped his hat. "Mademoiselle."

At any other time Eris Renard would have felt utterly stupid carrying on in such fashion while standing on the dam bridge in plain view of half a dozen fishermen and various others. He didn't feel stupid with Madeleine. He felt good. His chest expanded as he watched her drive away from him.

It was incredible how she made him feel about himself. He

would never get over the way she carried on about his smile. Or his eyes. She nearly had Eris believing he was handsome.

He *felt* handsome when she looked at him, when her eyes lingered and her hands couldn't stay away from his face.

He was beginning to see what she saw in the mirror, instead of what countless others had seen and shied away from. The scars were somehow less noticeable and his eyes looked different to him, warmer, browner, less hard. He saw his teeth more often, and he paid more attention to his hair because of her. He thought he would probably gain a few pounds, but a regular meal or two wouldn't hurt him. He found he actually preferred sitting down to eat.

After driving down below the dam to check licenses and chat with the fishermen, Eris went home and took out his wallet. Before he could lose momentum he punched in the number and held his breath. He listened to four rings, and then a woman's voice answered. "Hello?"

Eris opened his mouth and nothing came out. He cleared his throat and struggled, finally pushing a weak hello past his lips.

"Who is this?" asked the woman.

"My name is Eris Renard," he managed. "I'm calling to speak with Sara Bent Horn."

"My God," she said softly. "Your voice is so deep."

"Is this Sara Bent Horn?"

"It is. Is this my son Eris?"

"According to the adoption agency I am."

"Where are you?"

He cleared his throat again. "I work for the Kansas Department of Wildlife and Parks at Green Lake Reservoir."

"You're a game warden?"

"A conservation officer."

"Are you married? Do you have any children?"

"No." He couldn't believe he was having this conversation. Talking with his mother. It was unreal.

"When I turned forty last year I knew I had to find you," she said, and he was stunned into silence.

Forty last year? She was only forty-one now?

"I . . . how old were you when . . . ?" he asked.

"When I had you? I was fourteen. I don't want to talk about

any of this over the phone to you. I have to see you. Please don't say no, I've been waiting for this moment for so long."

No longer than I have, thought Eris.

"I can't get away," he told her. "I'm responsible for—"

"I'll come to you," she interrupted. "Just tell me the nearest major airport and I'll book a flight."

"Where are you?" asked Eris, picking up the phone number to look at the area code.

"Santa Fe, New Mexico," she said. "I'm an artist. I have my own studio and gallery here. Are you anywhere near Wichita?"

"A little over an hour away," he told her. "There's nowhere to stay around here. No motels or—"

"Would it be all right if I stayed with you?" she asked. "Do you have room?"

He did, but she was suddenly going too fast for him. He wanted to see her, yes, but he didn't know if he wanted to have her in his house. She was, after all, a stranger.

"You can stay with me," he heard himself say.

"Wonderful," she said, and he heard a break in her voice. "You don't know how happy you've made me. I can't wait to see you. I'm going to take the first available flight out, is that all right?"

"Fine," he said.

"Give me your phone number, so I can call you back with the flight details," she asked.

"It would be better for me to call you back later today," he said. "I'm never home to hear the phone ring."

"Yes, of course. Can you call me around three, your time?"

"I'll try."

"All right. I'll speak to you again soon. And Eris? This might sound like a stupid question, but are you angry? Have you been angry with me? I have to know."

"Yes," he said.

"Okay. We'll talk when we see each other. I have a lot to tell you."

When Eris hung up he felt numb. He looked around his house and suddenly realized he was going to need some furniture. A couch. A table, maybe, and something for her to sleep on.

His mother was coming. As quickly as she could.

He put his hands to his eyes and rubbed. Then he walked out

onto the porch to feed the baby hawk and wait for Madeleine to come home.

She frowned when she saw him come up the hill. She got out of the truck with a sack of groceries and handed them to him while she opened the door.

"What's wrong?"

"Nothing."

"Why are you still here?"

"I was waiting for you."

They went inside and Madeleine moved to put the groceries away. She was still frowning, waiting for him to go on.

"I contacted my mother this morning," Eris said. "She wants to come here. She's booking the first flight out."

Madeleine stopped what she was doing and stared at him. "You found your mother? Eris, that's wonderful. You've already spoken to her and everything?"

"She's coming here," he said. "She wants to stay at my house."

Madeleine moved to grip his hands. "I can't imagine what you must be feeling right now. What you must be thinking."

Eris gave her fingers a squeeze and said, "I won't be able to be with you while she's here."

"No, I suppose not," Madeleine said with a brief smile. "I was wondering myself how we would handle the weekend, with Manuel and Jacqueline here to guard my virtue. How long will she be staying?"

"She didn't say."

"Will I be able to meet her?"

"I don't know."

She fell silent and slowly removed her hands from his to go back to putting away groceries.

"I'm glad you found her," she said, not looking at him. "I'm sure it was important to you."

"Yes," he said.

"Where does your mother live?"

"Santa Fe, New Mexico. She has an art gallery and a studio there."

Madeleine stopped what she was doing again and turned to look at him. "My parents live in Santa Fe, your adoptive parents—"

"No," said Eris. "It wasn't Santa Fe."

"Oh."

They stood looking uncomfortably at one another, until Eris said he had to go.

Madeleine nodded and turned to finish putting away her things. Eris exhaled and moved past the counter to put his arms around her and pull her against his chest. She stiffened, and for a moment he thought he should let her go, but finally she relaxed against him and placed her arms around his waist.

"I'll bring her to meet you when I can," he said. "I want her to see you."

She lifted her head to look at him. "For a minute there I thought you were ashamed of me."

"Never." His mouth worked, but he couldn't begin to impart what she was to him. Instead he kissed her, then tore himself away and left the cabin.

He had to go and find a bed for Sara Bent Horn.

CHAPTER
TWENTY

MADELEINE COOKED HER MEATLOAF that evening and watched in curiosity as a delivery truck unloaded furniture at Eris's house. After thinking about it she knew he would need another bed. And maybe another chair, or something to sit on in the living room. Perhaps a small dinette.

When the meatloaf was finished and Eris showed no signs of coming, she picked up the phone and called the Birdys. Earl Lee and Gloria were delighted to be asked to dinner and hurried right up the hill, bringing a six-pack and a can of tomato juice with them.

Both went on and on about the cabin, and after dinner Earl Lee attached himself without hesitation to a sports channel on the television, leaving Gloria and Madeleine to walk outside and sit on the porch to enjoy the evening air. The black kitten played at their feet, gnawing on toes and chasing imaginary insects.

"Seen the digger man?" asked Gloria.

"We call him the Earthworm," Madeleine told her, and was gratified to hear Gloria snort with laughter.

"That's it. I'd heard it before but forgot it."

"Gudrun is Mole Woman," Madeleine added, and Gloria slapped her knee and laughed even harder.

Her short brown hair appeared red in the light from the porch.

The glass of tomato juice was right beside her, this time diluted with beer.

"I saw him last night as a matter of fact," Madeleine told her. "And he was on his way up to the cemetery."

"Why the hell didn't you call me?"

"I started to, but something else came up. How often does he do this disgusting thing?"

"No one knows for sure. Damn, I wish you'd called me last night."

"Maybe I should have," Madeleine said thoughtfully, staring down the darkened lawn at Eris's house.

Gloria flicked a pill bug at the kitten. "What did you say you do?"

"Do?"

"Profession."

"Oh. I'm a teacher—well, I'm not a teacher anymore. I'm back to being an anthropologist begging for a grant."

Gloria was impressed. "Any specific area?"

"Native-American languages."

"Huh. How does that grant stuff work exactly?"

"The begging part? I tell a university what I've done and what I want to do, and they discuss the merits of my application. If they approve, *voilà*, I get money and time to study and write."

"What do you write?"

"Papers, generally published in scholastic journals. A few years ago I wrote a book on variations in the Sioux language. It was published by a university press."

"Did it do very well?"

"It wasn't a bestseller, if that's what you're asking."

Gloria grunted. "Must've not had any humping in it."

Madeleine rolled her eyes and Gloria gave her a light pinch on the arm.

"Glad to know what you're made of. I can see you as an academic type, with the right clothes and that tight little bun you wear. You ever talk with Renard about his people?"

"Only briefly."

"He's a quiet one, Renard is. Earl Lee thinks the world of him. He once saw Renard cut his hands to shreds trying to loose a deer whose leg was caught in a barbed-wire fence. Renard had tranquilized the deer and he didn't know anybody was watching him. Earl Lee said he was as gentle with that deer's leg as if it were a human. That said a lot about him to Earl Lee."

Madeleine nodded, but she said nothing. She wanted to change the subject so the sudden thickness in her throat would go away.

"Earl's thinking about teaching next year," Gloria went on. "The folks over at the county community college want him to come and work with a criminologist on a course about the future of penal institutions."

"Sounds interesting," said Madeleine.

"I thought so." Gloria swirled her glass and then took a drink. "I bet the community college would be more than interested in you."

"How so?"

"You said you were a teacher."

"Not anymore. I'm finished teaching."

"Too many kids with shit for brains?"

Madeleine smiled. "You got it."

"Things are different in the country," Gloria said. "Kids aren't the same as they are in the city. They still know how to say please and thank you and they're grateful just to get off the farm or out of that small town and go to school."

"I don't know about that," said Madeleine. "I had kids from small towns in my classes. They fit right in with the rest."

"So they wouldn't stick out. Out here being courteous is the norm, not the exception."

"Have you told that to the jerk in the baseball cap?"

"He's a punk. Don't even consider him."

"You sound like you're trying to convince me."

"I am. I'd love to have a smart woman like you around all the time. I don't know that many smart women."

Madeleine chuckled. "I'm flattered, but I'm afraid my circumstances won't permit me to remain here beyond the summer."

"Out of money?"

"For starters. Second on the list is the fact that the cabin belongs to my sister and her husband, who only tolerates me because I'm family and because my sister loves me."

"It's a shame," said Gloria. "I can see us becoming cohorts in crime, nailing up pictures of the Earthworm wiggling his worm."

Madeleine burst out laughing, and she found herself laughing continuously over the next hour, because Gloria had just gotten started.

When the Birdys finally took their leave Madeleine was sorry to see them go. She enjoyed Gloria immensely and wanted to call her sister Jacqueline and say, *See? I have a friend.*

They made plans to see each other again soon, and Madeleine finally closed the door behind them. It was ten o'clock and Eris wasn't home. She refused to allow herself to stay up and wait for a glimpse of his mother, but there was no chance of sleeping once she was in bed.

The ringing of the phone startled her and she leapt out of bed to answer it, hoping it was Eris but figuring it to be Jacqueline. "Hello?"

"I can't believe you're fucking Renard. A piece like you spreading your legs for that ugly bastard. Makes me sick just to think about—"

She slammed the phone down and hurried through the cabin, locking all the doors and windows.

Someone really was watching her.

Her heart pounded in her chest as she glanced all around herself, wondering what she could use as a weapon.

Manuel and Jacqueline were going to love this. They would probably kick her out rather than wait for her to leave and take her troubles with her.

She had meant to tell Eris about the first call. She meant to tell him about the man in the baseball cap, too.

Madeleine's throat and mouth were dry as she picked up the phone and called the police. She would make a complaint. That was doing something.

The police were understanding and concerned, and they told her to keep her doors and windows locked. When Madeleine hung up she felt better, but only minimally. She went back to bed and lay shivering under the covers despite the warmth of the air. Already she missed Eris.

RONNIE LYMAN SAT BEHIND the wheel of his green Grand Prix and wondered what else he could do to Eris Renard. Following him, spying on him, and scaring his girlfriend wasn't enough. Renard hadn't led him to Sheila, as he had hoped. He knew the do-good sonofabitch knew where she was. He had to; Sheila had told him everything else.

His teeth clenched as he thought of what he would do to her when he found her. He had a hell of a time convincing the cops the whole scheme had been her idea to begin with. He asked them to watch the television tapes so he could show how she had been the one to do most of the talking. There was no way he could have coached her.

Despite his argument, Ronnie was taken into custody again. He wasn't put under arrest, but the same judge he had seen before demanded his presence, and he told Ronnie he was so disgusted he wanted to order a brain scan to see if there was any activity in Ronnie's head.

"How could you do that to your own little girl?" the judge had asked, his eyes stained red and bloodshot. "Don't you know that by perpetrating that hoax, you're just as guilty as the man who molested and murdered her? You delivered her into his hands, Mr. Lyman. How does that make you feel?"

"Pretty shitty, sir," Ronnie had said. "But I keep telling you people it wasn't my idea. My wife, Sheila, got crazy when we lost our house. She said we had to do something, anything, to get some money. So she cooked up this scheme to—"

"You couldn't dissuade her from it?"

Ronnie stared, confused. "What?"

"You couldn't change her mind? This woman you nearly strangled at your little girl's funeral? You couldn't sit down and talk her out of it?"

There was no reply. Ronnie knew when to keep his mouth shut.

The judge finally let him go. But he was on probation for three years, and he had to find a job. Otherwise, he was going back to jail.

Thanks to Sheila and Renard.

Sheila he couldn't do anything about, not right now anyway, but he could make life difficult for Renard until he found a job. Or until Renard led him to Sheila.

He was so good at following people he considered going into the collection business. Renard never once saw him as he went about his daily routine. Of course, Ronnie hung way, way back on the dusty dirt roads, but he never lost Renard once. After one day he was bored stiff, though, so he decided to watch what Renard did after he came home. That was a little more interesting, considering the pretty blonde who lived in the log cabin. Ronnie got the name from the mailbox and called up information for the phone number.

Easy.

Still, there had to be something else he could do. Some way to make Renard see what a man felt like to be cut off from his family and set adrift in a hostile environment. Let him know exactly what kind of mistake he had made by messing with Ronald James Lyman.

It was something Ronnie would have to think about. He started his car and drove away from the pay telephone at Diamond Bay. His headlights picked up the huge blood stain in the road and he stopped to look at it and wonder. Then he drove on, slowly.

CHAPTER
TWENTY-ONE

ERIS SWALLOWED UNCOMFORTABLY AS he stood at a gate in Mid-Continent Airport and watched people leave the plane. He knew his mother the moment he saw her. She was the only Indian on board. She was tall, like Eris, and slender, wearing a billowing blouse, a long skirt, boots, and a colorful beaded belt at her waist. Her black hair was held back by a beaded band that matched her belt. Her eyes, when they landed on him, registered shock. She strode quickly toward him and Eris stood where he was, his palms sweating.

"I didn't expect you to be so tall," she said. "Don't ask me why."

Then she put her arms around him. Eris swallowed again as he inhaled her scent. He gave her back a cursory pat.

She leaned away and looked into his face. After a moment, she said, "You look like him."

Eris cleared his throat. "Do I?"

"Yes." She released him and stood back. "I can tell you're uncomfortable with this, with me. I won't touch you again until we know each other better. Forgive me if I seem to stare. You don't look anything like I expected."

"Neither do you," he said. She looked too young to be his mother. She was too attractive, with her dark eyes and appealing smile. She was too vital, too warm, too much like nothing he had ever imagined when he imagined what his birth mother would look like. His resentment of her increased tenfold in those first moments.

"Let's get my bags," she suggested, and she waited for him to lead the way.

At the baggage claim he watched her as she stepped up among the other passengers. He watched the way people looked at her, and the way she ignored them, as if she were used to admiring glances and dismissed them as her due.

Eris was still having trouble believing he had actually sprung from that lithe body. He wanted to ask where his real mother was, the one who was round and gray and cried every time she thought of the baby she had given away. He wanted that mother of his imagination, with the plump, comforting arms and a soft sentimental bosom. Not this woman, who looked like an ad out of *Southwestern Art*.

She had brought three bags with her, and Eris lifted a brow when he saw their size and wondered exactly how long she was planning on staying with him.

"Don't worry," she said when she saw his expression. "I'm not moving in. I just like to be prepared for anything when I go somewhere."

Eris lifted two of the bags and carried them out of the airport. At his truck he loaded the bags into the back and threw a tarpaulin over them before unlocking the passenger door for her to climb inside the cab.

When he slid behind the wheel, she said, "The people you work for don't mind your hair?"

"No." No one had ever said a word to him about it.

"That's good. I'm glad to see it long. Have you always kept it that way?"

"No. Not always." He started the truck and eased out of the parking lot. He felt her looking at him.

"Who adopted you, Eris?"

"A military man and his wife."

"White?"

"Yes."

"I had hoped otherwise," she said, and before she could go on, Renard asked his question.

"Who is my father?"

"Was. He died in an accident on an aircraft carrier somewhere off the coast of Africa. His name was Daniel Birdcatcher. He was twelve years older than me. I lied to him and told him I was eighteen. He never knew about you. I never told him. He died before you were born."

"Your parents made you put me up for adoption?"

"No," she said, looking at him again. "They wanted to keep you. It was my decision to give you up."

"Why?" he asked, his throat dry.

"I was fourteen and had my whole life ahead of me. If I had kept you I would've had responsibilities no fourteen-year-old should have. I was young and stupid and I knew if I kept you my parents would end up raising you, and they were too old by that time. We were also incredibly poor, and I wanted better for you than what I could give. There was no access to abortion, but I wouldn't have had one anyway. I was too much in love with the idea of giving birth to Daniel Birdcatcher's baby. The idea became even more romantic after his death. I was carrying his seed." She paused then. "If all I'm saying sounds trite, then try putting yourself in the shoes of a frightened fourteen-year-old whose only knowledge of babies came from a government-sponsored film shown at school."

"Government-sponsored?" Eris repeated.

"Everything at an Indian school was government sponsored. It was a way of life. For many, it still is."

"You lived on the reservation?" Eris asked.

"Until I left. When my parents found out I signed the adoption papers they asked me to go. An older friend was heading for New Mexico, so I went with her. I've been there ever since, waiting tables, working in bars, selling jewelry and finally making a name for myself as an artist."

"Did you have any other children?"

"You have a brother who just turned twenty-one. His name is Clint."

"You're married?"

"Divorced. I was married for eleven years to a man who owns a ranch just south of Santa Fe. We were too different."

"Was he white?"

Sara Bent Horn laughed. "Never." Then she sobered as she

looked at her son. "The white people who adopted you, were they good to you?"

"For a time, yes. Then things changed. I left them when I was very young."

"And did what?"

"Went looking for you."

His mother turned to gaze out the windshield. "I'm sorry, Eris. I'm sorry for being so young and so stupid."

There was silence in the cab for several minutes; then Eris asked about his father again. "What was Daniel Birdcatcher like?"

"As tall as you, but heavier. I fell in love with him on sight. He was dancing in costume, dressed in feathers and scarves and beads, and he stole my soul at a glance. I was tall, too, of course, so it was easy to fool him into thinking I was older than I was. You have his eyes, Eris, and his mouth. I wish I had a picture of him to show you, but I don't."

"Does he have any people still living?"

"I don't know. I never kept up."

"What about your parents, are they still alive?"

"Oh, no, they died years ago. I have an older sister left, and a few cousins. Other than that, I'm it." She turned to him again. "Are your adoptive parents here in Kansas?"

"No. We moved to New Mexico when I was very young."

"New Mexico? Really? What made you come back?"

"I wanted to go to school here."

"You graduated college and everything?"

"Yes."

"I'm so proud," she said, smiling. "My son, the college graduate. Do you enjoy your job?"

"Yes."

"That's wonderful. You look very professional in your uniform. What about your personal life? Are you seeing anyone special?"

"Yes."

"Is it serious?"

He only looked at her.

"Sorry," she said quickly. "I'm going too fast again. I'm just trying to learn about you."

"We haven't been seeing each other long," he said. But as far as he was concerned, it was serious.

"I know half a dozen girls in Santa Fe who would fall all over themselves for you," said his mother. "Indian women seem to outnumber the men in New Mexico."

"Madeleine is white," said Eris.

"Is she?" said his mother politely.

"She's an anthropologist specializing in Native-American languages."

"Really."

Eris glanced at his mother. Her tone suggested sudden boredom with the subject. A second later she yawned and he told himself she was simply tired.

"I want you to meet her," he said, and his mother nodded and said of course she would meet her, and then she asked him about his adoptive parents again.

They talked for the duration of the drive, and by the time he reached the lake it was after midnight. He glanced at the log cabin as he passed by and saw a light in Madeleine's bedroom. It created a sudden ache in him and an urge to go to her, but he ignored it and removed his mother's luggage from the back of the truck and opened up the house.

He had purchased a sofa, another chair, a dining room set, a bed and a dresser that day at the furniture store. He didn't recognize his house when he walked inside.

His mother smiled when she saw the place and said something under her breath about the Spartan way bachelors lived. Eris placed her suitcases in the spare bedroom and asked if he could get her anything to eat or drink. She said no, and asked to be directed to his bathroom. Eris pointed, and while she was inside, he picked up the phone to call Madeleine.

It rang six times and he was about to hang up when she lifted the receiver and said a cautious hello.

"It's me," he said. "Can't sleep?"

He heard her sigh in relief. "I was reading. Did you just get home?"

"The plane was late."

"How is she? What's she like?"

He paused, then said, "Not what I expected. You'll see when you meet her."

"I could cook something."

"No. Don't do that. I'll call ahead to let you know when we're coming."

"Okay. I guess I'll see you soon then."

Both hesitated, neither wanting to hang up.

"I miss you," she said softly. "It's crazy, I know."

"Not crazy," he said, his voice low. Then he heard his mother come out of the bathroom. "I'll see you later."

" 'Bye," she said.

Eris's chest hurt as he hung up. He missed her, too. More than he ever would have believed possible. He wanted nothing more than to hold her in his arms and lose himself in her softness until things came clear again. There was a strange person in his house who called herself his mother and he wasn't entirely sure he liked her. A part of him wished he had never written that letter and another part of him was glad he had, because he was used to disappointment in life and this was just one more disappointment he would eventually get past. Still he was drawn to her, out of curiosity if nothing else.

He wanted to hear more about his father, everything she could tell him. He wanted to hear about his grandparents and their parents and everything he could think to ask from the storehouse of questions he had compiled over the years. He wanted to know where his name came from and why she had made certain he kept it. He wanted to know about Clint, and those cousins she had mentioned, and the older sister.

She possessed information that had made up the stuff of his private maunderings and most personal thoughts, and he told himself she owed him information if she owed him nothing else. It wasn't asking much.

She came into the living room and asked Eris what time he awakened in the morning. He told her, and she frowned.

"I'm sorry. It's biologically impossible for me to rise at that time. What time do you get off work?"

"Whenever," he said.

"Why don't you come by at lunch tomorrow and pick me up?" she suggested. "I can ride with you in the truck while you do whatever it is you do, and it'll give us a chance to talk more. Would that be all right?"

He wasn't wild about the idea, but neither was he inclined to leave her sitting alone in the house all day. He agreed and told her he would see her the next day. He went to his bedroom, she went to the spare room, and they both closed their doors.

Eris undressed and got into bed. Restless energy still thrummed through him, but he understood the source: it wasn't every day an adoptee met his birth mother.

He thought of the shock in her eyes when she first saw him and wondered what she had expected him to look like. He had seen her eyeing the scars on his face, but she said nothing. He was glad.

His lids grew heavier as his thoughts slowed, and he finally drifted off, wondering what her expression would be when she saw Madeleine.

THE NEXT DAYS PASSED slowly for Madeleine. She spoke to Eris on the phone several times, but she did not see him. He and his mother were busy becoming acquainted, and Sara was not yet ready to meet anyone else. Madeleine said she understood. On Friday morning she got in the truck and drove down to the swimming beach to look carefully around for any adversaries before taking out her beach umbrella and notebook. For her own entertainment she was making notes about the lives of the lake people, to make comparisons later, with the lives of people in similiar communities centuries ago. Little would have changed, she told herself.

Gloria Birdy would look right at home in a scarf and apron, swilling ale instead of red beers. Sherman Tanner would still be a digger, only with cruder tools. Madeleine smiled to herself as she wrote, pondering the intricacies of human behavior. In all her years as an anthropologist she had given little true thought to the vagaries of emotion and concentrated solely on development. For the first time she wondered why she had been so determined to avoid the heart of man as a species. The methods he used to learn and teach himself had always fascinated her, but why he felt driven to learn, what motivated him, had never been a true consideration before now.

She shook her head as she held her pencil and supposed she was entering another stage in her life, one centered on experiencing the very things that interested her now. Now that she felt the way she did about someone who felt the way he did about her. It amazed her how much more alive she felt, how much more aware of every breath, every sensation, every nerve she had become. It was a battle to keep from being swallowed by sensation. To keep herself somehow intact beyond and separate from the relationship.

She was no giddy teenager about to collapse into the identity of another, but all the emotional trappings and stirrings were being observed by the scholar in Madeleine even as she experienced them. The anxiety. The euphoric sense of elation. The overwhelming joy she experienced just to hear the sound of his voice on the phone when he called. The desperate loneliness she knew without him. The aching and yearning for his physical presence. His touch.

Perhaps she had never shown any interest in man's emotional side because she herself had never been exposed to emotion at such levels. Perhaps some cautious part of her had avoided it, been leery of the pain involved.

She sighed and continued writing. She wrote about Shelly Bigelow, and the fate that had befallen her. She wrote about Shelly's father, Bill, and the many friends he appeared to have gained through his generosity with the pontoon boat, including Denise and Tim Lansky. She wrote for two pages on the violent man in the baseball cap, and briefly compared him to Dale Russell. Dale Russell, she believed, would never actually harm anyone or abuse them physically, but the man in the ball cap apparently knew of no other way to salve bruised feelings. He would take what he wanted when he wanted and he would do it with force if he had to. His was learned behavior, Madeleine wrote, and in a sidebar she added what he had said about his father having dinner with the judge.

When she realized her arms and legs were becoming pink even with the umbrella shading her from the sun, she closed her notebook and packed up her gear. Windburn could do just as much harm as sunburn, and it appeared she had a good dose of it. She drove back to the cabin and looked with a start at the clock. It was almost four. She had been sitting out and writing much longer than she realized. She put her things away and went to the bathroom for some witch hazel to apply to her tender skin. She tidied her bun and applied lipstick, then she poured herself a glass of iced tea from a pitcher she had prepared earlier. She opened the door of the cabin and looked out in time to see Eris's truck stopping by his mailbox. A woman was in the cab with him, and both of them were laughing.

Madeleine stared. She had never seen Eris really laughing before. He looked as if he had known the woman beside him for years, instead of having met her just a few days ago. And the woman beside him looked too young to be his mother. Far too young.

While she was looking, Madeleine saw Eris lift an arm and gesture to her. He pointed to his mother, then to Madeleine. She nodded and went hurriedly to change. If he was bringing his mother now, then Madeleine needed to look less pink and wind damaged. She pulled off her top and shorts and put on a pale yellow sundress. She took her hair down and shook it loose, allowing the natural curls to fall around her face and neck. Before she could run to the bathroom and apply makeup, there was a knock at her door. She shoved her feet into slim strap sandals and went to answer.

Eris stood on the porch beside a woman only a few inches shorter than he. She was long and slim and darkly attractive, and her eyes revealed surprise when she saw Madeleine.

Madeleine greeted them and stepped aside to allow them to enter. Eris's eyes on her made her feel instantly warm. He was as happy to see her as she was to see him. When he came inside he surprised her by reaching for her hand. She gave it to him gladly.

"Madeleine Heron, this is Sara Bent Horn, my mother."

Madeleine extended her free hand. "I'm pleased to meet you."

Sara Bent Horn only touched her fingers. "Eris didn't tell me you were such a beauty."

"Thank you," said Madeleine. "I could say the same of you."

Sara lifted her head and looked around herself. "This is a nice cabin. What does your sister's husband do?"

"Manuel is a neurologist. My sister Jacqueline is an anesthesiologist. They work at the same hospital."

"Manuel is Hispanic?"

"He's from Mexico, yes."

"Do all the women in your family go for ethnic types?"

Madeleine's heated flesh went suddenly cold. She felt Eris's hand squeeze hers.

"I've never thought about it," she said, forcing herself to smile. "Would you care to sit down?"

"Eris tells me you're an anthropologist," Sara said, ignoring the invitation. Her dark eyes swept over Madeleine's form. "You look almost too fragile with your sweet pink skin and dainty little hands and feet." Madeleine glanced at Eris and saw him staring at his mother with a slight frown on his face. His mother saw the frown and quickly apologized. "I meant it as a compliment, of course."

"Can I get either of you something to drink?" asked Madeleine, forcing another smile.

"Nothing for me," said Sara, and Eris declined as well.

Before Madeleine could ask how Sara liked what she had seen of Kansas, Sara asked the question Madeleine dreaded.

"What are you doing here for the summer? Are you working?"

"It's a long story," said Madeleine.

"I'd like to hear it," Sara told her, her smile cool. "I'm interested in everything Eris is interested in."

"I'd rather not go into it," Madeleine averred.

"You don't have to," said Eris. He turned to his mother and told her they needed to be going if she still wanted to eat out that night.

"Aren't you going to ask Madeleine to join us?" she inquired, her fine black brows lifting into arches as she looked at her son. Eris looked at Madeleine.

"Jacqueline and Manuel will be here soon," she said. "They come up every weekend."

"You couldn't leave them a note?"

"I assumed you and Eris would want time alone together."

Eris squeezed her hand again and opened his mouth, but Sara said, "We've had time alone together, and we'll have plenty more to come. We're only just beginning to know each other, my son and I. And as I said before, if he is interested in you, then so am I. Surely you'll change your mind and your dress and come have supper with us."

"The dress is fine," said Eris, frowning at his mother again. He looked at Madeleine and she could see the confused irritation in his expression.

"I'll come," she told him, rising to the challenge. "Just let me put up my hair and write a quick note."

His nostrils flared slightly, and his hand held on to hers just a second longer when she would have tugged it away. She gave him a tender smile and left the living room to hurriedly pin up her hair again and write a note to her sister.

Sara Bent Horn's assessment was cool as Madeleine rejoined them. Madeleine propped up the note on the counter and grabbed a jacket and her purse before moving to the door and locking it from the inside. Sara went out, followed by Madeleine, and Eris pulled the door closed behind them. His hand slipped around Madeleine's waist and his lips brushed her temple as they walked behind his mother. Madeleine looked up into his face and told him with a glance how it felt to be near him again.

His eyes darkened and his hand on her waist tightened in response.

Inside his house Madeleine looked in surprise at all the new furniture and watched jealously as Sara Bent Horn tossed her things casually onto the sofa before removing herself to change. Eris, too, went to his room to change, and Madeleine was tempted to go with him, just to remain close to him. She forced herself to sit on one end of the new sofa and wait. When Eris came out he was dressed in dark indigo jeans and a navy pullover. Madeleine smiled in appreciation and he took her by the hand and pulled her out to the porch with him, closing the door behind them. They reached for each other before the screen door shut, and when they kissed it was as if they had been apart three months instead of three days.

Eris lifted his head when he heard the door opening, and Madeleine released him to wipe the lipstick from his mouth with her fingers. Sara looked outside and said, "I'm ready when you two are."

"We're ready," said Eris.

The three of them rode together in Eris's truck, with Madeleine beside him and Sara near the passenger door. He was taking them to a family-owned steakhouse near Emporia, and on the drive over his mother asked Madeleine endless questions about her education, career, and other aspects of her life. Madeleine could feel the tension in Eris building, and she deflected the questions as best she could and finally succeeded in asking a few of her own.

She complimented the woman on her colorful style of dress and asked if her clothes were made by Indian artisans in New Mexico.

"Everything I own is Indian-made," Sara replied. "With the exception of my car, which was made in Germany, but is maintained by an Arapaho mechanic."

"Have you always been an artist?"

"Have you always been an anthropologist?"

Madeleine smiled and tried again. "What I meant was have you always been interested in drawing and painting?"

"I was more interested in drawing and painting than I was in making dolls, jewelry, or doing complex beadwork. I felt there was more freedom of expression in painting, and obviously more money."

"You appear to have done well," said Madeleine.

"Yes, I have," Sara said honestly. "I have more money than I ever dreamed possible. White people just love to buy pictures painted by Indians."

Madeleine was not offended. During her years in the field she had become accustomed to the barbs and the thinly veiled insults. White intolerance of Indians and Indian hatred of whites were more examples of learned behavior, the same as any other intolerance passed on through ignorance.

"Maybe I even have enough money to entice Eris away from his job here and come to New Mexico," Sara said, her dark eyes shining as she smiled at her son. "I want him to meet his younger brother."

Eris only glanced at his mother.

Madeleine looked at him and said, "You have a brother?"

"Half brother," said Eris. "He's going to school in New Mexico."

"Right now he's working in my gallery," said Sara. "I'm sure you could find a position with the parks department in New Mexico. In several places they actually give preference to Indians."

Madeleine was silent, listening. She had been to New Mexico many times. Eris would probably like it there.

But she hated the thought of his leaving. In the back of her mind she had been toying with the idea of finding work—even teaching—and a place to live somewhere within a reasonable driving distance, so she wouldn't have to leave him. She had never considered the possibility that he might leave her.

His mother went on talking, telling him how big her house was and how little space she used. When Clint was home from college the two of them encountered each other only when they planned to do so. There were two spare bedrooms besides the one Clint used, so there was more than enough room for the three of them.

At that point Eris took one hand off the wheel and placed it on Madeleine's knee.

Madeleine felt Sara's look, heard a pause in her speech, and she tucked her hand beneath Eris's arm. She wanted to look at him, but it was unnecessary. He had spoken volumes simply by touching her and leaving his hand where his mother could see it.

Sara drew breath and continued, undaunted. She talked about New Mexico and its inhabitants until they reached Emporia and were out of the truck and approaching the doors of the restaurant. Once they were seated inside and had given their orders to the waitress, Eris's beeper sounded.

"Sorry," Eris said, and he got up to look for a phone.

As he walked away, Sara looked at Madeleine and said, "Dedicated, isn't he?"

"He is," Madeleine agreed. "Do you mind if I ask where you came up with his name? It's unusual."

Sara gave a brief shrug, as if it wasn't important. "I saw the name spelled with an A in a children's book and decided to do it differently." She paused, briefly. "What exactly do you want with my son?"

Madeleine looked up, surprised at the bluntness of the other woman's question.

"You're older than he is, aren't you?"

"Yes."

Sara leaned back. "You obviously have a thing for Indians. How many did you go through while you were in the field? One at each reservation? You must have missed it while teaching."

Madeleine stared at the other woman. "You're very wrong."

"I can't be," she said, shaking her head. "Don't play stupid with me, you know exactly what I'm getting at here. I'm his mother and I already love him, but he's no beauty."

"Wrong again," said Madeleine, her gaze unwavering. "You've known him only a few days."

"How long have you known him?"

"Long enough to know there is no one else like him."

"I want him to come back with me," said Sara. "Don't make it hard for him."

"You mean don't make it hard for you."

"He will come back with me," Sara assured her. "All Indian men go through a period of attraction to white women. But he needs to be with other Indians and I'm going to do everything I can to make up for all he lost when the whites took him."

"I was under the impression you gave him away," said Madeleine, and Sara's dark eyes turned cold with anger.

"You know nothing about it."

"True," Madeleine admitted.

Sara smiled suddenly. "This conversation is absurd, really, because I'm not going anywhere right away. Your hold on him is probably sexual, nothing more, and my presence here will put a damper on that. When the sex is over everything else will be over. It's nothing personal, believe me. You seem like a nice person."

Madeleine lifted a palm and struggled to make her voice light. "No offense taken, Sara. I've met dozens of Indians just like you and I'm used to it."

Sara's chin quivered angrily and she opened her mouth, but Eris came back to the table at that moment and apologized again.

"Well, what happens now?" Sara asked when he didn't sit down again.

"We ask for our food to be placed in take-out bags," said Madeleine.

Sara frowned. "What on earth has happened?"

"A possible rabid skunk," said Eris. "We've had four so far this year."

He went to speak to the waitress, and Madeleine and Sara looked at each other again, but neither said a word.

They remained silent on the drive back, Madeleine and Sara carrying their bagged dinners in their laps. Eris glanced over occasionally, but neither would meet his look. At the lake, Madeleine saw Jacqueline and Manuel's Jeep in the drive and asked to be let out at the log cabin. Eris stopped the truck in the road and got out, taking the dinner from her so she could slide over.

Once she was out she took the dinner, thanked him, and lifted herself on her tiptoes to brush his lips before turning and walking across the road. Not another word was said between Madeleine and Sara Bent Horn.

CHAPTER
TWENTY-TWO

ERIS WAS KEPT BUSY most of the weekend with call after call, but when he was able to go home, he talked and ate with his mother, who gave him the stories he asked for about his grandparents and their grandparents and regaled him with tales of Fox who lived long ago, the ones who fought the whites and won. She made him laugh when she attempted to show him a dance and teach him a song, and she told him his father would have taken cash prizes at every powwow in the state. Daniel Birdcatcher was the best dancer she had ever seen, she claimed.

Only occasionally would Eris's attention wander to the door or the window. He hadn't seen Madeleine since the night she met Sara and he wondered if his mother's rudeness had changed things in some way. The silence between the two women on the return drive had been an uncomfortable one, and he knew something unpleasant had occurred between them. One had to listen to his mother for only half an hour to learn how bigoted most of her views were. Eris understood some of it, having been to the reservation and seen the poverty and alcoholism for himself, but he didn't understand all of it. Particularly her reaction to Madeleine. Eris had been proud to show her off, the beautiful, intelligent woman who wanted him, but his mother's behavior had made him embarrassed for Madeleine and angry with Sara. He had no idea what to do now. He thought Madeleine would understand, having been exposed to white hatred before, but he still wanted to see her, talk to her.

On Sunday night, after he saw Jacqueline and Manuel leave, he told his mother he was going up to see Madeleine.

"Can't it wait?" she asked. "She'll be here for the whole summer. I won't."

Eris didn't know about that. She hadn't shown any inclination to leave so far. Hadn't even discussed it. Not that he was anxious for her to leave, but he didn't want to put his relationship with Madeleine on hold indefinitely.

"I'll be back," he said.

"Why not invite her down here?"

"I want to be alone with her," Eris clarified, and before his mother could argue further he opened the door and exited the house to walk up and knock on the door of the log cabin.

Madeleine seemed surprised to see him. She opened the door and peered past his shoulder, as if expecting to see someone behind him.

"Hi," she said.

"May I come in?" he asked.

"Yes, of course." She stood aside and allowed him past her. She seemed to hesitate before closing the door, and Eris asked if she was expecting someone else.

"No, I just . . . didn't expect to see you."

Something had changed. He could feel it. He moved toward her and saw her take a step backward.

It reminded Eris of when he had first met her. It hurt.

"How was your weekend?" she asked, clasping her hands in front of her.

"Busy," he said. "I wasn't home much."

"Me either. Jacqueline took me to Wichita for the day on Saturday. It was good to be in the city again. And to drive my own car. I wanted to bring it back here, but Jacqueline talked me out of it. It's an Audi."

Eris nodded. He could see her in an Audi.

"Madeleine," he said abruptly, "What did she say to you?"

"Jacqueline?"

"Sara."

Madeleine lifted her hands. "Nothing I didn't expect. She is your mother, after all, and she's looking out for her son."

"I can look out for myself."

"She thinks you need to be with other Indians. She wants you to learn everything I couldn't teach you."

"I'll decide what I need." Eris moved toward her once more and then stopped when she retreated from him again.

"Don't do that, Madeleine. You don't know what it does to me to see you backing away."

Sudden emotion clouded Madeleine's eyes as she looked at him. "You don't know what it's doing to me. I only want what's best for you."

"Goddammit." Eris slammed a frustrated hand against the wall. "Don't say things are going to change because of something that woman said to you."

Madeleine stared, and he could tell she was startled by his angry display. Eris swallowed and strode forth to take her by the arms. He pulled her to the sofa and sat down to draw her onto his lap and put his arms tightly around her. He held her as close as he could without hurting her, kissing and touching her face until she made a noise in her throat and lifted her arms around his neck to hold him just as tightly. "I gave you the chance," she said to him.

He breathed out in relief and lifted a hand to cup her head. The thought of losing her did strange things to him, now that he knew how good it could be, how it felt to have someone who cared about him. He had that with his newfound mother, he knew, but his mother had to love him because he was her son. Madeleine didn't have to care about him. She didn't have to cook dinners for him or kiss him or make love with him. She didn't have to throw herself into his arms when he came home from work, or look at him the way she did. Him, with his face, the face even his mother looked at with poorly disguised pity. His beautiful Madeleine was his because she wanted to be, and his feeling for her only intensified to realize how much she did not need him.

He put a finger under her chin and lifted her head to look at him. She closed her lids to his probing gaze and he touched her lashes to make her open them again. When she was looking at him, he said, "I used to have a Volvo."

Madeleine stared at him in confusion for several seconds. And then she laughed.

He smiled and leaned his forehead against hers. She laughed again, hugged him, and they looked into each other's eyes. After a moment their gazes turned suddenly sober.

There was an air of anticipation between them as they went on looking at each other for breathless seconds. Then Madeleine put her hands to his face, and in a broken whisper she said three words that made his eyes squeeze shut and his breathing stop. He wanted to say her name, but no words could make it past the thickness in his throat. He could only hold her to him and clutch at her arms and shoulders with his hands. For the first time in his life he felt like giving thanks. The first twenty-seven years had been pretty dismal, but here suddenly was a woman he adored telling him she loved him.

He felt her lips cover his and he opened his mouth to kiss her. Madeleine's hands still cupped his face, and she began to gently kiss him on his cheeks and chin and forehead, her lips soft against the pits and scars of his skin. Eris opened his eyes finally to look at her, and he saw the words she had spoken repeated in her gaze as she looked at him. A shiver passed through him and the skin of his arms and chest goose pimpled.

As one they left the sofa and moved down the hall to the bedroom, unbuttoning clothes and taking down hair as they went.

Minutes later her fingers were tangled in his hair and he was tasting the skin below her navel when he felt her jump. Then he heard the reason for it.

Someone was knocking on the door.

They looked at each other; then Eris got up and put on his jeans. He went to the door shirtless and barefoot, to let his mother know he wasn't planning on coming home that night. He swung open the door and saw Dale Russell standing on the porch. Dale Russell stared at Eris. His brows drew together in a deep frown. "What the hell are you doing here?"

"That's my business," said Eris. "What do you want, Russell?"

He smirked and moved down a step. "The same thing you just got, obviously. Guess I'm shit out of luck tonight."

Eris shoved open the screen door and grabbed Russell before he could leave the porch. Eris slammed him into a post and held him by the throat, telling him what he would do to him if he ever spoke that way again. Russell's face turned red and then purple before Eris finally released him. Dale Russell gagged and coughed and spat, and then he reached to the waist of his uniform and drew his gun. He pointed it at Eris.

"You sonofabitch," he said hoarsely. "I'll kill you."

"Bullshit," said Eris, and behind him he heard an intake of breath that said Madeleine was at the door and watching.

Dale's eyes darted to the door. "Now I know why I'm having such a hard time with you, Madeleine. My skin's too clear. And maybe too white, huh?"

"Put the goddamned gun away or I'll take it from you," Eris warned, and his eyes spoke to Russell as he stood holding the gun in his hand. Eris knew he could take it from him, and Russell knew it too.

He forced a laugh and holstered the gun. He laughed again as he walked to his truck and climbed inside. He was still laughing as he drove away.

"Asshole," Eris muttered under his breath, and he turned to go back inside. Madeleine stood just inside the door dressed in a robe. She was staring at Eris with a peculiar expression. Eris closed the door behind him and went into the kitchen for a glass of water. After he drank the water he found her still looking at him. He put the glass down and asked her what was wrong. She gave her head a small shake. "Nothing. I had no idea you were fearless."

Eris said, "If he was going to shoot me he would have done it rather than talk about it."

Madeleine swallowed. "How reassuring."

He took her hand and they returned to her room. "If he comes back to bother you while I'm not here, call the head office and tell them he's harassing you."

She agreed, and then haltingly began to tell him about the phone calls she had received, and her second meeting with Bruce Beckworth, the man in the baseball cap.

Eris sat down on the bed beside her and drew a deep breath. He wished it was Madeleine living with him instead of his mother. He was frustrated by his inability to protect her when he wasn't around. "Ask Gloria Birdy to go with you the next time you feel like getting out," he told her. "I'll feel better if you're with her."

Madeleine nodded and slipped off her robe to lie down again. Eris took off his jeans and moved in beside her. Then it occurred to him to ask about her diaphragm. He gave her a gentle nudge and asked if she was wearing it. She shook her head. "It won't stay in with you."

Eris blinked. "So you haven't been using anything?"

"I don't have anything else to use. I didn't think about it while I was in the city."

His heart rate quickened. "Are you concerned?"

She propped herself on an elbow to look at him. "Not as concerned as your mother would be if she knew."

He smiled at her and she smiled back at him. Then he took her in his arms.

THE NEXT MORNING ERIS rose early, kissed Madeleine on the nose, then returned to his house. Sara was up and dressed, surprising him, and she greeted him as he came in.

"I'd like to go out with you this morning," she said. "Puttering around here is truly a bore, and I always think of dozens of things to tell you that I can never think of again once you're home."

"It's not a good idea today," Eris told her, thinking of the incident with Dale Russell. "I have too many stops to make."

"Please," she said. "I really am dying of boredom, and I'm thinking of going home soon. I want to be close to you a while longer before I go. Your superior will understand, I'm sure."

Eris could see she wasn't going to give up. He sighed and then nodded before disappearing to take a shower and dress. In the shower he surprised himself by thinking that Madeleine was more like him than his own mother. Sara was clearly an extrovert, clearly uncomfortable spending time alone. Madeleine knew how to occupy herself, the same as Eris. He had seen the notebook she'd filled up with writing on her dresser. She was working whether she knew it or not.

He was glad to know she had struck up a friendship with Gloria and Earl Lee Birdy. They were good people and Eris liked them. He would never have imagined them to be Madeleine's type, but she always managed to surprise him.

Like the thing with the diaphragm. He suspected Madeleine was a bit surprised at herself over the matter. He wasn't certain he could actually sire any children, but then he had never believed he would find someone he wanted to have a child with. Not until Madeleine said she loved him. He was still reeling from that, and a part of him almost wished she hadn't said it, because now all he could do was wonder if she loved him enough to stay.

Just thinking about it made his eyes close and his breathing slow. He wanted to say it to her. Leave or stay, he had wanted to push the words past his lips. But something had stopped him. He figured it was the adopted kid in him, the one who had learned to trust, the one who believed, and then was burned by circumstance.

She knew how he felt about her, he told himself. She had to know.

After he finished in the bathroom he passed through the hall to go to his room and found his mother standing at the foot of his bed. Eris wrapped his towel firmly around his middle and told her he needed to get dressed.

"You want me to braid your hair?" she asked.

"No," he said.

She smiled. "Okay. Some do, some don't. Yours is awfully long. Did you already eat, or can I fix you something for breakfast?"

"A cheese and egg sandwich would be great," he said, and she frowned at him.

"What?"

"Fry an egg and put cheese and mayonnaisse on the bread."

"Ugh. The things you bachelors eat."

Eris closed the door firmly behind her as she stepped into the hall. He liked the cheese and egg sandwich Madeleine had made for him. It was quick and filling and didn't make much of a mess.

The sandwich his mother made for him wasn't nearly as good, but Eris ate it anyway and swallowed a glass of juice before heading outside to see about his hawk. His mother was still eating at the table.

The hawk was dead in its cage, speared through the middle with a long pointed stick. Eris drew a sharp breath and looked around himself, his eyes narrowed and his mouth tight.

His first thought was of Dale Russell, but anyone could have killed the hawk. The slimy kitten-killing Earthworm could have done it, he told himself as he eyed Sherman Tanner's house.

He put on some gloves and removed the hawk from the cage so his mother wouldn't see it. He placed it in the garage in a paper sack to take care of later.

Goddammit. He hated to see that. Someone being cruel to an animal just to be cruel to a human.

His mood was sour the first few hours that morning and it stayed sour in spite of his mother's attempts to change it. Finally she sighed and said, "Did you and Madeleine have an argument?"

"No."

"Then what's wrong? Are you always this moody?"

He only looked at her.

"You and Clint, the original silent brooders. I don't know where you come by it, unless it was from my father. He was a brooder to beat all brooders. Made my mother crazy. He'd spend hours sulking and expect everyone else's mood to be just as dark as his. He wasn't happy until he'd made everyone else unhappy. Then he would suddenly, miraculously cheer up again."

A smile tugged at the corner of Eris's mouth. He turned the truck down the county road where he had caught Bruce Beckworth shooting birds and listened to his mother go on about family peccadilloes until she had him chuckling.

Then a tire blew out.

Eris muttered under his breath and stopped the truck to get out and have a look. It was the left rear tire, and it was already flat. He hunkered down to examine it, and a hundredth of a second after he lowered himself, the rear glass of the pickup shattered and he saw his mother's head slump forward. Before he could turn around and look, a bullet slammed into his shoulder and then another struck him just above his shoulder blade, sending him into the tailgate of the truck and causing his vision to darken. Eris forced himself to flatten and roll under the truck. From far away he heard the sound of a door slamming and tires spinning in the dust. He twisted around to look, but the pain of the movement caused his vision to darken again and he could see nothing but the blackness of unconsciousness awaiting him. He took deep breaths, and when he was ready, he moved out from under the truck and pulled himself up with his uninjured side to ease himself to the open driver's door.

He checked over his shoulder as he moved, but there was no sign of the gunman. The pain streaked like fire down his body every time he moved his head and he gritted his teeth as he bent down to slide inside the cab. He reached with his good right arm to lift his mother's head, and his hand came away covered with blood. He saw a red horizontal line that started almost at the back of her skull and plowed through her left temple. Rivulets of blood streamed down her cheek. Eris checked for a pulse and found a faint one. Then he picked up his radio.

CHAPTER
TWENTY-THREE

MADELEINE'S LIP CURLED WHEN she saw Sherman Tanner come
hurrying up the drive to the cabin. She took her notebook inside
and made a point of slamming the door. He came and hammered
on the wood anyway.

"You'll want to hear this," he called from outside. "I just heard
something on my radio about our neighbor that might interest
you. He's been shot."

Madeleine's breath stopped. She rushed to jerk open the door.
"Eris? Eris has been shot?"

"That's right," said Tanner, pleased to be imparting such information. "The woman in the truck with him was shot, too.
They're both being flown to Wichita by helicopter, because it
sounds like the woman's injuries are critical and Renard didn't
want to leave her."

Madeleine asked if he knew which hospital and then nodded
when he told her. It was the hospital in which Jacqueline and
Manuel worked.

"Who did it?" she asked, thinking of Dale Russell. "Do they
know who shot them?"

"An unknown assailant, was all I heard," said Tanner with a
sniff.

"Thank you for telling me," Madeleine said, and she shut the door in his face to rush to the telephone and call Jacqueline. Her sister was in surgery, and Manuel was out of the office, so Madeleine quickly threw some things in a bag, scooped up the kitten, and locked the door to the cabin behind her. Her heart was pounding in her chest as she got in the truck and started the engine. She was fuming at Dale Russell, whom she knew had to be responsible. The man pulled a gun on Eris last night. She had seen him.

Worry made her teeth grind as she drove, and she began to pray as she had never prayed, asking for Eris to please be all right. For the first time in her life she was truly in love and the man she was in love with didn't need his mother to die right after he found her; she was important to him, and she could make him laugh and she could tell him things about himself he needed to know.

Her mental state made her reckless; she made it to the city in under an hour and sped through traffic to Manuel and Jacqueline's house to quickly drop off the kitten before hurrying on. She couldn't leave it in the hot pickup any more than she could have left it at the cabin to go hungry. She wrenched open the door with a key her sister had given her, *and saw Manuel naked on the sofa in the living room with a woman who was not Jacqueline.*

Madeleine's face went slack with shock and Manuel leapt from the sofa and reached for his pants. Madeleine put the kitten down and left the house, hurrying to the pickup to get to the hospital, a few blocks away. She shook her head in amazement and disgust as she drove away and didn't know whether she wanted to laugh or cry over all the time she had wasted envying her sister's marriage.

Her heart felt sick for Jacqueline, and she knew she would avoid her sister rather than seek her out once in the hospital. She wouldn't be able to look her in the face without blurting out what she had just seen, and Madeleine had other things to worry about at the moment.

She was given the runaround in the intensive care unit until she told them she was Eris Renard's fiancée and begged to be allowed to see him. A kindly doctor took pity and showed her to Eris's room, where he lay swathed in bandages, his eyes open and staring at the ceiling. His gaze lowered as she stepped in the doorway, and at the sight of her face he extended his good arm to her. The doctor nodded and told her to go on, closing the door behind her. Madeleine went to Eris and dropped her purse to put her arms around him. His arm came around her waist and she pressed grateful kisses against his face and mouth before looking him over to assure herself he was all right.

"I tried to call you," he said.

"Tanner told me. Is there any word on your mother?"

"She's still in surgery."

"Where was she hit?"

"In the head."

Madeleine sucked in her breath. It was too bad Manuel was fooling around at home. He was purported to be one of the best neurologists in the state.

"What about you?"

"Once in the shoulder, once beneath the shoulder blade."

She swallowed and he took her hand and squeezed her fingers.

"Shouldn't you be sleeping?" she said. "Are you in any pain?"

"They gave me a shot."

"What happened?" she asked. "Do you think it was Russell?"

"No." Eris's eyes shifted away from her. "Russell is no marksman. First a tire was shot out, and then the shooter went for a heart shot on me, but I was already bending down to look at the tire. I don't think he meant to hit Sara."

"Was she conscious? Did she speak to you?"

Eris looked at her. "She came around just as we were landing. She asked me to take her home."

"She did."

"She was frightened, and going into shock."

Madeleine held her breath. She would not ask. He would have to tell her.

"I told her I would," he said.

"Take her home."

"Yes."

"How much time will you have off?"

"A few weeks disability, and possible additional suspension for having her with me in the first place. I'll stay in New Mexico a week or two."

Madeleine nodded. "When will you leave?"

"As soon as she's able. It'll be up to the doctors to say."

She squeezed his hand; then she cleared her throat and said,

"I should go now and let you sleep. I'll come by later, if they let me in. I had to tell them we were engaged."

Eris quirked a brow and Madeleine dropped a final fleeting kiss on his lips before departing. She left the room and found the nearest elevator to take her down to the hospital cafeteria. She ordered a Diet Coke and sat huddled in a booth in the corner, unable to fight the feeling that once he left he would never return.

When she saw Jacqueline enter the cafeteria she thought of hiding, but it was too late; her sister had already seen her.

Jacqueline looked tired, but she smiled as she walked over to Madeleine's table. "What are you doing here?"

"Eris and his mother were shot today. I came as soon as I heard."

Jacqueline's eyes rounded. "Eris Renard? Who shot him? Why?"

"Nobody knows. He's all right, but his mother was wounded in the head. Last I heard she was still in surgery."

"Who's doing it? I'm not sure where Manny is today."

"He's at home," Madeleine said haltingly. "I saw him when I dropped off the kitten."

Jacqueline peered at her sister. "What's wrong? Why did your cheeks just turn red? Did you walk in on him in the bathroom or something?"

Madeleine covered her mouth and stared at her sister over the top of her hand. The mental debate of whether to tell her or not tell her lasted approximately ten seconds.

She had to. If the circumstances were reversed, Madeleine knew she would want to know.

"I walked in on him with another woman, Jacqueline. They were both naked on the sofa."

Jacqueline gaped soundlessly at her for nearly thirty seconds while her face went white. "You're lying," she said finally. "You're paying me back for everything I said to you. It's been eating you up thinking of a way to get back at me and you—"

Madeleine put her hands over her eyes and shook her head. She got up to leave the table, but Jacqueline snatched her by the arm and pulled her around.

"Tell me you're lying, dammit. Tell me."

Madeleine could only look at her and apologize with her eyes.

Jacqueline swerved away from her and bent over to grip the table and make a choking sound. Madeleine put a hand on her back, but Jacqueline knocked it away and collapsed into the booth, her eyes red and her shoulders already heaving in silent sobs.

"I never wanted to hurt you," Madeleine whispered. "I'm so sorry."

"Go away," said Jacqueline. "Just go away."

Madeleine stared dejectedly at her sister's bent head and wondered why doing what felt like the right thing never felt right once it was done.

Before she realized what she was doing she was in the truck and heading back to Jacqueline's house. She didn't go inside, she simply put the keys to the truck under the visor and hopped into her Audi, parked beside the drive.

She felt better driving the Audi. Once on the highway she opened up and flew down the road.

While driving she asked herself the real reason she told her sister what she witnessed. If she had kept her mouth shut things might have gone on the same for them, with Manuel only occasionally sampling other women and Jacqueline remaining blissfully unaware and still happily married.

Perhaps it truly had been something vindictive on Madeleine's part. Some desire to take retribution for all Jacqueline had said and to prove to her sister that even people who did good and never hurt anyone else got hurt themselves sometimes. Just because people were people.

She closed her eyes briefly as her thoughts shifted to Eris. She wished she hadn't told him how she felt about him. She had warned herself not to say it aloud, not to give in to her emotions when she was still unsure of his. Now she found herself feeling like Sam Craven must have felt the last two years of their marriage. The way her sister Jacqueline was doubtlessly feeling right now.

It was a terrible, desolate feeling.

The miles crawled by as she shifted gears and mashed the accelerator with her foot.

She had told Eris she would come by later, but she could not go back and face him that night. She had to get away from everyone. Including herself.

*　　*　　*

RONNIE LYMAN SPENT THE day following a man in a baseball cap driving a Blazer. He had seen the man shoot Eris Renard earlier, and he giggled himself into a fit when he realized the guy was staggering drunk. It was too good. It was just *too* good. Ronnie had been following Renard and hanging way back, wondering who the woman in the cab with him was and what he could do to her, when he saw the whole thing happen. Renard's truck had gone down the road, kicking up dust, and the Blazer pulled out two hundred yards behind it. There was a moment of hesitation, and then the Blazer fell in behind Renard's truck. In a flash the man had leapt out of the Blazer and thrown open the door to begin firing, as if the decision had been made and acted upon in an instant. It took him two shots to blow out a tire, and Ronnie was impressed at the man's marksmanship. Renard would be dead right now, splattered all over the road, if the man hadn't been so drunk. Ronnie was sure of it.

The guy had balls, he gave him that. But now Ronnie was wondering what else he had. He followed him all the way back to Fayville and saw the Blazer turn off in a drive a half-mile long that led up to a house the size of a damned shopping center.

Ronnie hung in there, watching to see if the place was maybe the house of a girlfriend or someone else, but the Blazer stayed there for hours. Long enough for the guy in the ball cap to sleep off his morning drunk, Ronnie guessed. An hour after dark, just as Ronnie was preparing to leave, he saw the lights of the Blazer suddenly come on again. He started his own car and made ready to follow.

The Blazer headed northwest again, and Ronnie trailed him as he picked up a couple buddies along the way. Then the man in the baseball cap and his two friends headed for a public hunting area, where they began to drink beer, spotlight deer, and take turns shooting.

The guy obviously figured he didn't have to worry about Eris Renard that night.

Ronnie stayed back and watched until the trio decided to leave. They drove to the reservoir and trolled the bays before stopping to join a party in progress at a private dock. When the three men left the Blazer, Ronnie took a tiny penlight from his glove compartment and hurried over to have a look inside. He wanted to see what kind of rifle had been used on Eris Renard and the luckless deer that night. The rifle was in the back, and Ronnie picked up a cartridge rolling around on the floorboard. .270 cartridge.

The gun was a Remington 7400. Semiautomatic. A play toy for a rich boy.

Ronnie slunk back to the car and made himself comfortable. The party went on until nearly three in the morning, and Ronnie was fighting sleep by the time they stumbled to the Blazer. Someone from the party came out and told the man in the baseball cap to leave the beer he was taking with him. The man in the ball cap put down the beer and kicked the other man in the balls, then hit him over the head with his fists locked when he doubled over. Somebody shouted, somebody else screamed, and the guy's friends dragged him away and shoved him in the Blazer, leaving the beer in the grass.

Several guys from the party came running, but the Blazer took off after a shuddering start and weaved down the road away from the pursuers.

Ronnie frowned as he started his car and fell in behind. He wondered if he should even mess around with this guy. The asshole was clearly unstable.

But a second look at that big house changed his mind, and he thought he even glimpsed a Jaguar in the garage when the driver put the Blazer inside for the night.

Everything that had been driving him the last two weeks, the need to find Sheila and his daughters, the urge to harm Eris Renard and scare his pretty blonde girlfriend, were swept away like leaves in a gutter as Ronnie considered that Jaguar.

He knew what he would do. He would bypass the guy in the ball cap entirely and go directly to the owner of that Jag. Without knowing it, the owner of the Jag would pay for all Ronnie had lost. For Kayla, for Sheila and the girls, and for the aggravation, jail time, and the thirty-second report on television that Eris Renard was responsible for about the hoax perpetrated by Ronnie. Ronnie's mother couldn't show her face in public because of him. Even the lowlifes at the bingo hall were shunning her. And unless Ronnie changed his name or stumbled across someone who hadn't seen the telecast or a newspaper, no one was going to give him a job doing anything but picking fruit or hauling furniture.

But maybe, Ronnie thought, just maybe, the owner of the Jaguar could see his way free to help Ronnie out. Then Ronnie wouldn't need a job. He could just skip the state altogether and say a fond farewell to everyone he knew in Kansas. Including his good friend the judge.

And he would deal with Sheila later, when and if he ever found her.

Ronnie rummaged around in the car until he found a pen. He used a white hamburger wrapper to write on. He wrote down the rifle make and the cartridge he found and added that he had watched the man in the baseball cap jump out of his Blazer to shoot conservation officer Eris Renard in the back. A woman in the cab was hit in the head.

He finished by writing that he would take one hundred thousand dollars not to tell anyone what he had seen.

Ronnie was sure he had misspelled conservation, and maybe a few other words as well, but he wasn't worried. He idled up to the mailbox and saw the name Beckworth, and was about to put the note inside when he changed his mind. He drove instead the rest of the way to the house and then left his car to stick the note in the storm door. The minute he made a step toward the door a security light came on, and as he snatched at the handle to open the door and shove the note through the crack, an alarm sounded somewhere.

Breathing hard, Ronnie jumped away from the door and raced for his car. He crawled behind the wheel and was speeding down the drive before the front door of the house opened.

Tomorrow he would give Beckworth a call.

CHAPTER
TWENTY-FOUR

ERIS SLEPT BADLY IN the hospital. He had many hours to lie awake and wonder who had shot him and for what reason. There were so many possibilities he could not begin to narrow it down. Every man who walked in the woods with a firearm disliked and distrusted a conservation officer. It might have been someone Eris nailed for killing game out of season the year before, afraid to get caught again or still pissed off about the first time. It was impossible to say whether the person meant only to wound or to kill, but the placement of the shots suggested the latter, which further suggested to Eris it was someone serious with intent, or a drunk who was otherwise a damned good shot.

When he tired of thinking about it his mind wandered to other areas of his life and to the changes that had occurred and were still occurring so rapidly. He tried to think when it had all begun, when things started changing, and he found himself remembering a night when he stood in his yard eating a sandwich and watching a woman take off her clothes in the bedroom of the log cabin above him. That was it, he told himself. The first time he had seen Madeleine.

It worried him that she hadn't come by to see him again. He sensed she was troubled by his decision to return to New Mexico with his mother, but he had no choice. He felt responsible for what had happened to Sara, who had remained unconscious for many hours after surgery before finally coming around. The eyesight in her left eye was damaged, as well as the hearing in her left ear, and there were miniscule pieces of floating bone fragments the surgeons had been unable to reach, but all agreed the prospects for recovery were good.

Eris saw her first thing the next morning; he was taken to her in a wheelchair by a nurse's aide. She cried to see him and asked how he was feeling.

He had asked the hospital to call Clint after Sara was out of surgery, and they had complied. Eris called the number for her while in her room, so she could talk to her other son herself and tell him she was all right.

When he ended his visit with his mother and returned to his room he found Jacqueline just leaving. Her eyes were swollen and her face was pale, but she gave him a brief smile and asked how he was feeling.

"Good," he told her.

"How is your mother?"

"She'll be all right."

"I'm glad. I was shocked to hear what had happened. Do you have any ideas about who was responsible?"

"Could've been anyone," said Eris. Then he asked if she had seen Madeleine.

"No, uh, actually, I thought she might be in here. It surprised me to find her at the hospital yesterday. I had no idea she'd become so friendly with your mother. My sister doesn't make friends easily."

Eris looked away from her. It was obvious Jacqueline knew nothing about Eris's relationship with Madeleine.

"If you see her," Jacqueline continued, "please tell her I need to speak with her."

"Did she stay with you last night?" Eris asked, and Jacqueline shook her head.

"I stayed here. Will you please tell her?"

He nodded. "If I see her." He was beginning to doubt he would, and a tightening sensation in his chest caused him sudden discomfort.

"Are you all right?" she asked before leaving.

He nodded again and looked at her. "Are you?"

"No," she replied; then left the room.

Eris picked up the phone and called the cabin. He let it ring twelve times before hanging up. As he put the phone down, his superior entered the room, and Eris spent the next hour listening to how these disastrous consequences could have been avoided if he had obeyed the rules of common sense and left his mother at home. Eris answered the questions he was asked, but he didn't volunteer any information, and his superior shook his head in disappointment. "You're a damned fine CO, Renard, but if she had been anybody but your mother, we'd be getting sued right now. I'm going to suspend you without pay for three weeks."

"On top of my disability?" asked Eris.

"You want Russell handling things that long?" came the reply.

"No," said Eris.

"Me either. Take what time you need, then get back to work as soon as possible." He started out and then stopped. "The shell casings found in the road were .270s. Make copies of all your reports and give the police a list of everyone you've offended for the last two years."

With that, the man left. Eris stared after him and silently thanked him for coming in person instead of simply calling on the phone. Then he got out of bed.

He was still weak. And dizzy. Everything on his left side ached, and it hurt to move his head.

He got back into bed and went to sleep.

THE RINGING PHONE WOKE him, and he picked up the receiver. "Hello?"

"How are you?" asked Madeleine."

"Better. Where are you?"

"At the cabin. Sorry I didn't make it back last night."

"Run into trouble?"

"No, I just . . . didn't make it back. How's your mother today?" He told her all he knew, then he paused.

"That's good news," she said. "You must be very relieved."

There was a brief silence between them. Finally he said, "I want to leave here tomorrow. Can you drive over and pick me up?"

She was surprised. "Surely they're not ready to release you."

"I can't stay here."

"What about your mother?"

"She'll be all right. I'll drive back in a few days. Will you come and get me?"

"Your legs wouldn't fit in my Audi. I guess I can take it back to Jacqueline's house and get the truck again."

Eris told her about Jacqueline's visit to him that morning, and her request.

Madeleine's voice lowered. "Okay. I'll call her. What time should I come tomorrow?"

"Around noon."

"All right. See you then."

He hung up confused and disappointed. Something had changed again. Something in her voice was different. He figured it was the impending trip to New Mexico. He thought briefly of asking her to go with him, maybe settling her with her folks while he stayed with his mother, but they would still be apart.

Eris didn't know what to do. He knew how he would feel were she to leave him, but it wasn't the same. He was coming back.

Late that afternoon he went to see his mother again, and he sat quietly in her room looking at her face until she awakened. They talked awhile, and he told her he would be going home the next day, because staying in the hospital made him crazy. She said she understood. She didn't mind. He was coming back to New Mexico with her and that was all that mattered.

When he returned to his room, Madeleine was waiting. She ran to him, sliding her arms around him and pressing her face against his chest. Eris closed his eyes and held on to her with his good arm. After a moment he sat and pulled her down next to him, on his good side.

"I hate talking to you on the phone," she mumbled into his hospital gown. "It makes me miss you so much."

He kissed her forehead. "I was worried when you didn't come last night."

"I couldn't," she said. "I was such a mess."

She went on to tell him about Manuel and Jacqueline. She had just come from seeing Jacqueline, who had forgiven her after a screaming confrontation with Manuel, who denied nothing, said it was his right as a male and he assumed it was something Jacqueline understood. Jacqueline didn't. When Manuel said

women in his country understood, Jacqueline told him to go back
to his country. She would take the house and the car, he could
have the Jeep, the cabin, and his precious boat. Manuel had said
fine. He would need a week to vacate the house, but he wanted
the troublemaking Madeleine out of the cabin immediately.

Madeleine was to go back that evening and pack all her things.
Jacqueline had moved to a hotel in the city in the meantime and
said Madeleine was free to come and stay with her.

"It's time to get serious about finding a job," Madeleine concluded. "I haven't heard a word about any of the grants I applied
for."

Eris thought a moment, opened his mouth, shut it, opened it
again, then took a deep breath and said, "Come and stay with
me."

"Now that you have furniture?" said Madeleine, the corners of
her eyes crinkling.

He smiled and looked at his bandages. "I'm going to need some
help for a day or two."

"Just a day or two?"

"After that you may be the one who needs help. I'm off work,
remember."

Madeleine smiled and then glanced away. "What happens
when you go to New Mexico?"

"You stay."

"Until you come back?"

"For as long as you want."

She looked at him, and her hesitancy matched his.

"Do I take it you like my cooking?"

Eris squeezed her waist in reply, his hand warm and even a
little moist. Madeleine put her arms around his neck and kissed
him.

As if on cue, an aide stepped into the room and asked Eris if
he was ready for a bath.

Madeleine circumspectly lowered her arms and moved aside.

"I'm sure you have other things to do," she said to the aide. "I
can help him with the bath."

The woman eyed them in disapproval, but she apparently did
have other things to do, because she left the pan, the sponge, the
towels, and a fresh gown behind her as she turned and exited
the room.

"Jacqueline says this hospital is incredibly understaffed when it comes to nurses and aides," Madeleine explained as she moved to close the door.

"Lucky me," said Eris, and he reached behind himself to untie his gown.

Madeleine filled up the pan in the bathroom with warm sudsy water and brought it to him. Then she proceeded to give him his first sponge bath ever, slow and unhurried, taking her time with each limb and massaging as she soaped, being careful to avoid any areas that were painful to him.

Her lips and fingers followed the sponge across the marks on his back and chest and Eris found himself stirring just watching her.

The aide ducked in once, just to see how the bath was coming, and Madeleine threw a towel over Eris's middle to hide his state of arousal. When she was gone they looked at each other and grinned like naughty children.

She gently toweled his skin dry and helped him into a fresh gown. Then she took a small brush from her purse and loosened the band on his long black hair. She began to brush slowly, moving upward with each stroke, until she was brushing from the scalp down. Eris's entire body goose pimpled as she went on brushing and brushing, causing his scalp to tingle.

He smiled as he felt her pick up his hair and band it again without braiding it. When she was finished, she moved in front of him and looked into his face.

Eris matched her gaze for a long moment before placing a hand on the back of her neck and pulling her close. She put her arms around him and met his lips, opening her mouth to him and making a noise low in her throat as their breathing slowed and the kiss deepened. Eris heard the whisper of the door opening again and he ignored it, hoping the aide would go away, but a throat being loudly cleared caused them to draw slowly apart.

A start went through him, and he felt Madeleine flinch when they looked and saw Dale Russell standing in the room, his handsome mouth twisted in disgust.

"You've got nerve," Madeleine said, low and angry.

Russell lifted a hand. "I didn't shoot anybody. I came to let you know that. You can believe it or not, but I'm telling you it wasn't me."

Eris only looked at him.

Russell shifted his feet, put his hands on his waist and shook his head. "Madeleine, I can't get over this. You and him."

"Get out," she said.

"I'm going. Just wanted to come by and proclaim my innocence, in case either one of you were thinking of tattling on me for anything." Eris and Madeleine remained silent. Russell smirked and left the room, shaking his head again as he went.

"I think I'll stay with Jacqueline tonight," said Madeleine when he was gone. "I'll come tomorrow to pick you up and we'll go back to the cabin together."

Eris nodded. He thought it was a good idea.

DALE RUSSELL WALKED THROUGH the hospital in search of the elevator. What he really wanted to find was a place to throw up. Seeing Madeleine kissing Renard had actually made him sick to his stomach.

A group of student nurses passed him in the hall, and he felt them all stop and gape at him. Females often did that, stopped whatever they were doing to stare admiringly at him. It didn't happen as often as it used to, him being stuck out at the lake all day, and he missed it in a way, because he knew something inside him fed off the attention. He didn't do anything about it, of course, but that wasn't the point.

He was beginning to think his problems stemmed from all the time he was spending alone. It hadn't been as bad the year before, but that was the first year, when the job was new and he was concerned about doing everything right. This year he pretty much knew what he was doing, so his mind grew idle during all the long boring hours and he found himself thinking about things he hadn't thought about in years. Like little girls.

Madeleine. His focus on her kept him straight, as long as she kept saying no to him. But it was also driving him crazy, because no woman had ever said no to him as firmly and consistently as she did. She honestly wanted nothing to do with him, and Russell was completely stunned and utterly confused to find her with Eris Renard, of all people. The bastard was so ugly. All those horrible marks all over him.

But even Dale had to admit there was something about Renard. Seeing him in Madeleine's house with his hair all wild and wearing nothing but old blue jeans was almost scary. He reminded Dale of some animal just out of a cage, the way it looked when the door first opened, as if it was deliriously happy to be free at last and was doubly prepared to tear your arm off if you went near it or threatened its newfound freedom in any way.

Renard. If anyone out there unnerved Dale, it was him. Renard didn't give a shit about the governor or the governor's nephew. He proved it when he jumped Dale at the cabin. Dale had spent the night and part of the next day thinking of ways to get Renard fired—until he heard he had been shot. Then Dale became uneasy because of what had happened the night before and he ducked out of sight for the next twelve hours. Eventually he decided the best way to play it would be to confront Renard and tell him he hadn't done it.

One look at Renard's face told him Renard knew he wasn't the one who shot him, and Dale found himself feeling insulted rather than relieved, particularly since he had walked in to find Renard doing what he was doing with the one female who looked at Dale like she recognized what he was inside and knew all his dark, twisted secrets. More than anything else about Madeleine Heron, he thought it was that, the hidden knowledge of him she seemed to possess, that made Dale keep coming back to her again and again. He wanted desperately to have her in a situation where he could see if he was right.

He wished it wasn't so important to him, that feeling he felt when he was doing something society regarded as "wrong." He wasn't a rapist. Rape didn't appeal to him, because he imagined most of the women he touched would wind up enjoying it once they got a good look at him. There was no gratification in being wanted by a woman. Being wanted was empty.

What he enjoyed most of all was a look of trust betrayed. Like the look Kayla Lyman had given him as he pulled down his underwear and made her open her mouth. Something about that look made him feel powerful and confident and sexy beyond belief. He came for fifteen minutes into that mouth.

Dale shuddered as he finally stumbled into an elevator. He had to stop thinking about it. Concentrate on Madeleine again. She was much bigger game, and years older, but that same sense of excitement trilled in him when he was near her, danger and elation mixed with anticipation. Only thing was, he had to make her trust him again, and how he was going to do that he had no idea. Small children were no problem, but grown women, particularly keen, intelligent women with big tall boyfriends, were a different matter.

Still, Dale had to cling to her, had to keep focused on the challenge she presented, if only to keep himself out of trouble and away from any more little girls.

CHAPTER
TWENTY-FIVE

WES BECKWORTH SOLD COCAINE and marijuana for nearly twenty years before going into real estate. The change of vocations was a wise decision for him, since most of the people who had supplied him or bought from him were now either dead or in jail. Wes took the money he had made, which amounted to several hundred thousand dollars, and bought every acre of pasture land and riverfront property he could get his hands on. The next twenty years were even more profitable for him, leasing, selling, and developing, and Wes Beckworth became known as a man with a gift for making money.

His twenty-five-year-old son did not share his gift. Bruce wanted to do nothing but drink beer, drive his boat, fire his guns, and fight with other drunks. Wes would have included women on the list, but Bruce was so obnoxious none would even get close to him. A friend of Bruce's told Wes he had seen his son pick up a hooker in the city, abduct her, drive her out to a county road and beat the hell out of her—without ever having sex with her.

Wes was not surprised. Bruce had a problem with rejection that started with his mother, who had married Wes only because he could supply her with all the drugs she needed. Wes put her in the hospital a few times, but the night he broke her leg with an axe handle she decided she had had enough. Bruce, who was around six or seven at the time, had screaming fits of anxiety for years after her departure.

Wes had finally married again in January, and Bruce had been acting like an asshole ever since, getting into trouble every other day by smashing up the Blazer, beating up people, and getting arrested.

Now Bruce had shot a conservation officer, wounding him and seriously injuring a woman who had been riding along in the cab of the truck.

It wasn't the first time his son had shot at Eris Renard, Wes heard. Renard came very close to catching Bruce and his spotlighting buddies a time or two. It was only by shooting at him that they were able to escape.

Of course Bruce denied shooting Renard. A lie sprang to his lips as easily as the word hello. But he had told his friend about it, and the friend told Wes. Bruce's friend was paid a lot of money to tell Wes things. Wes never trusted his son's version of events, and he had learned early to bribe Bruce's friends into giving him the truth.

The witness to the shooting had the deer rifle and the cartridges right, but any hunter in the woods could carry a Remington 7400 and use .270 cartridges.

After learning of Bruce's guilt, Wes's first instinct had been to get rid of the rifle and destroy the evidence.

But that wouldn't make the blackmailer go away, and that's what he would need to get Bruce completely off the hook this time.

There was no question of whether he would do it, but it wasn't necessarily loyalty to his son that made him want to see Bruce remain free. Wes loved the challenge of pitting his mental skills against the system. He had been doing it all his life, and so far he had won. He wanted to keep winning.

When the blackmailer called, Wes was ready for him. It was important to turn the tables quickly and become the aggressor rather than the defender, the hunter rather than the prey, and shift the advantage.

If the blackmailer was the average dumbshit, he would lose confidence immediately and begin to negotiate rather than demand.

"This Beckworth?" asked the voice on the phone.

"Who is this?"

"The man who saw your son shoot Renard. You give me what I want, I go away forever."

"What do you want?"

"A hundred thousand."

"Dollars?"

"No, a hundred thousand dick slickers. Of course I'm talkin' about dollars."

"Or you'll do what?" asked Wes, smiling to himself.

"Make another phone call, this time to the cops. I'll even testify if I have to. I saw him do it."

"You testify and I'll slit you open from your balls to your gizzard," said Wes in a mild tone.

There was a pause; then, "I bet that works on most people. It don't work on me. I'm gonna want the money by Friday. I'll call again later and tell you what to do with it."

The man hung up and Wes took the phone away form his ear to put it on the base. He leaned back in his chair and fingered the edges of his desk while his mind worked. He considered giving the man what he wanted and then dealing with him later, after he knew his name and where he lived, worked, whatever.

He got up from his chair and walked downstairs, to where Bruce was sprawled in a chair, drinking beer and watching an X-rated video tape. Wes looked at the screen a moment, then he took the beer bottle out of Bruce's hand and hit his bald son over the head with it, breaking the glass and causing Bruce to leap from his chair in an aggressive stance a second before his eyes rolled up and he fell forward onto his face.

Wes watched the tape a moment more, then he turned off the VCR and the television and walked upstairs to find his wife.

JACQUELINE OPENED THE DOOR of the hotel room and Madeleine carried her purse inside. Things were still awkward between them, but Madeleine sensed her sister's anger and hurt were no longer directed at her so much as at Manuel.

"It's not a suite at the Marriott, but it'll do," said Jacqueline as Madeleine looked around herself.

"It's fine," she said. "How are you feeling?"

"Suicidal. How are you feeling?"

"Penitent."

"Don't. I would have done the same."

"Would you?"

"Yes. I take it you're not going to the cabin until tomorrow."

"Do you think Manuel will mind?"

"Fuck Manuel. Everyone else has."

Her brows lifted, and Madeleine eyed her sister. She wondered if perhaps she should stay with Jacqueline after all.

"Jacqueline," she said, "have you called Mom?"

"Not yet." Jacqueline flopped onto the bed. "She'll drop everything to come running out here. I don't want them to worry."

Madeleine went to sit down beside her. It had been Jacqueline who called their parents to relay the news of Sam's death. They told her not to worry about Madeleine; she was as tough as they came. Things would be different with Jacqueline. Those who gave more needed more, and Jacqueline had always given more than Madeleine.

She drew a deep breath and said, "Eris asked me to come and stay with him. If you need me, I won't go."

Her sister blinked and looked at her. "Renard?"

"Yes." Madeleine's brown-green eyes were steady.

"Oh," said Jacqueline. "To help him until he can operate with two arms again?"

"No. To live with him."

Jacqueline stared again. "You're joking."

Madeleine was silent.

"What are you saying?" asked Jacqueline. "Are you telling me the two of you have been seeing each other? You and Eris Renard?"

"Yes."

Jacqueline made a face. "Madeleine, he's . . ."

"What?" Madeleine asked, daring her to finish.

Her sister blinked again. Her mouth worked. Finally she said, "You haven't known him six weeks."

"I won't go if you need me," Madeleine said again. "Will you be all right on your own?"

Jacqueline slowly nodded. "I'm still trying to . . . how did the two of you ever connect? He's so . . . so stiff and always looks so awfully forbidding."

Madeleine looked away from her sister. "I don't see the same Eris the rest of you see."

"Apparently not," said Jacqueline, her voice suddenly quiet. She reached over to bring Madeleine's chin around. They gazed into each other's eyes a moment; then Jacqueline said, "I see a lot of potential for hurt in there. Maybe as badly as I hurt right now. Sure you can handle this so soon after Sam?"

"There's no comparison," said Madeleine.

"Meaning you're in love this time."

Madeleine looked down at her hands. Jacqueline shook her head and fell back onto the bed. "I've seen everything."

After a moment Madeleine moved to the other side of the bed and pulled the pillow from under the coverlet. As she lay down, she said, "I think you should call Mom."

"Stop worrying about me."

"I want to. That's why I think you should call Mom, so she can worry about you for both of us."

In spite of herself, Jacqueline smiled. Then she sighed and closed her eyes. "How do things get so screwed up, Madeleine? Please tell me."

"I wish I could."

"I thought my life was perfect. I had to pinch myself every day. There I was, married to a handsome, talented doctor, living in a beautiful home, working at a job I loved and having it all."

"That would have made me suspicious from the start," Madeleine murmured.

"What? What would have made you suspicious?"

"The perfection. It just doesn't happen, Jacqueline. It never will."

"Spoken like a true realist."

"I try to be."

"You'll have to be."

Madeleine turned her head. "What does that mean?"

"Eris Renard is an adoptee who's just found his birth mother. Isn't that what you told me?"

"So?"

"So nothing. You know what you're up against. He's an Indian and she's an Indian and you're not."

Madeleine knew. "I've got to find a job," she said.

"Go back to Wichita State."

"I can't. I can't go back there."

"Then take some money from Sam's parents."

"No, thanks." She rolled over on her side to face Jacqueline. "Is there a big and tall shop around here somewhere? I need to buy something for Eris to wear home tomorrow. His uniform was ruined."

"Near Towne East, I think. He is pretty tall, isn't he?"

"He's six-four."

"Maybe you have something there, Madeleine. Find a man who looks like Renard and you know he'll never—"

"Shut up before you say something to make me hate you," Madeleine interrupted, her voice tight.

Jacqueline was silent for some moments. Then she apologized. A moment later she started crying, and Madeleine moved over to put her arms around her. If Jacqueline didn't call their mother in the morning, then Madeleine was going to do it.

MANUEL MADE IT IMPOSSIBLE for her to take the truck, so Madeleine was forced to drive her Audi to pick up Eris. She moved the passenger seat back as far as she could and hoped for the best. She went to the big and tall shop and used the money Eris had given her to buy jeans and a shirt she thought he would like; then she hurried to the hospital with her purchases and raced into the elevator, her pulse thrumming with sudden unnamed excitement.

He smiled when she rushed into the room, and Madeleine had to stop as she reached the bed and simply look at him. How was it that no one else saw the wild beauty of him? she wondered. How could anyone escape the warmth and intelligence in his eyes, the fine, straight nose, or the sensuality of his lips? What were they looking at when they saw him? she asked herself.

She opened her mouth and said a greeting to him in the Sauk-Fox language, one or two simple phrases she could remember from the books she had borrowed. It felt good to use the language, feel the texture of it on her tongue and against her teeth.

His brows drew together slightly, and she leaned forward to brush his lips before handing him the sack.

"What did you say to me?" he asked.

"I said it is a new day, let us greet it together."

Half an hour later Eris was dressed and being wheeled out of the elevator by an orderly.

"I moved the seat back in the Audi," Madeleine told him, "but you're still going to be cramped."

He was cramped, but not as bad as she had imagined. As they drove away from the hospital, Eris looked at the Audi and then at her. "How long have you had this car?"

"Several years. I bought it when I decided to teach."

"After your marriage?"

She glanced at him. "Before." Then she asked if he had seen his mother that morning.

He nodded. "She's doing well. The bruising and discoloration are bad at the moment, but it'll pass."

"Did you tell her I'm coming to stay with you?"

"Yes," he said.

They were silent for several minutes, until Eris looked at her and asked, "Where did you meet Sam?"

She blinked. "Why do you want to know about him?"

"Because I want to know about you."

Madeleine considered, then said, "If I tell you, will you answer some of my questions?"

"If it's important to you," he said.

"Knowing about Sam is important to you?"

"Yes."

"Because I'm moving in? Because the last man I lived with happened to shoot himself and you're just mildly curious as to the reason why?"

Eris's mouth twitched. "Because I want to know."

"All right. I met Sam in a bank shortly after I came back to Wichita. I was on the escalator and noticed a blond man staring at me. He dropped what he was doing to come after me, and that's how we met."

"Did you like him right away?" Eris asked.

"Yes. He was charming and aggressive and had an ebullient personality. He seemed to be either laughing or smiling all the time, and after what I had just been through with the silent and sullen Sioux, Sam was a refreshing change."

"Did you marry him soon after meeting him?"

"It seemed like it," said Madeleine, and then she looked at Eris. "No, I never really loved him. I didn't even take his name. Yes,

I was running away from what happened to me and hurrying to immerse myself in a normal life before the age of thirty because it seemed stupidly important to me at the time. Afterward, I told myself I was happy and I made myself believe it, but Sam eventually made the error more than apparent."

"Were you ever attracted to any Indians?" Eris asked, and Madeleine's mouth tightened.

"Is this you asking me, or your mother?"

"It's me," he said.

Madeleine glanced at him again. "I've been attracted to Indians all my life, Eris. When I was four years old I drew pictures of Indians riding horses and shooting arrows at buffalo. I read everything I could find about Indians, and dreamed of having long black hair and wearing buckskin dresses. My love affair with Indians has been lifelong, but you're the only Indian I've ever slept with."

He was silent a moment. Then he asked, "Why me?"

Madeleine took her eyes off the road once more.

"Because you're you."

He looked at her, and Madeleine's breath caught when she saw the narrowing of his dark eyes. Suddenly she knew she was right; his mother had been talking to him that morning. "Don't," she breathed. "Please don't let her make you doubt me."

"I don't want to," he said.

Madeleine was tempted to stop the car. Instead she pushed down on the accelerator and said, "Is it so hard to believe anyone could love you, Eris? Is it so hard to believe I could fall for you just because you're you? You're everything I could ever want. You're pure and brave and honest and strong; you're quick and intelligent and dedicated. You take nothing for granted and yet you live life on your own terms. If all of that isn't enough, we can talk about what you do to me physically, but I'm sure your mother has already talked to you about that."

"She has," Eris agreed, his jaw rigid and his gaze focused straight ahead.

Madeleine sighed but said nothing further, only concentrated on her driving. After a while, Eris said, "She thinks you're going to hurt me."

"Jacqueline thinks you're going to hurt me," Madeleine replied.

"You told her."

"Of course."

"I wondered if you would."

"What does that mean? Am I supposed to be ashamed of you? Is that what your mother suggested?"

"No. Her suggestion was to ask you to marry me, just to see what you would say. I told her it was too soon. She wanted to know why, so I told her about Sam, and why your sister offered you the cabin to begin with."

Madeleine briefly closed her eyes. She felt him looking at her, but she couldn't meet his gaze.

"When you came in my room this morning I almost asked you anyway," he said.

"Why didn't you?" she whispered.

"What would you have said?"

"What do you think?"

She heard him swallow and she glanced at him. The hand on his thigh was trembling.

Madeleine waited for him to speak, but he said nothing. She fell into disappointed silence and forced her attention back to her driving. They soon reached the reservoir and Madeleine had to slow down while driving over the rutted lake roads. The Audi inched along and finally they made it to the cabins. She helped Eris into his house and then walked up to the log cabin to begin packing her things.

She wondered if she shouldn't just throw everything into her Audi and drive out again. She felt like it. She hated having to defend herself against Sara Bent Horn's insinuations. The more she thought about it, the angrier she became.

She moved her things in piles to the porch and gave the cabin a quick swipe with a rag before closing the door firmly behind her. She reached in the pocket of her shorts for her keys and walked with purpose down to get the Audi. Eris came out on the porch and stood looking at her as if he knew what she was thinking of doing. Madeleine ignored him and headed for the car. When she reached for the door handle, his hand was suddenly there to cover hers. She looked up into his face, and his eyes were black as he said, "I made room in my closet and dresser for your things."

Madeleine's chest lifted with her breathing. Her mouth opened to make a terse reply, but she made not a sound. The expression on his face prevented her from speaking or making any movement. She stared at him as long as she could, and then lowered her head finally to look at their hands on the Audi's door handle.

"I'll be with you in a minute," she murmured, and she pulled open the door. She went to pick up her things and bring them down to unload at Eris's house. He helped her where he could, then he sat down on the bed and watched as she filled up his closet and the drawers in his dresser. When Madeleine was finished, she went to the kitchen to make him a sandwich. She carried it into the bedroom and found him sound asleep on the bed.

She put the sandwich on the nightstand and pulled off his boots before sliding onto the bed beside him. She put his good arm around her and stared at him a long time before closing her eyes.

CHAPTER TWENTY-SIX

RONNIE LYMAN SAT ON the road by the cemetery and pondered as he stared down the hill at Eris Renard's home. The safest place for a drop would be the place least expected to be named, namely, Eris Renard's front porch.

After thinking about it for hours, Ronnie knew he was right. The location of the drop was sure to unnerve Beckworth, who was certain to be watching the area closely after leaving the money. But what could he do to Ronnie in a cop's front yard?

Ronnie drove to Diamond Bay to find a pay phone to call Beckworth. The man's speaking voice was a growl that had at first intimidated Ronnie, until he remembered why he was calling. Beckworth's voice grew even rougher when he heard Ronnie's nasal tones that night. Ronnie decided to cut through all the threats and promises of bodily harm and simply tell the man what he required.

"Put the money in a brown grocery store sack and take it to Eris Renard's house. Put it on the porch at exactly six o'clock."

"What kind of—" Beckworth began, but Ronnie hung up before he could get started. The man was nothing like what he had expected, and he regretted not going directly to his son. A drunk would have to be easier to handle, even a violent drunk. He knew that from dealing with his own mother and father.

Not that he would give a shit about his mother or father or anybody after Friday. He wouldn't. He was headed south, down Texas way, to see what he could see. His mom thought she was going along, but Ronnie had news. No way was he taking her with him. She could stay here and rot. It was partly her fault Kayla got taken, and Ronnie wasn't forgetting that anytime soon.

Women had screwed around with his life long enough, and he wasn't going to let another one latch on if he could help it. After all he had done for Sheila, given her three beautiful little girls, all so she could treat him like shit and wipe him from her feet at the first opportunity. She probably had another man now. Yeah, Ronnie could see that. He could see her doing her hair up real nice and putting on a pretty dress and some lipstick for some brainless bump stupid enough to date a woman with two children.

Ronnie's teeth ground in his head as he thought about it. Bitch better not ever let him catch her. He'd fix her so no man would ever look at her again.

ERIS AWAKENED TO FIND Madeleine curled up beside him. He attempted to stretch and grunted with the discomfort it caused him. Madeleine shifted and raised her head slightly, causing him to relax again and look at her while she slept. Her lashes were dark brown and curled at the tips. Her mouth was slightly open. He could see faint traces of lines around her eyes and mouth, and a light mole just above her upper lip.

He inhaled as he studied her smooth white skin, and thought of Sara. She had told him to ask Madeleine to marry him, and if she said yes, then he would know things were moving too fast between them. If she said no, it was a better sign.

"These romances that flare up like a flame on a match last just about as long," she told him. "You want something that starts off slow and burns a long, long time."

"Like you had with my father?" he wanted to say. "Or with Clint's father?"

But he said nothing. Women hadn't exactly been knocking down his door before Madeleine came. But neither had he made himself generally accessible. If Madeleine had not been so aggressive he wouldn't have more than a nodding acquaintance with her.

He caressed her hair and thought of all the wonderful things she had said about him, all the qualities she said she saw in him. His chest had swelled to hear her. He hadn't expected her to say any of what she did, and the fact that she had, and that she was so hurt by the inferences in his conversation made him regret giving credence to anything Sara said about her.

When he thought she was going to get in her Audi and leave he nearly lost control. He came close to wrenching her hand off the door handle and pushing her away from the car to keep her with him by force if necessary. It had been a struggle to keep his touch light and his voice normal.

He watched her now, her face sweet and slack with sleep, and wished he could lean down and kiss her lips; but since he couldn't move his head without suffering pain, any kissing and other activity would have to be handled by Madeleine.

His mother was wrong about that, too. His relationship with Madeleine was not based solely on sex. She gave him much more than just simple physical gratification.

He smoothed her hair again and rubbed a strand between his fingers. He hoped Sara didn't spend the entire time he was in New Mexico trying to convince him how wrong Madeleine was for him. He told her in the hospital that morning he didn't want to hear it, but she kept on and on, needling with her questions and finally prompting a few doubts. The worst part had been when she bluntly told him to look in the mirror and tell her what he saw. Eris got up out of his wheelchair and left the room.

And then Madeleine had come rushing in to see him, radiant as sunshine and looking at him with something like awe and wonder in her eyes, as if he were every bit as beautiful as she.

Eris touched her lips and she opened her eyes. She looked at him and kissed his fingers. He caressed her cheek and chin, and she slid a hand under his pullover to run her palm over his chest and stomach.

"Did you find your sandwich?"

"Didn't look for one."

"Bread's probably hard now. What time is it?"

He looked at the clock on his dresser. "Almost eight."

She blinked in surprise. "I didn't think I'd sleep so long. How long have you been awake?"

"A few minutes."

She lifted herself to look at him. "Do you need anything? A pain pill? Something to drink?"

"I'm all right," he said.

She propped her head on one hand and went on sliding her palm over his stomach while she closed her eyes again. After a moment she began humming a song, and Eris recognized it as a tune from *Man of La Mancha*. "The night you were in my wallet," he said, and she opened one eye to look at him. Then she smiled and lifted herself up to kiss him. He pressed her to him with his good arm and returned the kiss with a sudden, fierce hunger.

Her hands moved behind his head, and as she undid his hair she looked into his eyes. Then she pushed up his shirt and unzipped his jeans. She kissed his mouth again, and then his chin, moving down to his neck and chest and over his stomach, where her hands pulled down on his briefs.

When she took him into her mouth, Eris shuddered and swallowed convulsively. Her name came out but he wasn't aware of saying it. He was aware of nothing but sensation and his fingers clutching the sheets with the need to hold on as long as he could so it wouldn't end.

Later, as they held each other again, Eris reached over and picked up the sandwich she had made for him.

"Is it stale?" she asked. "I can make you another."

"It's fine," he said. "Don't move."

She didn't.

Early the next morning they drove to Otter Creek and got out to walk and talk about the wildlife they saw. Eris showed her a red-tailed hawk that might have been the parent of the young hawk he had found. Madeleine was dismayed to hear how the bird had been killed. She immediately blamed Tanner but couldn't say why.

On Friday, as they were driving over to pick up his truck from the repair garage, she began to ask about Eris. He looked at her with a lifted brow and she reminded him that he had agreed to answer her questions.

He remembered.

She started off by asking about his adoptive parents and

why he had left them at such an early age. Eris briefly told her what he remembered. She asked another question, and another, and he soon found himself telling her most of what he preferred not to talk about, or even think about, including his days at the diner in the bus station, the ugly rented rooms, and the construction jobs he had held.

"Did you ever have a girlfriend?"

"She saw what the chicken pox did to me and hit the ground running," he said.

"Was she white?"

"Hispanic."

Madeleine turned her head to look at him. "How did you get along? Did you ever get lonely?"

Eris took a deep breath and then released it. "I got along by minding my own business and staying out of everyone else's. Not too many people cared about a tall Indian kid with no parents. I didn't let anyone care, because I stayed out of everybody's way."

"Weren't you lonely?" Madeleine repeated softly.

"Yes," he said. "I was lonely. But I got along."

She looked at him again. "Were you lonely when I met you?"

"I outgrew it," he said. "You get used to being alone and you don't notice being lonely so much anymore."

Madeleine stared straight ahead and stopped asking questions. Eris was faintly surprised. He had expected her to either go on inquiring or start sympathizing. She did neither. She simply concentrated on her driving.

When they reached the garage she put a hand on his arm and leaned over to kiss him. "I'll see you at home later. Drive safely."

He took his left arm out of the sling and got out of the car. He was going to see his mother at the hospital as promised, and it would be the first time he had driven since his injury.

He looked after Madeleine as she departed in her Audi and saw several of the mechanics in the garage looking at her, too. Their glances quickly shifted when Eris turned to them. He asked about his truck, and the nearest man pointed. Eris signed the ticket and walked over to the truck to get inside. The blown-out tire and the shattered back glass had both been replaced. When he slid inside the seat he found no trace of blood or glass in the interior. He started the engine and backed out of the garage. It felt good to be behind the wheel again, though he did find himself listening for blowouts the first half-hour or so.

Sara was glad to see him. Her bruises had faded to a yellowish green color and the swelling had lessened considerably. She held out her hand as he entered the room, and Eris briefly took it before sitting down in a chair in the corner.

"I didn't know if you'd come back," she said, her one visible eye watching him steadily.

"I told you I would," he said.

"You were angry when you left here the other day."

"Not angry," he said.

"What then? Hurt? It was only an attempt to make you think, Eris. Right now you're not thinking, and I've been there, believe me. I'm asking you to consider how you'll feel when she wakes up someday and sees the pits in your skin instead of the sparkle in your eye."

Eris stood. "I think you're capable of returning home on your own, Sara."

"Don't do that," she said immediately. "You have to come and meet Clint. He's dying to meet you. I never told him about you until I turned forty, and he's been as anxious to find you as I was. He's always dreamed of having a brother."

"I want to meet him," said Eris. "But unless you stop attacking Madeleine it's not going to happen."

Sara exhaled and looked at her hands. "I'm not attacking her. What I'm trying to do is save you from certain heartache when she decides to end the fling."

"Why are you so certain it's just a fling?"

"Eris, be realistic. Please."

He stared at her. "Are you trying to make me dislike you?"

She looked shocked. "No. My God, is that what I'm doing? Do you dislike me?"

Eris surprised himself at the anger that erupted from him. "I'm not some ugly piece of human refuse from a reservation who doesn't know enough to think for himself and needs someone to tell him how to get by. I don't need anyone to think for me. I'm not stupid, and I'm not being led around by the nose."

"No, I'd say it's definitely not your nose she's got hold of."

Eris shook his head in disappointment and felt a twinge of pain. "Does insulting me make you feel better about yourself,

Sara? Are you trying to justify your attitude by making me into some simple deluded fool in desperate need of a mother's guidance?"

"I am not insulting you, dammit," she said angrily. "I'm only telling you what I know to be true."

"On half an hour's acquaintance with her? How can you possibly make such a judgment?"

"She's the one who passed judgment. I'm just another Indian to her, and she's met dozens like me. She said so herself."

"She's met dozens of white-haters," Eris clarified, and because he felt the need to defend her to his mother, he went on to tell her what had happened to Madeleine during her last year in the field.

Sara listened, but was unmoved. "So she ran away from Indians and became a teacher because a group of youngsters beat her up and painted her white."

"They left her to die, Sara."

"She didn't."

Eris stared at his mother again and considered for the first time the possibility that he had been lucky she gave him away.

"What does my name mean?" he asked suddenly.

"What?"

"Where did you get my name?" He wanted to know before he walked away from her.

Sara paused and her mouth softened. "Eris was the name of Daniel Birdcatcher's great-grandfather. Daniel said it meant 'quiet like the dawn.' You were so quiet when you were born, didn't cry or anything, and you came out just minutes before dawn, so I called you Eris. I asked the people at the adoption agency if you could keep it, and they said it would be up to the adoptive parents. I'm glad they kept it."

Eris nodded and made a move as if to leave, but his mother held out her hand again.

"Don't go. I'm sorry. I truly am. I know she's important to you and I won't say any more. I'm glad she makes you so happy. I want you to be happy, Eris. That's all I've ever wanted for you."

He stood looking at her but made no motion to take her hand. After a moment she dropped it.

"The doctors said I can leave tomorrow. I'd like to make flight reservations for tomorrow afternoon. Is that all right with you?"

It wasn't. Eris wanted more time alone with Madeleine. He enjoyed having her near him in the small house and already felt comfortable with her in a way he had never felt when his mother was there. He and Madeleine could sit alone in companionable silence and read without feeling the need to make conversation. They made love when they wanted to, touched when they needed to, and slept peacefully in each other's arms at night. He wasn't ready to leave her yet.

"Eris? Is tomorrow night all right with you? I can make it Sunday if you like and come and stay with you and Madeleine tomorrow night."

"No." He didn't want her in the same house with Madeleine. "Go ahead and make reservations for tomorrow. I'll be in around noon to pick you up."

"Fine." She smiled. "I'll see you then."

Eris left the hospital and sat in his truck in the parking lot for nearly twenty minutes while he was thinking. Finally he came to a decision, and he started the truck. He wasn't sure what to do, or how to go about it, but he knew he would need a ring.

CHAPTER TWENTY-SEVEN

MADELEINE COULDN'T BELIEVE SHE had already missed a period. She peed on her hand twice before finally placing the tiny plastic wand exactly where it needed to be. She got up and flushed and then washed her hands before rereading the steps listed on the instructions of the home pregnancy test.

There was no way she could stand and wait for five minutes, so she walked around the house tidying up things and looking out the windows. She stopped when she saw Manuel's Jeep parked outside the log cabin.

He had come to check up on her, she guessed. See if she had gotten her things out. Madeleine was tempted to walk up and apologize for ruining his party, but then the door opened and out came the woman Madeleine had caught him with on his sofa. Madeleine stared as Manuel followed the woman out, his white teeth gleaming in a smile. The jerk.

She was glad Jacqueline wasn't here to see this. But Jacqueline was safely ensconced in the arms of their parents, who had come right away, as Madeleine had known they would.

Madeleine said she would see them when Jacqueline took possession of the house. That would happen any time now, she deduced, since Manuel was at the cabin with his new girlfriend.

She wasn't exactly looking forward to seeing her parents, but it had been several years since her last visit.

And boy will I have news, she thought to herself after she walked into the bathroom and checked the test.

Madeleine picked up the thing and stared, overcome by sudden emotion. Her eyes began to sting and she shook her head in disbelief as she took out the other test in the package and went through the process again. She wanted confirmation of the first results.

The second results were the same and Madeleine sat down on the edge of the tub and hugged her abdomen while she cried. She hadn't expected this or had any idea she would feel this way. She experienced a moment of genuine happiness that rocked her and made her quake at the intensity of the feeling. She had a sense of being on the threshold of an entirely new purpose with a vastly different perspective.

She couldn't wait to see Eris. They hadn't planned it, but they hadn't avoided it either, and she knew somehow he would be as delighted as she. Maybe even more so, she thought, remembering all he had told her that morning. He had lived such a stark life. Madeleine wanted to stop the car and put her arms around him, but she sensed he would regard it as pity, and pity was something he wanted no part of for himself.

Madeleine understood. She felt him look at her in surprise when she said nothing further, but by then she was already thinking of finding a pregnancy test and seeing if the abrupt absence of her all-too-regular period meant what she thought it meant.

Six months ago she would have quailed at the idea of being pregnant. Pregnancy was what happened to other women, women who weren't careful.

Six months ago she didn't know Eris Renard.

She passed the afternoon doing laundry and folding clothes. Madeleine wondered how she could feel so good about doing something she had once found so menial. She had hated doing Sam's laundry. She loathed folding his socks and T-shirts and underwear. It was a task she would have gladly paid someone else to do could she afford the fee. Everything with Eris was different. She enjoyed folding his garments and stacking them neatly in his drawers. She would have to get some more towels for the bathroom, she decided, because he didn't have enough for the two of them. As soon as she got a job she would see to that, she told herself.

Madeleine decided to go over to the community college Gloria Birdy had mentioned to her. It was the first week of July and there was still time to plan a course should they decide they wanted her. Or she could fill in where needed until the next semester. She wanted to be busy again, and she wanted to be where she could better research her project on lakeside communities.

Returning to the field was out of the question now. She was ready to become a part of everything she had studied and flow into the culture around her instead of merely observing it.

She was going to add to the population of her species by one, and the importance of protecting and providing for the baby growing in her womb would teach the anthropologist what a thousand studies in the field of human nature could not. Madeleine was looking forward to the lessons.

AROUND SIX O'CLOCK SHE walked to the window to look for any sign of Eris returning. Instead she saw a man walking onto the porch and bending to pick up a paper bag. She called in a loud voice for him to stop. The man jerked, started, and dropped the bag back onto the porch as he looked up to see Madeleine. She looked at the man, the man looked at Madeleine, and then he was scrabbling for the bag again and running hard away from the porch to jump into a green car parked up the road.

Eris pulled up in time to see Madeleine running toward him, shouting and pointing. He hopped back inside his truck and started the engine, and she rushed to throw open the door and jump inside.

"Get out," he ordered immediately.

"You're off duty," she replied. "Who was that?"

"It was Ronnie Lyman. What the hell was in the sack he took?"

"I thought YOU knew."

Eris backed out and took off across the lawn.

They didn't have to go far to find Ronnie Lyman. The front of his green Grand Prix had disappeared into the side of the man in the baseball cap's Blazer, and the man in the ball cap was dragging Ronnie out of the car to hit him in the head with a tire iron when Eris and Madeleine came upon the scene.

"Beckworth," Eris said under his breath, and Madeleine grabbed for his arm when he would have gotten out of the truck.

"You're unarmed."

Eris freed himself and got out. Madeleine looked again and cringed at the amount of blood covering Beckworth's hand and arm as he repeatedly struck the other man.

"Asshole!" Beckworth screamed. "You ruined my fucking wheels!"

Eris walked over and caught the tire iron on the back swing. He wrenched it from Beckworth's hand and threw it to the side of the road. When Beckworth twisted to see who had dared to touch him, Eris hit him once, hard. Beckworth flopped backward over Lyman's inert form and lay still. Madeleine's eyes were round as she got out of the truck. She thought to call a warning about the other two men in the Blazer, but they weren't doing anything, just staring as Eris bent over Ronnie Lyman.

Eris looked up as Madeleine approached. "Get back in the truck and radio for help. Tell them we need an ambulance."

As she hurried back to the truck she saw people moving in from all sides. Tanner and his wife walked eagerly up to see, and a man in a sleek Jaguar came cruising slowly by, inching along through the people in his path.

Madeleine blinked at sight of the Jaguar and climbed into the truck. She turned the radio on and started asking anyone who was listening for help. Dale Russell answered immediately and said he would take care of everything.

She got out of the truck again and approached Eris, who still squatted over Ronnie Lyman and was surrounded by a ring of people he told repeatedly to stay back. He looked expectantly at Madeleine and she told him she had made contact with Russell. Eris nodded grimly and looked at Ronnie Lyman again.

Beckworth lifted his head and got slowly to his feet. He snarled when he saw Eris, and Madeleine shouted when she saw his intent. Eris twisted around in time to receive a vicious kick to the chest. His lips disappeared in a grimace and the left side of his shirt began to blot with blood as his wounds opened up and began to seep. Beckworth danced around and moved in to swing, but Eris caught one leg and gave a yank, sending him sprawling to the ground. The breath left Beckworth in a whoosh and Earl Lee Birdy stepped through the crowd and put one large foot on his ribcage. "You ever want to breathe again, you stay put."

The cap fell off Beckworth's head, and even as he fought for breath he scrabbled to replace the hat. A minute later Dale Russell was on the scene and looking important as he smacked Beckworth on the head a few times and cuffed him before calling the police. He checked the vital signs on Ronnie Lyman, and he and Eris exchanged a look that confirmed what Madeleine had already suspected. Ronnie Lyman was dead.

When the ambulance arrived, the sheet went over Lyman's face and a murmur went through the crowd. As Beckworth was taken away in the back of a police car, Madeleine saw the Jaguar leave the side of the road and fall in behind the sheriff's officer. The driver of the Jaguar was smiling, Madeleine noticed.

An attendant from the ambulance wanted Eris to ride along to the hospital, but he shook his head. Madeleine told the attendant she would bring him in the truck. The entire side of his shirt was covered with blood and his face had gone pale.

There was no talking on the way to the county hospital. She sent a hand over to squeeze his thigh, but his eyes were closed and did not open until she stopped the truck in the hospital parking lot. Madeleine walked inside with him and watched worriedly as interns came to take him away from her. She tried to follow, but they asked her to please stay behind and give the front desk what information she could.

Just before ten o'clock, they allowed her to go in and see him. The bleeding was stopped and the wounds had been stitched a second time. When she went in she was surprised to find him sitting on the edge of the bed. His left arm was in a sling again, and he held out his right arm to her.

Madeleine went to him and held on tightly. "Are they going to let you come home?"

"Not tonight. They want me immobile. I never got a chance to tell you my mother is being released tomorrow and wants to leave immediately afterward."

"Tomorrow?" Madeleine said. "You're leaving tomorrow?"

His arm tightened in response.

"Eris . . ." She wanted to ask him to wait. She had so much to tell him. They had so much to talk about, so many plans to make.

"The sooner I go, the sooner I'll be back," he said into her hair. "I'm going to meet my brother."

Madeleine swallowed and nodded. "You want me to come for you in the morning and take you to Wichita?"

"If you don't mind."

"Shall I pack for you tonight?"

He nodded. "Jeans and shirts, socks and underwear. And throw in my Nikes, if you think about it."

Madeleine said she would take care of it. Then she decided to leave—it was that or fall apart in front of him—and let him get some sleep so he could be rested for his trip. She kissed him and started away, but he pulled her back and held on. He pressed her against him and rubbed her neck with his fingers as he kissed her temple. "I'm going to miss you," he said.

She closed her eyes. "I'll miss you, too."

"I'll call."

Madeleine nodded.

They looked at each other a moment, then he put his hand to her face and said, "Tell me you won't go anywhere."

She placed her hand on top of his. "Tell me you won't listen to her about us."

They gazed at each other again and tenderly kissed.

As she left the hospital Madeleine didn't feel at all strong. Her hands shook and her lip quivered all the way home.

CHAPTER
TWENTY-EIGHT

DALE RUSSELL WAS FED up with the justice system and the way things operated. He had sent Bruce Beckworth to jail the day before on charges of manslaughter, and the little bastard was already free on bail. Dale called up his aunt, the governor, to complain, and learned that Wes Beckworth had donated twice the legal amount of dollars to her campaign and she wouldn't do jack shit about his son the habitual criminal. Furthermore, Russell was to stay as far away as possible from him.

"I'm not the one who'll be testifying against him in the trial," said Russell. "There were half a dozen witnesses who saw him beating the guy to death."

"The autopsy will say what killed him," came the reply, and Dale could just imagine the conclusion of the report: *The injuries sustained by the decedent were a direct result of the impact of the crash.* Or some such bullshit. It made Dale sick to think of the people like Bruce Beckworth running around all over the country beating and killing people because their fathers were rich enough to keep them out of jail by buying off politicians like his aunt. It made a person ashamed to be part of such a system.

Dale went on maundering about it until the irony in his thinking threatened to break through the self-righteousness he had cloaked himself in. When that happened he simply shifted gears and thought about Madeleine Heron.

She was at Eris Renard's cabin now, he knew. He had seen Manuel Ortiz with a woman who was not his wife, and since Madeleine was the sister of the wife, and she was in the truck with Renard, there was only one place she could be. He dropped by the cabin on his way home that evening so he could tell Renard about Beckworth's release from jail and see if Madeleine had moved in.

Madeleine was there alone. She told him Eris was gone at the moment, and Dale lifted his brows.

"Is he still in the hospital?"

"No, he was released this morning. I'll tell him you came by."

Her voice was dull and her eyes were puffy. Dale put up a hand when she would have shut the door. He wondered what was wrong with her.

"Madeleine, I want to apologize to you. I've been a real jerk, and after watching the way you handled things yesterday I found myself admiring you and Renard. You look like you make a good team."

Madeleine nodded. "Thank you. Goodbye."

Dale let her go. His plan was to move slowly, let her gradually grow to trust him again.

As he left the drive he realized Renard's truck was in the garage and Madeleine's Audi was parked out front. So where was Renard? And how did he get wherever he was?

Suddenly he remembered Renard's mother. He bet she was gone, too, and Renard was probably with her, leaving Madeleine temporarily alone.

Dale had the urge to turn around and go back, just to see if Renard came home. Dale was certain he was right, and he wondered suddenly if the puffy eyes and sad face were because of Renard's absence.

He drove down to Diamond Bay and was nearly run over by a Jaguar speeding over the bumpy road. Dale's lip curled when he saw who was behind the wheel.

Bruce Beckworth smiled and flipped him the bird as he sped away, and Dale flipped it right back at him.

Goddamned criminal, he thought to himself in disgust.

*   *   *

BRUCE WASN'T SUPPOSED TO have the Jag. His old man had forbidden him to drive it, ever. Bruce didn't care. He had no wheels
and the Jag was there. If the old man wanted to go somewhere,
let him drive his wife's Lexus. She never went anywhere but the
tanning salon, anyway. And the nail place, where she had those
long fake nails put on, the kind that curled under slightly and
looked really spooky under the right kind of light. Bruce hated
her. She hated him, too, and did everything she could to stay
away from him.

She was pissed because she had gotten drunk once and done
it with Bruce. The old man had passed out upstairs, and she had
come downstairs looking for some. Bruce gave it to her and she
had hated him ever since. Couldn't stand to look at him.

He loved to taunt her with it, but it wasn't so much fun anymore. Her repugnance didn't stem from guilt so much as disgust,
and Bruce knew enough to feel insulted. The more she avoided
him, the more he felt the need to seek her out.

Earlier that day, when he got home from jail, he heard her
screaming at his father to just get rid of him. Send him away or
let him go to prison, but get him out of the house and out of their
lives. Bruce had listened long enough to hear his father tell her
everything was going to be all right. He would work things out.
Those words sent him down to his father's office to find the keys
to the Jag. Beside the desk was a paper sack, and after he opened
it Bruce had to sit down.

The sonofabitch was going to do it. He was going to pay Bruce
off and tell him to get out.

Bruce carried the sack out to the Jag with him. He spent the
next six hours just driving, finally ending up at the lake and in
search of a party. When he couldn't find anything that suited
him, he drove to the home of one of the guys who had been with
him in the Blazer the evening before. His friend seemed shocked
to see him, and Bruce laughed as he sat down in a lawn chair
and opened his first beer of the day.

"Is it me you're surprised to see, or the Jag?"

"Both, man. You really screwed up yesterday."

Bruce laughed again. "Did I? I'd say the guy that's dead

screwed up more than I did. You realize who that was? That was the guy who freaked everybody out when he said his little girl was missing."

"I heard. You out on bail or what?"

"Yeah. I ain't worried."

"Your old man."

"My old man is an expert at workin' things out. He's gonna work me out next."

Bruce's buddy looked at him, and Bruce said, "She can't handle me in the house no more. Can't look at me without thinking about me sticking my dick up her ass. She wants me out." He drank down the beer and looked at his friend. "I got a Jag and a sack full of cash. Before I leave here I'm gonna burn down a house and kick the shit out of the CO who cuffed me yesterday. You comin'?"

His buddy shook his head. "Too much for me, man. Whose house?"

Bruce opened another beer. "Read about it in the paper tomorrow, puss."

He picked up his friend's twelve-pack of beer and carried it to the Jag. His friend said not a word. When Bruce was gone the friend went into the house to call Wes Beckworth and tell him everything that was said. Everything but the part about Mrs. Beckworth.

Bruce drove to the swimming beach at Vista Bay and sat drinking beer and watching swimmers until the light faded from the sky and the beach became deserted. When the moon was high and the stars were bright, Bruce started the Jag and purred slowly over the road toward Briar's Cove and the cabins on the hill.

DALE RUSSELL SQUINTED HIS eyes and blinked when he saw a lone figure skulking around outside Renard's cabin. At first he thought it was the man he had seen walking his dog up the road, but this person was bent over in a crouch and carrying something large in his hand. Dale looked for a car parked somewhere near but saw nothing.

A burglar? he wondered, and he immediately pictured himself rescuing Madeleine from a thief.

No, he decided, as he sat in the dark interior of the truck's cab and watched. This guy was splashing something around the front and sides of the house.

What the hell was he up to? Dale wondered. Was he trying to kill Renard's plants?

He eased himself out of the truck to get a closer look, and a second after the door clicked, a loud whooshing sound and a bright splash of light made Dale jerk his head around.

Flames engulfed the entire house. Dale spied a figure to the side of the house, saw his smiling face clearly, and the man saw him at the same moment. Beckworth pointed his finger and then rushed Dale, charging with furious intent.

Dale's bladder leaked when he saw that face, but his hand reached for his gun, and before he realized what he was doing he had emptied his firearm into the chest of the man running toward him. He heard shouts that sounded very far away, and his head lowered as if in slow motion to look at Beckworth, still twisting on the ground in front of him.

Dale dropped his gun and forced himself to lift his head. A man was yelling in a high, whiny voice, and another huge man, as tall if not taller than Renard, came running up the road to throw himself at the door of the burning house. It seemed he was inside for hours, but it was actually only a minute before he came carrying Madeleine out the door. She was coughing and choking and gasping for breath, and Dale suddenly remembered himself when he saw her. He strode over to check her condition, and then he walked with purpose back to his truck to pick up his radio and call the fire department. And the police.

Manuel Ortiz ran down to see what was happening, and he appeared stunned to find Madeleine on the ground, gasping for air. He checked her over and instructed the huge man to carry her up to his cabin. Madeleine protested, but Manuel insisted. Dale watched her go and wanted to rush over and tell her what he had done, how he had saved her, but he had other things to worry about at the moment, like justifying the use of deadly force to the hordes of official personnel soon to descend upon him.

He didn't know what the hell he was going to tell his aunt.

Farther up the hill toward the cemetery, no one saw the man get out of the Lexus and slide behind the wheel of the Jaguar. The woman behind the wheel of the Lexus heaved a huge sigh of relief as she looked in her rearview mirror at the scene below.

CHAPTER TWENTY-NINE

MADELEINE PROTESTED WHEN MANUEL wanted to sedate her, but he told everyone it was for her own good and did it anyway. She slept for twelve hours, and when she awakened she found Manuel standing over her.

"What did you give me?" she asked.

He gave a small shake of his head, as if to say it was not important.

"I'm pregnant," Madeleine said. "It better not have been anything that will hurt the baby."

Manuel lifted both brows in surprise. "I'm sure it will not. Who is the father?"

"Eris." She raised herself. "I have to call him. I'm not even sure what happened last night."

"Renard," said Manuel, his voice thoughtful. He nodded his head then. "He is a good choice for you, Madeleine."

Madeleine blinked and looked at him. He was the last person on earth she would have expected to recognize that.

"A person named Beckworth was responsible for the arson," Manuel told her. "He is now dead, shot and killed by Dale Russell, who has been suspended pending an investigation."

Madeleine swung her legs over the side of the bed. "I have to get in touch with Eris. He's in New Mexico."

Manuel extended a hand. "Feel free to use my phone."

She paused, suddenly wary. "Why are you being so nice to me, Manuel? You don't even like me."

He smiled. "Of course I like you, Madeleine. My anger was only momentary. You cost me much and I reacted."

"You cost yourself," Madeleine replied, and he nodded in agreement.

"I did, yes. But I will win her back, if I so choose. She is not like you, Madeleine."

"Meaning?"

"Meaning that Jacqueline will be willing to forgive." He turned and left her then, and Madeleine heard the door to the cabin open and close. She was alone.

A couple of minutes later she was listening to the ring of the phone at Bent Horn Gallery. It was the only number listed, her only means to contact Eris, and no one was answering. She cursed softly and hung up. She went to the window to stare down at the blackened house below. The sight of it made her squeeze her eyes shut and shake her head. She could not imagine Eris's reaction. She tried calling for another two hours and gave up as Manuel came back.

"Any luck?" he asked. She shook her head.

"Where is your girlfriend?" she asked.

"She is just a woman I know, who preferred not to stay when I told her who you were."

Madeleine quirked a brow, and before she could comment, there was a knock on the door. Manuel answered and she saw Dale Russell outside, dressed in jeans and a T-shirt.

"Hello. Just checking to see how Madeleine is today. I thought I'd go inside the house and see what can be salvaged, if anything."

"Is it safe?" asked Manuel.

"Should be," said Dale. "Is Madeleine all right?"

"I'm fine," Madeleine called from the living room. "Wait for me."

"Madeleine," Manuel cautioned. "It is not wise for you to be in the house."

She paused and thought of the possible fumes. "You're right. I'll stay outside and use the hose to clean anything that can be saved."

"I'm going out in the boat," Manuel told her. "I'll leave the cabin door open for you."

Madeleine glanced at him, and though it was difficult for her to say, she thanked him for his generosity.

Dale was full of tender concern and gentlemanly conduct as he walked her to Eris's blackened house.

"Were you able to reach Renard?" he asked.

"No. Not yet."

"Is he with his mother?"

"Yes."

"When's he coming back?"

"Soon."

"Going to be a shocker," Dale murmured.

The rest of the day was spent sorting clothes and other items into piles that were salvageable and piles that were not. Most of the new furniture had been ruined beyond repair. The fire trucks and huge hoses had destroyed the yard. Madeleine's throat thickened in dismay each time she thought of Eris coming home to see the place.

Dale worked hard all day and didn't want to talk about it when Madeleine tried to ask about his suspension. She dropped the subject. Her stomach was growling and she was just beginning to think about eating when she saw Denise Lansky come driving down the road. Madeleine stepped out and waved, and Denise stopped the car.

"Good lord, what happened here?"

Madeleine briefly told her and they discussed it for several minutes before she finally asked what Denise was doing back at the lake.

"Here for the Fourth. Brought a few of the kids with me again. But I'm not here to talk about that. Have you heard word on a grant yet?"

"Nothing," said Madeleine, and out of the corner of her eye she saw Dale Russell inconspicuously watching and listening to them.

"Any other offers?" asked Denise, and Madeleine lowered her voice to tell her about the community college.

"Don't go there," Denise said immediately. "I've got something better. Something you are absolutely perfect for. It's grant money, all right, but not the kind you're used to."

Madeleine took her arm and walked away from the house with her, out of Dale Russell's earshot.

Denise went on to tell Madeleine about an acquaintance in the city who was having a slight problem in keeping a director for a Head Start program.

"Head Start?" Madeleine was already shaking her head. "I'm not qualified for that."

"It's the Head Start program for Indian children. They can't find a director willing to work with the parents. They can't find anyone even remotely familiar with the various cultures. I told them I knew just the person."

Madeleine found herself smiling. "You thought of me. Because I helped you with the kids."

"No, I thought of you because of your extensive background in Native-American tribes. The way you handle kids was only a secondary concern. This job is perfect for you. You've got so much to offer."

Madeleine couldn't stop smiling. She was more than interested. It would be an opportunity for her to make her knowledge of language and culture available to any who were interested in learning. She was so excited she wanted to grab the smiling Denise and hug her.

"When do they want me?" she asked, and Denise began to laugh.

"Are you serious? Are you really interested?"

Madeleine nodded. "Very much so."

"I told them I'd call after I talked to you, but you could walk right in there Tuesday morning and tell them you're ready to start."

"I'll do that," Madeleine said, and her firm tone made Denise laugh again.

They chatted for a bit longer; then Denise made Madeleine promise to come see her and waved as she left.

When Madeleine walked back to Dale he smiled and asked if she would be leaving the lake soon.

"I will, yes," she said.

"Did I hear her say you were getting a grant?"

"That's right." Madeleine wasn't going into it with him.

"Well, that's good news, isn't it?"

"It is," she agreed. "I appreciate everything you've done here today, Dale, but I don't think there's much more we can do."

He looked at the piles on the grass. "What do you want to do with those?"

"I'll take care of it. Thank you, really, for coming out to help. Eris will be grateful, I'm sure."

Dale lifted his hands. "Okay. I'll get out of here now. Need to clean up and get something to eat. Can I buy you some dinner?"

Madeleine's growling stomach was tempted, but she shook her head. "No, thanks. I'm fine."

"All right. Be seeing you."

She waved to him and watched until he was in his truck and heading up the road toward the cemetery. She felt someone watching her and turned to see Sherman Tanner come sauntering across the grass.

"What are you going to do with those?" he asked, pointing to the piles of ruined clothes and other items.

"Call someone to come and haul them off," she said. "The rest I'm going to load into my car and Eris's truck."

"Where is he?" asked Tanner.

"Away," said Madeleine and excused herself.

Madeleine returned to the cabin and tried the gallery again. Then she called information and begged for the unlisted number of Sara Bent Horn. "This is an emergency," she insisted. "His house burned down and he doesn't even know."

"I'm sorry," the voice told her. "I can't release the number."

Madeleine slammed down the phone just as Manuel walked through the door.

"Still no luck," he surmised. He went to the refrigerator and drew out a bottle of beer. "Have you eaten, Madeleine?"

"No," she said, and she looked at herself. Her clothes were grimy. "I'm too dirty to go anywhere."

"Jacqueline has some extra clothes in the dresser," he told her. "I'll cook the fish if you prepare a salad."

Madeleine exhaled. His kindness to her was driving her crazy.

They ate dinner together and talked more than they had talked in the entire time Manuel and Jacqueline were married. Manuel told her of his family, nine brothers and two sisters, and of his father, a politician in Mexico.

She got up from the table and put her plate in the sink. Manuel brought his plate and she swiftly washed up while he sat and watched.

"Are you staying tonight?" he asked.

"No." She needed to get what clothes she had to the nearest washing machine.

"Will you be seeing Jacqueline?"

"Yes."

"Will you tell her you spoke with me?"

"Yes, Manuel. And I will tell her of your many kindnesses. I'll be back tomorrow to pick up Eris's things."

"Come and tell me how she is. Will you do that?"

Feeling slightly like a traitor, Madeleine agreed. She picked up her singed purse and fished around inside for her keys. Then she left him to his silent cabin and walked down the hill to get in her Audi.

CHAPTER
THIRTY

SARA SAW TO IT that Eris didn't have a chance to call Madeleine until Monday morning. From the moment they landed in Albuquerque's airport she and Clint took command of his existence and chauffered him around in the back seat of a red Mercedes. In the first twelve hours they introduced him to dozens of people who all struggled to hide the same look of shock Sara had worn the first time she saw him. As for Sara, she presented him as if he were a piece of dark but reaching artwork she had recently completed.

Sara put together a small dinner party Sunday evening and Eris met several more people, all of them Indians, all of them terribly concerned with Sara's injuries, and all of them wondering why Eris was still living in Kansas. Everyone assumed he either aspired to move to New Mexico or was already in the planning stages.

"We're creating a new West," a woman from the Institute of American Indian Arts Museum said to him. "We're seeing a resurgence of pride and spirituality unsurpassed in this century. It's important we band together and keep it alive."

"And nonwhite," Sara added. Everyone smiled.

Eris awakened earlier than his mother and his brother the next morning. After showering and dressing he moved through her huge adobe house to stand on a tiled veranda and look out over the mountains in the distance. A piece of a rainbow provided a colorful arc across the gunmetal gray sky. The land in the foreground appeared lush and green, not at all like the desert he had expected.

Nothing in Santa Fe was as he expected. The people were all chic and sophisticated, and the buildings were all uniform. It was a beautiful place, wonderful to look at, but Eris didn't feel he fit in.

It took him ten minutes to find a telephone.

A minute later he was staring in consternation as a recording told him service at his number had been temporarily disrupted. Eris called again and heard the same message. He hung up and walked around the huge house counting rooms before trying again. Then he called the lake office.

"Renard?" said the officer who answered. "Damn, I'm glad you called. We were beginning to think you were in your house when it burned down."

After an extensive pause, Eris heard himself demanding to know what the hell the man was talking about.

"Bruce Beckworth torched your house Saturday night. Dale Russell shot and killed him and is on suspension right now."

"What about Madeleine?" Eris asked immediately. "Is she all right?"

"Who?" the man asked. "Oh, yeah, the blonde. She's okay. Smoke inhalation, Russell said."

"Where is she?"

"I don't know. Russell came by a little while ago to make some copies of his report and he said he went to see her, make sure she was all right. He said she got a grant, whatever that means. You haven't talked to her?"

"No." Eris felt suddenly sick. "She can't call me. I need to talk to her. Can you find out for me where she is?"

"I would, but the way Russell talked, she's already headed out. He sure felt bad about your house, and he tried to look after her for you, but he said she was acting a little spacey after getting rescued from the fire. She'll probably call you when she gets to where she's going, so I wouldn't worry too much about it. I would, however, get my butt home. Because of Russell the chief cut your suspension short. He needs you back here."

"I'll be there when I can," Eris told him, and he hung up. He stared blankly at the paintings hanging on his mother's walls before putting his head in his hands and rubbing harshly at his eyes. "Goddammit," he muttered.

"What's wrong?" his mother asked from behind him. "Madeleine not answering?"

Eris's nostrils flared. "Please shut up. You don't know."

"I know you're upset," she said in a calm voice. "Talk to me. What's going on?"

"I have to go back," he told her. "Someone set fire to my house on Saturday. Madeleine was inside."

"Was she hurt?"

"I don't think so."

"Then why run off? Call your insurance agent from here and find out all you need to do. We can fax the forms from my office."

He stared at her. "I just told you my house burned down and you want me to stay and meet your friends?"

Sara was unperturbed. "My point is there's very little you can accomplish by rushing back."

"I'm needed back at work. And I want to talk to Madeleine."

"Where is she?"

He hesitated before admitting he didn't know. "No one can tell me."

His mother spread her hands, but before she could say anything, Eris said, "She doesn't know how to contact me."

"Obviously."

"I told her I would call her. I haven't had a chance before now."

"Surely your superior doesn't expect you to come running back. Your shoulder hasn't even begun to heal."

Eris exhaled. "I want to go back."

"To work, or to Madeleine?"

He looked at his mother and said, "I need her more than I need to be here."

"You don't mean that," Sara argued. "Eris, we've waited all our lives to meet."

"And now we've met." He picked up the phonebook from under the end table and began thumbing through it, looking for the number for the airlines.

Clint walked into the room, sleepily rubbing his bare stomach. "What's going on?"

"Eris is returning to Kansas," Sara told him. "A man burned his house and his girlfriend was frightened."

"Damn," said Clint. "Your house burned?" Then his brows lifted. "Is it the blonde Mom was telling me about?"

A voice in Eris's ear asked if she could help him and Eris told her yes, he needed to get back to Wichita as soon as possible.

"What about the dermabrasion?" Clint asked his mother, and Eris stared at the two of them as he was placed on hold.

"The what?"

"Dermabrasion," said Clint. "For your skin. Mom said she was going to give you a new face for a late birthday present."

Eris's nostrils flared again. He turned his back on his mother, who stared stonily at Clint.

"What did I say?" asked Clint. "What?"

When the reservations were made, Eris hung up the phone and asked his brother to take him to the airport in Albuquerque. Clint looked at Sara and shrugged. "Sure, I'll take you. I'll throw some clothes on while you get your things together."

Sara stood motionless, her attractive mouth a thin, tight line as her sons brushed past her to go into the hall.

Eris told her goodbye as he left the house, but she had nothing to say to him. He figured it was just as well, the story of their short acquaintanceship, one of them forever leaving the other behind.

Clint chuckled as he got in the car. "Man, is she pissed. It ain't often she gets thwarted, O brother of mine."

Eris said nothing.

Undeterred, Clint continued. "Anyway, it gives me a chance to ask about your girlfriend without Mom hearing. I hear she's really pretty."

"She is," said Eris.

"Older than you?"

"A few years."

"And white."

Eris looked at his half brother. "You're Fox on Sara's side and what on your father's? Chippewa?"

"Yeah."

"The Fox and the Chippewa used to be bitter enemies. They warred constantly."

"Until the white man appeared on the continent and they warred against him."

"Right," said Eris. "What if the white man had never come?"

Clint smiled. "The Fox and the Chippewa would, in all likelihood, still hate each other. I see your point. Mom, however, would not. She sees what she wants to see, and what she does not want to see is a white woman attached to the arm of her oldest son."

Eris turned his face away. "What she wants doesn't concern me."

The ring shoved into the recesses of his wallet proved it. He had wanted to give the ring to Madeleine on Saturday at the airport, but the wheelchairbound Sara gave them only seconds to be alone before she rushed him off to go and sit aboard an unmoving plane for forty-five minutes.

It had taken him several hours to find a ring he liked. When he finally stumbled on one he wanted, he didn't blink an eye at paying the steep price. It was the ring he wanted for Madeleine, and it was the only one he was ever likely to buy. Eris wasn't a traditionalist, but he wanted everyone who looked at her to know she was spoken for. All he needed to do now was ask if she would wear it.

As if reading his thoughts, Clint said, "Don't bother sending an announcement to Mom. She'll piss nails for a week."

"She knows how I feel about Madeleine."

"Madeleine. Nice name. All Mom ever called her was 'that blonde.' "

Eris looked at him. "Sara is a racist."

"Yeah, I know. I get tired of listening to it myself. And I damn sure don't tell her about my friends back at school."

They rode on in silence for several minutes, until Clint looked over and said, "It was really good to meet you, Eris. I mean it. I wish we had more time together."

Eris nodded.

"I understand how you feel," Clint said. "I'd want to get back and check things out. You think you'll be back anytime soon?"

"For the dermabrasion?"

Clint's face colored slightly. "Hey, I never meant anything, you know. Mom made such a big deal out of it and all. I thought you wanted the procedure and it was something the two of you had talked about before coming."

"I've learned to live with it," said Eris.

"If Madeleine doesn't care, why should you? Sounds like you're a lucky guy."

Eris wanted to agree, but until he knew exactly where Madeleine was at the moment, he couldn't say if he was lucky or not.

When they reached the airport he was disgusted to find all flights either delayed or canceled and all traffic being rerouted due to a collision and widespread fire on the runways. His flight wouldn't be rescheduled for another four or five hours, and he had nothing to do but sit and wonder about Madeleine.

Unless he could find some way to call her sister, Jacqueline.

JACQUELINE'S MOUTH QUIVERED AS she stared at Madeleine.

"You ate dinner with him? You actually sat down and ate dinner with Manuel?"

"I was starving," Madeleine said in defense.

"How could you?" Billie Heron asked of her older daughter.

Frank Heron shook his head.

"He helped me after I was pulled out of a burning house," Madeleine said to the three of them. "It wasn't like I slept with him."

"I don't know that, now do I?" snapped Jacqueline.

"Yes, you do," Madeleine answered quietly.

"Oh, that's right, because you're in love with Eris Renard. How stupid of me to forget."

"Who is Eris Renard?" asked Frank, her father.

"A conservation officer at the lake," answered Jacqueline.

"Oh," said Frank, as if that explained everything.

"How could you?" Billie asked Madeleine again. "Sam hasn't been dead six months."

Madeleine looked at her mother. "Sam has nothing to do with this."

"Did his parents ever contact you? They sent us a check a few weeks ago and asked us to make certain you got it. They said they were sorry for all the debts he left you, and they wanted to help. We kept meaning to send it. Frank, have you got that check?"

Frank took out his wallet and pulled out a folded piece of paper. "Here. It's for twenty-five hundred dollars."

Madeleine looked at her father. Twenty-five hundred. Sam left her strapped for ten times that amount. And she had paid off every cent.

She took the folded check from her father's hand and stuffed it in the pocket of her jean shorts. Pride was no longer an issue; she would need the money for a temporary place to stay. There was no way she could remain with Jacqueline and her parents.

She walked downstairs to collect all the laundry she had done, and she carried it out to her car while her family watched.

"Where are you going?" Jacqueline finally asked.

"I don't know," Madeleine answered. At the moment she didn't care if she ever saw any of them again. She just knew she was going.

"Madeleine," Jacqueline said firmly. "Where are you going?"

Madeleine ignored her and got in the car.

Minutes later she was flying down the road on her way to the cabin to pick up Eris's things.

AN HOUR AFTER MADELEINE departed, the phone rang at Jacqueline's house. Billie Heron answered. She listened, and then turned to Jacqueline. "It's a man asking for you. He says his name is Renard."

"Tell him I don't know where she is," Jacqueline said, her mouth tight.

Billie told him, and then said, "I'm sure she'll call you once she lands somewhere. Madeleine is like that. She always has been." She listened again, then said, "This is her mother. No, none of us know where she's going. She didn't bother to tell us." When she hung up, she looked at Jacqueline. "He sounded very angry. Renard is the man she's been seeing?"

"Yes," said Jacqueline, her face sullen. "Among others."

CHAPTER
THIRTY-ONE

DALE DROVE AIMLESSLY AROUND the lake and wondered how he was going to live. His frantic killing of Bruce Beckworth had made his aunt livid. She called him crazy. Stupid. Dangerous. She wanted nothing further to do with him, and she was going to see to it that he lost his job as a conservation officer. She told him to go back to school and become a goddamned landscape architect or something equally useless so she would never have to set eyes on him again. She also threatened to have him put away if she heard about any dead or abused little girls within a hundred miles of him.

She hadn't believed him about Kayla Lyman after all. The old bitch had simply chosen to ignore it.

After hearing all she said, Dale was tempted to tell her what a hypocrite she was, but he didn't let himself do it. She would make good on her promise to have him taken into custody and hold him in some dark, dismal place for months while he awaited psychiatric evaluation.

He lived in Augusta, but he avoided returning to his apartment out of fear of hearing the telephone ring. He couldn't be fired if no one was able to tell him. He was suspended, yes, but he wasn't fired yet. Officially, he was still a member of the Kansas Department of Wildlife and Parks.

When he saw Madeleine's Audi make the turn from the highway onto the access road he inhaled deeply.

For a moment, he considered leaving her alone. He had other
things to worry about. It had surprised him that Renard hadn't
come running home once he learned about his house, but it soon
became obvious he didn't know yet, so Dale had gone scattering
a few seeds of suspicion and distrust at the lake office, knowing
the office would be the first place Renard called when he couldn't
get through at home. It wasn't as if he lied. Madeleine did say
she had received some sort of grant. And she was in fact leaving
the lake area.

Dale turned and went after the Audi. Pursuing Madeleine was
something to do at the moment, and Dale figured he had absolutely nothing to lose.

MADELEINE DROVE UP BEHIND Eris's truck and loaded the bags
out of the truck bed into her Audi. She then went into the house
to take a final look and found her throat thickening all over again
as she gazed at the blackened mess.

She turned and walked outside and saw Manuel on his porch
beckoning to her. Madeleine walked up to the log cabin. "Good
morning, Manuel."

"You still haven't spoken to Renard," he said.

She shook her head.

"You saw Jacqueline?"

"Yes." Madeleine told him of the scene with her family that
morning.

He smiled and shrugged. "Would you like to come in and try
to reach Renard again?"

"Could I?" Madeleine had tried the gallery from Jacqueline's
house with no success.

"Of course." Manuel put on his fishing hat. "Thank you for
talking with me. And Madeleine, you and Renard feel free to use
the cabin until you can make other arrangements. The key is on
the kitchen bar." When Madeleine stared at him he lifted a hand.
"I will not be returning for some time."

"Manuel . . . thank you. I keep feeling like I should apologize
for what I did, but somehow I just can't. Do you understand?"

"Perfectly," he said. He stooped to kiss her on the cheek, and then he stepped off the porch to go fishing.

Madeleine shook her head in confusion and went inside to pick up the phone. She listened to six rings and was about to hang up when she heard a click and a voice that said, "Bent Horn Gallery."

"Sara?" Madeleine asked uncertainly.

"This is Sara Bent Horn. Who is this?"

"It's Madeleine Heron, in Kansas. Sara, I need to speak with Eris. Can you please tell me how to reach him?"

There was a pause then, "No, I'm afraid I can't. He's gone off with his brother Clint and I haven't seen them for hours. I think Clint had a girl he wanted Eris to meet."

Madeleine ignored the last. "It's extremely important that I reach him. Eris's house has—"

"Burned down, yes, we know. Eris learned about it early this morning."

"He knows?"

"He spoke with someone where he works."

"Oh," said Madeleine. "I . . . please tell him how sorry I am—"

"You'll have to excuse me, Madeleine," Sara said to her. "A client just walked in. Goodbye."

"Wait," Madeleine said quickly, but it was too late. The dial tone droned in her ear.

"Damn you," Madeleine whispered as she replaced the receiver. She sat at the kitchen counter and stared out the window. She wanted desperately to speak to him, tell him how sorry she was about his house and how badly she missed him and how much she needed him right now. She wanted him to come home.

Madeleine stuck the key in her pocket and walked dejectedly out of the cabin. She trod down the steps and watched her feet as she walked down the hill to the Audi. When she looked up, she saw Dale Russell standing in front of his truck, parked so it blocked the drive. He was smiling.

CHAPTER
THIRTY-TWO

THE MOMENT MADELEINE ENCOUNTERED Dale's sickly smile, she sensed something wrong. She spoke to him, he spoke to her, and there was nothing suspicious about what he said, but there was a hint of desperation in his demeanor that set off warning bells, and the quivering of his nostrils and visible tension in his body sent adrenaline rushing through her veins. Inexplicably, Madeleine believed herself to be in danger.

She responded by picking up a piece of charred wood and throwing it at him as hard as she could. The missile took Dale by surprise and hit him directly above the left eye. Madeleine didn't wait to see anymore; she spun on her heel and ran as hard as she could for the log cabin. Once there she fumbled the key out of her pocket and opened the door. Then she slammed it behind her and shot home the dead bolt. She ran to the phone to pick it up, and while she was listening to a ring at Gloria Birdy's cabin, the line went dead in her hands.

Madeleine dropped the phone with a clatter and ran to each window and door throughout the cabin to make certain it was locked. She thanked Manuel for the security bars on the windows and then had a sudden vision of Dale Russell attempting to burn her out, thought perhaps it had even been him at Eris's cabin. Then she heard him knock politely on the door.

"Madeleine? We need to talk. I know you're not coming out, and you obviously don't want me to come in, so I'll just stand right outside here on the porch and talk to you. Can you hear me? . . . I think you can hear me. What the hell were you thinking of back there? You could have seriously wounded me with that chunk of wood. What made you throw it at me? Am I that threatening to you?" After a moment he continued. "Madeleine, I'm standing here asking myself what could possibly have provoked you. You know I would never do anything to hurt you, and it really bothers me to know you're so frightened of me."

Madeleine couldn't stand it anymore. "Why did you cut my phone line?" she demanded.

"What?" he asked. "Why did I do what?"

"You heard me."

"Your phone line? Madeleine, I don't know what you're talking about. Is there something wrong with your phone?"

"You *bastard*," Madeleine said through gritted teeth. "Get the hell away from me."

"Not until you calm down and tell me what the problem is," he said. "Just what is it that's got you all upset and afraid of me."

"It's not fear," she told him. "It's disgust."

Dale was silent for some time, and Madeleine's adrenaline began rushing again. Her head jerked from one window to the next; she expected to hear the shattering of glass any second.

Finally he said, "Well, I can't say I didn't suspect as much. You've tried to tell me in several ways, haven't you?"

"Get away from me," Madeleine repeated. "Leave me alone."

"No," said Dale. "I'm going to sit here all night if I have to and we're going to talk about just what it is that bothers you about me. I really want to know, dammit. You have no idea how important it is for me to know."

"Bull," she said. "You're just another bullshit artist who can't understand why everyone doesn't love him."

"I understand more than you think I do," he said. "I could tell you things about me, Madeleine. Things I'm not proud of, but it might make me more human to you."

"You're already incredibly repulsively human to me," she said.

A hard thump on the door made her jump. "God, you're hardheaded. What makes you think you're so fucking noble?"

"I never said I was. I've never claimed to be anything but what

I am, and I've been straight with you from the beginning. I want nothing to do with you. Not now, not ever."

"Which only makes me want to shove my dick in your mouth that much more."

Madeleine swallowed. Had he said what she thought he said?

"Eris is on his way home," she said loudly.

"I doubt it," Dale responded. "He thinks you're gone. I told the people at the lake office you were headed out, got a grant. I'm sure they passed the information on to Renard when he called in."

"I talked to him today," Madeleine lied. "He's coming home."

"Now why don't I believe you?" he asked. "Could it be the utter dejection in your steps when you were walking away from the cabin earlier?"

"You can't sit there all night," Madeleine said.

"Yes, I can. Because if I'm not sitting out here, then I'm going to be inside with you."

Madeleine's palms were sweating. "Dale, why are you doing this? Why won't you leave me alone?"

"Because chatting with you takes my mind off other problems, and Madeleine, my dear, I have plenty of those."

"Problems?" she said, a challenge in her voice. "Like the way you killed Bruce Beckworth? What is that act of cowardice going to cost you?"

"Hell, I don't even remember shooting the man. One minute he's rushing me and the next he's lying at my feet pissing his pants. The whole thing is a blur to me."

"What were you doing out here that night?"

"Watching to see if Renard came home. I knew he was gone, but you didn't say so. You wanted me to think he was away for only an hour or two."

"You're sick."

"You women always say that. In high school and college I was even worse, but you know the shit guys can get away with. High school drunks and fraternity pranks. And my aunt was pretty high profile even back then. A real hotshot attorney."

He fell silent and Madeleine was instantly aware. She liked it better when he was talking and she could track his movements. The silence unnerved her. She didn't realize she was holding her breath until her vision began to darken. She sucked in air and listened, her ears straining for any sound.

Finally she heard what sounded like a yawn. Then Dale said, "You know, I just realized I might be one of those guys who's been pushed around by strong women all his life and suddenly shows his resentment by whacking somebody off. What do you think, Madeleine?"

"You mean Bruce Beckworth?" she asked.

"No. I mean Kayla Lyman."

Madeleine stared at the door. "What?"

"You asked."

"The little girl? You killed the little girl?"

There was another long moment of silence, and then he began to chuckle. "Had you going there for a minute, didn't I? Yeah, it was big bad old Dale. Yup, and it was me that run down ole Shelly Bigelow, too. Creamed her shit good. What else did I do that you'll believe? Let's see . . ."

"You really are sick," said Madeleine.

Dale chuckled once more, and he fell silent again for a long time, long enough to make Madeleine think he was actually falling asleep and then waking up again, leaving her trapped inside, wide awake and terrorized.

Madeleine closed her eyes as a brief image of Kayla Lyman resurfaced in her mind. The sodden yellow sweatsuit. The floating hair and bloated features. She thought of the emptiness in Dale Russell's voice as he said the little girl's name in response to her question, and suddenly Madeleine began to wonder. Her imagination introduced her to a perverted, remorseless drowner of children on the other side of her door. And suddenly there was no longer any wondering in her as she saw in her mind's eye the image of him holding the little girl and heard him saying, "*Which only makes me want to shove my dick in your mouth that much more.*"

WHEN THE SUN CLEARED the trees, Madeleine had a huge knife in her hand and was prepared to use it. She heard Dale talking, asking how she had slept, but Madeleine did not answer. Her eyes remained glued to the door.

Dale staggered to his feet and kicked at the door in an effort to stretch his cramped limbs. She wasn't answering him, but he knew she wasn't asleep. He cursed himself for saying what he had. He ought to go now while he wasn't in too much trouble. No one could say he had done anything but aggravate her. She couldn't prove anything, and he had the cut over his eye to use against her. He kicked the door one last time and said, "You keep an eye out for me today, Maddie. You never know where I'm going to turn up."

He left then, got in his truck and drove out past the cemetery. Madeleine watched through the window and breathed out in relief. She threw back the locks and opened the door to run out of the cabin as fast as she could to the Birdys'. Halfway across the lawn she was tackled from behind, and she twisted to see a scarlet-faced Dale Russell holding her and laughing. She shouted as loud as she could and received a fist in the face for her efforts. He dragged her back to the cabin and hauled her up the steps to push her inside, one hand reaching behind himself to close the door. He sat on her chest on the living room floor and hit her again when she fought and tried to unseat him. He unzipped his pants and she screamed in rage at him and told him she would bite.

"You do and I'll kill you," he said calmly.

"You're going to kill me anyway," she said, and panic made her buck furiously again to get him off her.

Dale hit her again, hard, and held her quiet with his hands wrapped around her neck, choking off her air. A sudden pounding at the door made his head jerk up. One hand left Madeleine's neck to cover her mouth and nose.

"Madeleine?" asked a familiar voice outside, and she squealed and took advantage of Dale's surprise to bite down hard on his hand and scream for help when he jerked it away. In the next instant the lock on the door was released and the knob was turning. Dale leaped off Madeleine and looked wildly around himself for some way to escape. He ran to the mudroom door and yanked at the locks, leaving the cabin through the back door just as Eris entered through the front. Eris was stunned into momentary paralysis at the sight of Madeleine's battered face. Then he spat a vicious curse and followed her pointing finger out the mudroom door to race after Russell. He caught him at the cemetery road as he was trying to get in his truck. Eris's eyes were black with fury as he swung a fist that landed in Russell's stomach and made him double over in search of air. Dale sent out an arm to hold him off, but Eris knocked it away and hit him again, plowing into the side of his jaw and sending him to the ground with darkening vision. Dale got to his knees and held up both arms this time, begging for mercy. Eris hissed between his teeth and hit him twice more, opening up the cut above his eye and rendering him unconscious.

Dale slumped to the ground and Eris stood over him a moment, his chest heaving. Then he turned to walk back to the cabin.

Madeleine came out to meet him, and the pain in his shoulder caused him to stumble as she threw her arms around him. He held her tightly a moment then moved with her into the cabin to sit down. She buried her face in the hollow of his neck and clung to him so fiercely he found it difficult to breathe. Eris put his arm around her and held on. "Are you all right?"

She tightened her hold on him and blurted, "Don't ever leave me again. I'm pregnant."

Eris's jaw fell. Dale Russell was momentarily forgotten.

But he wasn't gone yet. The sunlight pricking at his lids brought him around, and Dale rolled awkwardly to his feet. The blood in his eye was about to blind him, and after Renard's last blow he was so dizzy his sense of direction was slightly askew. He made his way to where he thought his truck was parked, telling himself everything he was going to do to make Renard's existence a miserable one. He stopped in confusion and found himself in the middle of the road. He turned to search for his truck and saw nothing but the headlights and grill of a dented brown station wagon barreling toward him at thirty-five miles an hour.

The impact with the vehicle threw Dale fifteen feet into the dense brush and growth that bordered the road.

Sheila Lyman hit the brakes in the station wagon and stopped screaming at her little girls about the bubble gum on the car seat so she could look and see what she had hit. She had come to see Eris Renard and thank him for treating Ronnie so nice even though Ronnie hated his guts and wanted to hurt him. Sheila had heard how Renard stopped the man who killed Ronnie, and she wanted to offer to take Renard to dinner or maybe even go out on a date sometime. The sight of his burned-out house had nixed that idea. Sheila figured Ronnie was probably the one who had burned it.

She craned her head and couldn't see any dead animals behind her, but she did see a CO's truck, and the idea of having hit one of those scared her worse than Ronnie ever had. Sheila's tires kicked up dust as she sped away.

Eris and Madeleine moved to the window at the sound of the loud thump. Neither recognized the driver of the station wagon tearing up the road.

"Where do you suppose Dale went?" Madeleine asked, her voice worried. "The truck is still there."

"I don't know." Eris led her back to the sofa. He couldn't stop looking at her. "He won't come near you again."

"Did you hurt him?"

Eris's nostrils flared. "I hope so."

He touched her bruised face and saw her wince.

"Shouldn't we call someone about him?" she said. "I want to press charges."

"He'll probably call someone about us."

"I believed him, Eris. What he said about Kayla Lyman."

Eris nodded, and they were both silent for several moments. Then he lowered his head to kiss the tip of her nose and one swollen cheek. "Why didn't you tell me, Madeleine?"

She looked up at him. "I thought you might see it as an excuse to keep you here."

"Russell told someone at the lake office you got a grant."

"I told him I did."

"Did you?"

"No. I'm supposed to go and see some people today about a job."

Eris's pulse quickened. "Where?"

"In Wichita."

"Is it what you want?" Eris asked, watching her face.

She heard something in his voice and touched him on the chin. "Yes. Almost as much as I want this baby. Do you?"

He swallowed and reached behind himself to take out his wallet. He opened the leather, withdrew the ring inside, and put down the wallet to pick up her left hand. Eris put the ring on her finger, and then he looked at her, his dark eyes searching her face.

Madeleine sucked in her breath as she stared at the simple, elegant cut of the diamond. Finally she lifted her gaze to Eris, who was waiting.

"Don't say no," he croaked. "I lost the receipt."

Her lips curved upward and she lifted his left hand in hers and pressed a kiss on his bare ring finger.

His heart thudded in his chest and he pulled her to him. In a strangled whisper he said what he had been longing for some time to say, and he was rewarded with a tiny noise of joy and a deep, lingering kiss. When she finally pulled away from him she asked, "Where are we going to live?"

"Somewhere else."

CHAPTER
THIRTY-THREE

SHERMAN TANNER HEARD WHAT sounded like a moan as he walked his dog up the road that evening. His dog heard it, too, and it wanted to investigate the source. Sherman let the dog have its head, and it leapt into the brush, its leash snaking along behind it. Sherman followed, and his nose immediately picked up the scent of blood. His nostrils widened and he filled his lungs.

Then he saw a blood-covered arm jutting up, white bone sticking out where the flesh was torn. Sherman moved closer, and closer yet, until he could see all of the injured man.

Extensive, Sherman told himself as he looked over the man's arms, legs, and trunk. The right leg was twisted unnaturally and was obviously just as broken as the arm that jutted up. Even the neck appeared bent at a strange angle.

Sherman looked hard at the man's face and finally recognized him. It was the other conservation officer. The good looking one. Used to be, anyway.

His dog was getting close to that torn flesh, sniffing at the white bone, and Sherman called it away. Another moan sounded, as if the injured man knew someone was near, and Sherman leaned down to look into his face.

"How long have you been here?" The man's lips opened and dark red blood streamed out of his mouth. "Oooh," said Sherman, and he shook his head. Things didn't look good. There were obviously internal injuries as well as broken bones. Sherman guessed he'd have to cut his walk short and go back home to call someone about the broken CO.

Or would he?

He had already turned to call the dog when the thought struck him. He looked up and down the deserted road, then turned back to stand over Dale Russell. He unzipped his pants. As he reached in his underwear he said, "I do this to remind dead things where the source of life comes from. I like to think it gives one more taste of life to something already dead. And now I have the opportunity to say my farewell to a passing life."

The injured man's head moved half an inch, as if he were trying to turn away, and when Sherman Tanner ejaculated, Dale Russell's chest heaved one final time and then was motionless.

Sherman zipped his pants and waited, watching for nearly ten minutes before being certain the man was in fact dead. Then he ran back to his house to find his wife, Gudrun. She was going to have to help him get the man to their backyard.

This time they would need their shovels.